"Yo   **ett,**

Ebon
her fa
someone? Engaged? Married?" *No sense in making the same mistake twice,* she thought, checking his left hand. No ring.

"No, I'm as single as they come," Xavier replied.

"Then why won't you go out with me?" Ebony cringed at the sound of her voice. She sounded desperate, pathetic and needy. Clearing her throat, she tried again. "What could be wrong with two single, attractive people enjoying dinner?"

His eyes twinkled in amusement, which was all the encouragement she needed. Now she knew two things about Xavier Reed—he found her attractive, and he thought she was amusing. Both were very good things.

"I'm an excellent judge of character, Ms. Garrett, and I seriously doubt we'd have anything in common."

Ebony nailed him with a look. The articulate and well-spoken jerk had obviously been blessed with good looks, but he was about as warm as an icerink. She took a step forward to leave, but the sting of his insult pushed her to ask, "How do you know we have nothing in common when you don't know anything about me?"

He shrugged one shoulder. "Call it intuition."

Books by Pamela Yaye

Kimani Romance

Other People's Business
The Trouble with Luv'

PAMELA YAYE

has a bachelor's degree in Christian education, and has been writing short stories since elementary school. Her love for African-American fiction and literature prompted her to actively pursue a career.writing romance fiction. When she's not reading or working on her latest novel, she's watching basketball, cooking or planning her next vacation. Pamela lives in Calgary, Canada, with her handsome husband and adorable daughter.

The Trouble with Luv'

PAMELA YAYE

KIMANI™
ROMANCE

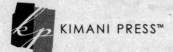 KIMANI PRESS™

ISBN-13: 978-0-373-86039-5
ISBN-10:   0-373-86039-0

THE TROUBLE WITH LUV'

Copyright © 2007 by Pamela Sadadi

www.kimanipress.com

Printed in U.S.A.

Dear Reader,

I once heard a youth pastor say, "Church is no place for hookups!" That got me thinking, love has no boundaries or restrictions. You could meet your soul mate anywhere. At the gas station, on an airplane, in court, even at church. And what better place to connect than in the house of the Lord?

Ebony Garrett is one of my favorite characters. Fun, feisty and gregarious, she puts everyone around her at ease. Well, everyone *except* Xavier Reed. At first he thinks he's ill-equipped to handle the sexy boutique owner, but after a disastrous date, he sees another side of the self-made woman. A quintessential gentleman, he showers Ebony with tenderness, respect and unconditional love. Despite the obstacles the couple face, they discover that when it comes to true love, there's no problem at all.

Thanks for reading *The Problem with Luv'*. I enjoy hearing from readers and promise to respond to all e-mails. Just be patient with me—I'm a new mom! Contact me at PamelaYaye@aol.com. I look forward to hearing from you. Happy reading, and be blessed!

With love,

Pamela Yaye

Acknowledgment

Being an author is a dream come true, a dream God placed in my heart and faithfully brought to pass. Thank you, Lord, for all your blessings on me!

To my husband, **Jean-Claude**: You make me laugh, you make me smile, and for the last six years, you have made me one very, very happy woman. I love you, papito!

Baby Aysiah: Thank you for taking two-hour naps and for sleeping through the night. You are my number-one girl, and mommy loves you very much.

Mom and Dad: Words can't describe what you mean to me. You are everything I want and ever hope to be. Thank you for inspiring me, believing in me and encouraging me to pursue my dreams.

To the most beautiful woman I know: Bettey, you're the best sister a girl could have. Intelligent, funny and caring, you continually show me what it means to be loved. Only God knows what I would do without you.

Kenny: You're the best big brother a girl could have. Your ambition is admirable, and I know you are just steps away from even greater success.

To the lovely Sha-Shana Crichton: I never imagined I would find an agent I not only like and respect, but consider a friend. We are going to have a long and prosperous relationship because I'm never, *ever* letting you go!

To my editor, Mavis Allen: You are talented beyond measure, and working with you has helped me refine my skills. Thank you for your insight, your dedication to this project and your invaluable contributions.

Marsha and Delroy McCormack: God brought you guys into my life when I really needed a friend. Thank you for everything you've done. I never would have finished editing this book if it wasn't for you!

Chapter 1

"Wake up, chile! I can't believe the day is half done and you're *still* lazing around in bed. Humph! It's a wonder you ever get anything done keeping such peculiar hours."

Ebony groaned. Cradling the phone under her chin, she forced her eyes open. She didn't know what time it was, but she knew it was too early for this. Sunlight streamed through the partially opened window, warming the cold, dark room. Birds chattered and a light wind ruffled the lavender satin curtains.

Reluctant to leave the comfort of her bed, Ebony dragged the duvet cover over her face. *I don't want to get up now. I'm tired. I want to sleep in. Is that too much to ask?*

It must have been, because the next thing she knew, aunt Mae was roaring in her ear. "Are you listening to me, chile? I said, *'wake up!'*"

Emerging from beneath the covers, Ebony peered at the alarm clock perched on the edge of the dresser. Blurry eyes prevented her from making out the numbers, 9…1…2. That can't be right, she thought, groping around the nightstand for her wristwatch, aunt Mae said it was noon. The silver hands on her diamond Rolex confirmed the accurate time. "It's only after nine," she croaked, shaking her head in disbelief. "Aunt Mae, I'm—"

"Listen," Mae ordered, cutting her off midsentence, "I'll be dressed and ready to go at five, so don't be late getting here. I'm part of the setup crew so it's important I'm at church on time. People are depending on me, Ebony."

"For what?"

Mae released a heavy sigh. *What was the matter with young people these days?* she wondered, taking a sip of her tea. When she was a child, she listened when grown folks spoke. It was either that or get smacked upside the head. Her niece, as intelligent and as educated as she was, didn't know how to listen. And the few times she did, she still got it wrong. "Tonight is the spring banquet at Jubilee Christian Center, remember? I mentioned it to you last Thursday when you came over for dinner. You agreed to buy a ticket and you promised to invite Opal and Kendall, as well."

Ebony yawned. She didn't recall saying any such thing but she could have. She was prone to agree with her aunt Mae whenever she was put on the spot. Ebony loved her aunt to death, but the woman yakked too damn much. It was difficult keeping up with all the rambling she did. For the sake of argument, Ebony agreed with her aunt's memory of events. "Okay, I'll buy a ticket to show my support. I'll even drop you off at the church tonight, but I'm not staying for the dinner. I have far too much work to do, aunt Mae."

"That's not good enough, Ebony. The good Lord expects more from his children than their money. You could make all the money in the world, donate it to the church, and it still wouldn't be enough. *He* wants your time. This banquet is about Christian fellowship. Meeting new people. Making new friends. There will be singing and eating and mingling and…"

Ebony was too tired to argue. If she couldn't outargue her aunt when she was sober, she'd be no match for her in her present state. She wasn't going to the banquet, and there was nothing aunt Mae could say to change her mind. She didn't have time for fellowship. Or to meet new people. Or to make new friends. She had a business to run. And if she ever got aunt Mae off the phone, she was going to take a shower, get dressed and head straight over to the office.

"It sounds like this, ah, banquet thing is going to be fabulous, aunt Mae, but I can't go. Work calls," she sang, her voice suddenly suffused with cheer. Ebony loved everything about her job. Discreet Boutiques was her life and she wouldn't trade the long hours, the pressures that came with being a CEO or her unbelievably high expectations for anything. "I expect to be at the office before noon and I plan to be there for the remainder of the day," she told her aunt matter-of-factly.

After some shuffling sounds, and incoherent mumbles, Mae said, "That's ridiculous! Preposterous! Working on a Saturday? What's the matter with you, chile?" She didn't give her niece any room to reply. "There is a time and place for everything, Ebony. A time to work and a time to play. A time to be serious and a time to have fun. It won't kill you to attend the banquet. Your work isn't going anywhere," she pointed out, the exasperation in her voice evident. "It will be there when you go into the office on Monday."

That's what I'm afraid of, Ebony thought, forcing herself to sit up and face the day. Going back to sleep was out of the question now, because when aunt Mae got started on something, there was just no stopping her. The sharp-witted Southerner had never been to law school or taken the bar exam, but she could argue a point better than O.J's illustrious Dream Team.

"…that's why you don't have a man, chile. *Work. Work. Work.* Who lives like that?" Mae queried, her tone one of incredulity.

Ebony didn't answer. She didn't expect her aunt to under-stand. Fifty years ago, single women aspired to be wives and mothers, not career women. *Of course she thinks I'm a work-aholic! I should be tending to a husband and breast-feeding babies, not running my own business.* Ebony chose her words carefully. The last thing she wanted to do was affront her aunt. They had an excellent relationship and she appreciated her guidance and wisdom. But not when it came to her career. "You don't know how much time and energy goes into run-ning a successful business, Auntie."

"Maybe I don't," she conceded, "but I do know that you're working yourself too hard. You eat, breathe and sleep work. When you're not at the office you're driving there. You have a beautiful house you barely spend time at, a fancy sports car you hardly drive and piles of money you don't spend. What kind of life is that? It's sickening what you're doing to your-self, Ebony. Just sickening!" Mae did nothing to conceal the contempt in her voice. She didn't want her niece to get mad at her but this had to be said. "Working fourteen hour days, six days a week is not healthy for anyone, Ebony." After pausing to ensure her words sank in, she added, "Even George takes a break from time to time. He goes down to that little ranch of his and rides horses and fishes and—"

"George?" Ebony frowned at the phone. "Who's George?"

"The president of the United States! He was reelected, remember?" Mae's voice reached an ear-splitting pitch. "See, you've been working yourself so hard you've forgotten who your president is!"

Ebony burst into laughter. Mae was a hoot. She had enough fire in her five-foot frame for five women and a tongue on her that would make her church friends blush. Upsetting aunt

Mae was never a good idea, but Ebony had to make it clear that she wouldn't be attending the banquet. "Maybe next time, aunt Mae. I have a lot to accomplish today, and when I get home from work I'm going to prop my feet up on the coffee table and watch a good movie. Dressing up and socializing with a bunch of church-folk after putting in a full day at the office is the last thing I'd want to do." Smothering a yawn with her hands, she tossed off the sheets and crawled out of bed.

Ebony glanced at the wall clock, amazed at how early it was. On the weekends, she rarely got out of bed before noon. *From now on I'm going to turn the ringer off the phone before I go to bed,* she thought, stretching her hands leisurely above her head. This was the third consecutive Saturday she had been stirred from her sleep by the insistent ringing of the phone. Aunt Mae was like a mother to her, but unless she was calling to tell her she won the state lottery, she didn't want to hear from her before noon.

"Are you sure you won't change your mind?" A short pause, then, "There'll be good-looking men there, Ebony. Doctors. Lawyers. Engineers. Professional people like you. Won't you come, suga? I really want you there."

Ebony didn't miss the disappointment in her aunt's voice. But if she wavered, even for a nanosecond, Mae would pounce on her like a fox on a squirrel. She had to remain strong. "The truth is, Auntie, I'm just not the churchgoing type."

"'I'm just not the churchgoing type,'" she mimicked. Ebony could see her aunt shaking her head and rolling her tongue over her lips like she was prone to do whenever she was about to lose her patience. "Hogwash! That's plain ole' nonsense, chile. *Everyone* is the churchgoing type!"

Mae smacked her forehead with her hand. *Now I understand. How could I have missed it? It's staring me right in the face!* Setting out to resolve the "situation," she stood and bustled into the bedroom. She flung open the closet door and combed through her church clothes. Her hands stopped at a polyester green two-piece. Too flashy. She continued on with her search. "I know what this is all about, Ebony. You don't have anything to wear! No worries, chile. I can lend you one of the new outfits I picked up at Lane Bryant. Got them for fifty percent off *and* I was able to use my senior discount card, too," she said, sounding proud.

Mae took out a modest-looking pink dress from the back of her closet and inspected it. Holding the outfit at arm's length, she spoke as if Ebony were in the room rather than on the phone. "I know this frock is too big in the chest and has a loose fitting waist, but I'll pin it from the inside and nobody'll be the wiser."

Ebony chuckled. She would swim in one of aunt Mae's size twenty dresses.

Mae went on as if the matter had been settled. "If you don't want to wear one of my outfits that's fine, but wear something appropriate to church. Don't come to the house of the Lord dressed in one of your party getups," she warned, her voice stern. "My friends from the Lakewood Bingo Hall will be there and I don't want them laughing at you."

The phone beeped.

"There goes my other line. Looks like I have to run." Mae spoke at a rapid pace. "The banquet doesn't start until six-thirty so that gives you the entire day to laze around in bed if you so please."

"But—"

"Enjoy what's left of the day!"

"But I—"

"Don't be late picking me up!"

"I'm not go—"

"See you at five!"

Before Ebony could object, the phone line went dead.

* * *

Where were the "good-looking" men aunt Mae said would be here? Ebony thought, as her eyes scanned the well-dressed crowd. She saw short and pudgy, tall and lanky, seedy-looking and average, but no good-looking men anywhere.

Then she saw him. The light-skinned man with the sexy dimples. He was nothing short of gorgeous. Oblivious of the lovesick expression on her face, she trailed him with her eyes around the room like a lost puppy in search of its owner. His vanilla colored suit, matching silk tie and designer shoes confirmed that he had good taste and a strong sense of style. Ebony loved handsome black men who moved with confidence, and Mr. Man was swimming in it.

Licking her lips aggressively, she shifted in her seat to get a better look at him. *Dimples are hot! Nice smile. Perfectly shaped head. Size twelve feet, maybe thirteen. And those eyes!*

Ebony was eyeballing him so hard, she feared she might pop an eye vessel. But she didn't have the power to turn away. It was as if his eyes were reaching across the room and seizing her attention. And he had other impressive physical attributes as well. A cocoa butter complexion that looked as smooth as a baby's bottom. Well-rounded chin. Thick eyelashes. And a traffic stopping smile that set hearts aflutter.

Over the next thirty minutes, Ebony watched the gorgeous stranger move around the room, socializing with the other guests. His classic good looks garnered him the attention of every single woman in the room, and a few who were taken as well. A constant stream of ladies had been approaching him since his arrival, but he didn't seem the least bit impressed in what any of them had to offer.

The lusty grin on Ebony's face slid away when a model-thin woman with feline features cornered him near the men's washroom. She watched them shake hands, contemplating whether or not to go and rescue him from the woman's clutches. He looked trapped and the terse expression on his face suggested the conversation was not going well. But before Ebony could stroll over there and send Jezebel on her way, the emcee took to the stage and asked guests to be seated. Smiling in satisfaction, she watched the twosome separate and return to their rightful seats.

Ebony helped herself to a buttered biscuit and took a generous bite. Taking a momentary look around the room, she sized up her competition. She wasn't the most beautiful woman in the room, but no one else had her charisma or sexual confidence. That, she was sure of. Most of the women in here looked sexually repressed, she thought, chuckling to herself. *And one thing I know for sure is that men adore sexually liberated women.* Ebony knew men inside and out. They enjoyed being with females who played by their own rules, lived in the moment and were free to do whatever, whenever, wherever. Ebony was as free as a jaybird. Few hang-ups. Open to try anything at least once. And when it came to sex, she had no inhibitions. None whatsoever.

Ebony set her sights back on the stranger with the killer smile.

"Handsome, isn't he?"

She tore her eyes away from him long enough to give her best friend a smile. "That's an understatement. Handsome doesn't even begin to describe how scrumptious he is."

Opal laughed. "But he doesn't meet your height requirement," she teased.

Ebony licked her lips in an exaggerated fashion. "Every now and then a brother comes along who forces me to make an exception of my rules." She flicked her head in his direction. "And there he is. He doesn't clear six feet and he's more of a caramel shade than dark chocolate, but he's the best-looking man in the room and there are several cuties in here tonight."

In the last hour, the room had finally started to fill up with some good-looking men. There was a six-footer with curly hair resting against the back wall. He was positively adorable, but he didn't look a day over eighteen. Ebony was all for the older-woman, younger man craze, but dating junior would be robbing the cradle. Or rather, the womb. The casually dressed man sitting at the table to her right looked like a low-budget version of Usher, but his mustard-colored dress shirt was speckled with lint and he had a protruding Adam's apple. An older gentleman, who looked like he slept on silk sheets and had weekly manicures and pedicures, was giving her the eye, but he had stained teeth. *With all that money, you'd think he could get his teeth whitened,* she thought, turning away from his sleepy gaze. No, the prize for the finest man in the room definitely went to Dimples.

Ebony's eyes darted around the room. The well-spaced banquet hall was a cluster of tables set with lace place mats, ivory bone china and triangle vases filled with trumpet-shaped daffodils. Diffused lights and classical music provided an intimate and peaceful setting. Guests were in the process of being served, and latecomers moved around the hall, hunting down any available seats.

"Who knew all the hotties were hiding out in church?" Ebony asked, before returning her attention to the object of her affection. Everything about the man was delicious, from the gleam in his eyes to the way his lips curved into that disarming smile of his. As she stared, one word turned over and over in her mind: tas-ty.

"He reminds me of Gavin," Opal confessed, sorry the moment the words left her mouth. "Sorry. I didn't mean to—"

Ebony waved off the apology. "I was the one who broke things off, remember? I'm fine, Opal. Besides, life's too short for regrets."

Her no-strings-attached relationship with Gavin Taylor, a promising investment banker, had been running smoothly until he had ruined things by getting serious on her. While basking in the aftermath of a toe-curling lovemaking session, he had announced that it was time to take their relationship to the "next level."

"We're not getting any younger," he'd said, nuzzling his chin against her shoulder. "Most people our age are already married." He said he wanted kids. Two, maybe three. With a sedated expression on his face, he had hugged her to his chest and rubbed a hand over her stomach. "Why don't I sell my place, move in here and we start working on that family?"

Ebony had retreated like a soldier caught in a cross fire. Settling down and having kids was not in her blueprints; operating the most profitable lingerie franchise in North America was. It was her first and only aspiration. Gavin Taylor was a terrific guy—articulate, intelligent, dependable—but Ebony would rather swim in shark-infested waters than get married and have babies.

Three lonely months had elapsed since the demise of their relationship and Ebony was yet to find someone to take his place. Living a sexless life was starting to have adverse effects on her. She was moody. Irritable. Short-tempered. And she found herself thinking about sex twenty-four-seven. During board meetings. On the phone with important clients. Waiting in line at the grocery store. At the bank. And every time a semiattractive man looked her way, she undressed him with her eyes. Sex toys had never appealed to her, but things were getting so bad, she was thinking about buying a battery-operated "friend." It had been so long since she had been intimate with a man, she had started to wonder if it would ever happen again. But from where she was sitting, things were definitely starting to look up.

"Gavin has nothing on that man. Nothing at all." Ebony winked. "But I'll give you all the dirty details in the morning."

Opal's mouth dropped. Her earrings tinkled harshly as she swung her head back and forth. "Ebony Denise Garrett," she began, in a hushed tone of voice. "I *know* you're not about to proposition that man. He—" Opal broke off her sentence when she realized the elderly woman beside her had stopped talking and was watching her. Opal put on a warm smile, and when the nosy grandmother returned to her meal, she jammed her elbow hard into Ebony's ribs.

"Ow! What did you do that for?"

"You can't take home some brother you met at church! You should be ashamed of yourself for even entertaining the thought," Opal hissed. "I have half a mind to leave you sitting here by yourself."

Ebony fought back a laugh. Sometimes Opal was worse than a great-great-grandmother. The tiger print dress hugging her voluptuous figure suggested she was gregarious, reckless and impulsive, but Opal Sheppard was as straight as a ruler. She was responsible and organized and planned every second of every day. There was no room in her life for any funny business or spontaneity. If it wasn't on her daily agenda, it wasn't happening.

Lips curled with disgust, Opal tried fruitlessly to hold Ebony's wandering gaze. Put off by the grin dancing on her friend's face, she laid down her fork, which had been suspended in midair, and folded her hands in front of her like she was about to drop a bombshell. "I can't believe the things that come out of your mouth sometimes! It's like you think with your…your…your private parts instead of using your brain." The mother in her said, "You need to get it together. It's time for you to grow up and quit—"

"Dang, girl! I was just playing!" Ebony said, finally giving in to her laughter. She hugged Opal with one hand, and was relieved when the miserable frown on her face fell away. "I just wanted to see what your reaction would be. *God,* you're such an easy target." Ebony resumed eating, but not before she added, "I'm not going home with anyone tonight, so don't get your panties in a bunch."

"Don't joke like that, Ebony. It's not funny." Opal finished what was left on her plate, and then signaled the waiter over. Dissatisfied with the tiny portion of food she had been given, she asked for another helping of baked chicken and shrimp fried rice. Opal didn't need a second helping of food, but she believed in getting her money's worth, and so far, she hadn't even eaten forty dollars' worth of anything. Since the New Year, her waistline had been growing at an alarming rate, but she wasn't going to let that stop her from filling her stomach.

Opal cast her eyes back at Ebony, and was surprised to find her still ogling the man at table number twelve. "Is he *that* fine?"

A roguish smile curled the corners of Ebony's mouth. In a dreamy-sounding voice she purred, "Girl, I think he's making love to me with his eyes."

Chapter 2

That woman is trouble in three-inch heels, Xavier decided, as the statuesque woman with the smoky eyes and mocha-brown skin approached. Her auburn hair was short, trendy, and bounced restlessly as she walked. The stylish cut showed off her delicate neckline and gave her a bold, edgy look.

She is sin waiting to happen! Xavier watched the woman weave her way through the crowd, like she was on a mission. Everything about her was tempting—the seductive curl of her lips, her sensual walk, the way she moved through space. Her mischievous smile set him on edge, but there was no denying it; the woman had a Lord-have-mercy-body. Her crimson V-neck dress clung to each and every luscious curve and drew attention to her figure. She had a smile that shone brighter than headlights, and the glint in her eyes hauled him in like a fisherman with the catch of the day. Her flawless skin was the most beautiful shade of chocolate, clear and smooth.

The woman had the ultimate bad-girl face and when she brushed past him and requested an iced tea from the portly man working the refreshment bar, Xavier concluded that her sexy, throaty voice could seduce even the most God-fearing man.

Tea in hand and an affable smile on her face, Ebony turned to greet the man to her right. "Having a good time?"

Xavier turned at the sound of her voice. His eyes lingered on her full, pouty lips and ultrawhite teeth. Her chandelier earrings shimmered under the soft lights, and jingled every time she so much as batted an eyelash. Gawking was indecorous and made the doer look asinine, but Xavier couldn't help himself. And when her smile expanded, revealing a perfect mouth, he felt like someone was squeezing his heart with both hands. She had the whitest teeth he had ever seen. Teeth so white it looked like food had never passed her lips. But the sugar in her smile, the honey on her red-hued lips and the dangerous slope of her hips told him otherwise.

Xavier took a sip of his drink before responding to her question. "I'm having a good time, thanks."

"The food was wonderful, wasn't it?"

He could listen to her deep vixenish voice all night. Rolling his eyes toward the ceiling, he patted a hand over his stomach. "The women's fellowship committee really outdid themselves this year. The main course was scrumptious, the desserts heavenly and the overwhelming turnout is a testament to all their hard work."

He smiled kindly, those dimpled cheeks enhancing his nice-guy appeal. He exuded masculinity and strength and though they stood shoulder to shoulder, Ebony felt elfin standing next to him. It was a welcome change. Most men were intimidated by her size; it was refreshing being with a man who wasn't dwarfed by her five-eight frame.

Ebony extended her right hand. "Ebony Garrett. And you are?"

"Xavier Reed. It's a pleasure to meet you, Ebony. I've never seen you at Jubilee Christian Center. Did one of our members invite you?"

"I came with my aunt. She visits Jubilee from time to time."

"Have you ever attended one of our services?" Xavier asked, inhaling her sweet perfume. The scent made him hanker for fresh fruit.

"I don't have much free time during the week, so I like to hit the clubs on the weekends. I use Sundays to catch up on sleep." *Stop babbling,* Ebony chided herself. *Be engaging and witty and let him know you're both interested and available.*

With a pensive expression on his face, he said, "You don't know what you're missing out on, Ms. Garrett. Church is where we feed the soul." He paused briefly, unsure of whether to share a page from his autobiography. "Back in the day, I thought there was nothing better than running the street with my boys and partying the night away. But after my best friend died, I knew I had to make some serious changes in my life. I gave up that reckless lifestyle years ago and started attending Jubilee. That was the best decision I ever made."

"Nothing wrong with having a good time," Ebony countered, troubled to learn about his wild past. "After putting in twelve hours or more a day from Monday to Friday, I need an outlet. I need to unwind. I'm not much of a drinker," she pointed out. "I go to the club to dance. Dancing is a great way to relieve stress. *You* should try it sometime."

"Maybe *you* should cut back on your hours so you won't be so stressed."

Ebony bit her tongue. She wanted to tell him to mind his own damn business, but didn't. In the corner of her eye, she caught sight of the flamboyantly dressed emcee swaggering toward the stage. He had a program in his right hand and a microphone in the other. She turned back to Xavier, her lips fashioned into a smile. His eyes were the lightest shade of brown she had ever seen and the overall image he projected was one of extreme confidence. Yes, he was just the kind of man she was searching for.

They talked for a few minutes about the church and then a long, painful silence settled in between them.

There was an air of shyness about him Ebony hadn't picked up on initially. If she waited for him to build up enough courage to ask her out, they could be standing there all night, and time was of the essence. "Have you heard of *A Taste of Venice?*" Ebony asked, tilting her head to the right. Her stance gave him an unrestricted view of her cleavage.

Xavier kept his eyes on her face. *She couldn't be more obvious,* he thought, refusing himself a glance at her chest. "That's the new upscale restaurant on Hennepin and Ninth, right?" She nodded, and he continued. "I've been meaning to check it out, but I haven't had the time."

So far so good, Ebony thought, brushing a lock of hair away from her face. She paused, when a trio of long-haired, blue-eyed blondes approached the bar. Each woman was making googly eyes at him. *How desperate can you be?* she wondered, when the thinnest one in the group tossed some hair over her shoulder and winked. *Heifer.*

Ebony waited until the women slithered away before she spoke again. "Are you free for dinner this Friday? Say, eight o'clock. We can meet at the restaurant if you'd like." She opened her clutch purse, pulled out a business card and had started to hand it to him when he politely declined. The smile slid off her face. "No, you're not free this Friday or no, you don't want to have dinner with me period?"

"Both." His eyes smiled, belying his harsh words.

The vacant expression on his face caused self-doubt to take up residence in her mind. *Is he for real?* she wondered. Ebony pushed for more details. "I don't understand why you don't want to go out with me. It's just dinner."

Xavier downed the rest of his soda. It was time to bring this conversation to a close. The entertainment portion of the program was set to begin any minute now and he didn't want to miss anything. His friend Liberty Williams was singing "Amazing Grace" and he just knew she was going to blow the roof off the church. "You seem to be a lovely woman and all, Ms. Garrett, but I can't go out with you."

Ebony was stunned by his brusque reply, but her face remained inexpressive. "Why? Are you dating someone? Engaged? Married?" *No sense in making the same mistake twice,* she thought, checking his left hand. No ring. In fact, aside from his watch, he wore no jewelry at all.

Xavier's eyes raked the room. This was one of those situations where his bogus wedding band would have come in handy. A few years ago, he had taken to wearing a gold ring on his wedding finger, but it hadn't been the deterrent he had hoped it would be. Women had descended on him in droves. They slipped business cards into his pocket, scrawled their phone numbers on napkins and told him his wife would never have to know. "No, I'm as single as they come." Xavier left it at that. He had a feeling that if he said anything else, she might use it against him later.

"Then why won't you go out with me?" Ebony cringed at the sound of her voice. She sounded desperate, pathetic, needy. Clearing her throat, she took a mouthful of soda and tried again. "What I meant was, what's the harm in two single, *very* attractive people going out for dinner?" His eyes twinkled in amusement, which was all the encouragement she needed. Now she knew two things about Xavier Reed: he found her attractive and he thought she was amusing. Both were very good things. "I'm paying, Xavier. It won't cost you a thing if that's what you're worried about."

"That's not it." Xavier chose his words carefully. It wasn't his style to hurt people's feelings, but there was no way he was going out with this pushy woman. "I'm an excellent judge of character, Ms. Garrett, and I seriously doubt we'd have anything in common."

Ebony nailed him with a look. The articulate and well-spoken man had obviously been blessed with good looks, but he was about as warm as an ice-rink. She took a step forward to leave, but the sting of his insult pushed her to ask, "How do you know we have nothing in common when you don't know anything about me?"

I know you're aggressive and bad news. Xavier decided to keep his observations to himself. He shrugged one shoulder. "Call it intuition."

Ebony studied him. Low-cropped hair. Chiseled facial features. Sculptured physique. There was a distinguished almost regal bearing about him. He couldn't be more than thirty, if that, but he was incredibly serious. Much too serious for a man so young. And handsome. Used to dating sociable, engaging men, not judgmental, ice-cold ones, Ebony quickly concluded that Xavier Reed would bore her to death and she was better off not going anywhere with him.

"Well, it was nice meeting you." He put his empty glass on the bar, smoothed a hand over his blazer and admonished her to enjoy the rest of her evening. Xavier turned, but was hampered when she coiled a hand around his arm.

Ebony hated rejection. It was an incurable virus that could break someone down. Play with their mind. Taunt them when they least expected it. Xavier Reed might be stern-faced and aloof, but after a few drinks, and some laughs, he'd be putty in her hands. But first, Ebony had to convince him to go out with her. Then, and only then, would she seduce the pants off him. "Are you sure you won't reconsider?" she purred, batting her eyelashes. "We don't have to go to A Taste of Venice—we can go anywhere you want. When it comes to things like that I'm not fussy. I'm *easy*."

I bet you are, he said to himself. Xavier slapped a smile on his face, in the hopes of screening the irritation he felt. Six years ago, he would have jumped at her offer. Easily swayed by glamorous women oozing sex appeal, he would have taken her out for an expensive meal, worked it off at one of Minneapolis' trendy nightclubs and then whisked her back to his place for a night she'd never forget. But Xavier wasn't the man he used to be. Gone were the one-night stands, meaningless relationships and bad-boy ways. Xavier had known it was time to quit playing the field when his closest friends had started dropping like flies.

First, Dominick had moved in with his girlfriend; then commitment-shy Lemar had gone off and gotten himself engaged; and these days, Juan was so consumed with his new lady love, two weeks had passed since they last spoke. The all-boys club had dismantled quicker than a female R&B group. He had lost his boys to women, and although he was happy for them, it made him hanker for a relationship all his own. He was saving up to buy a BMW, but aside from owning a temperamental, banged-up jalopy, every aspect of his life was in order. He owned a three-bedroom home in one of the city's developing areas; had a substantial amount of money tucked away in low-risk investments; traveled two, sometimes three times a year; cooked, cleaned and washed better than most women and he had no baby mama drama to complicate his life. Returning to graduate school to earn a master's degree in psychology was a long-range goal, but for right now, he was content being a high school guidance counselor and part-time economics teacher. All he needed was the right woman to complete the picture. He had played the field long enough and at thirty-two he was ready to start a family of his own. Xavier was in a settling-down frame of mind, and the woman clinging to his arm was not "the one."

I wonder if I'll ever find Ms. Right, he thought, as his eyes skimmed the banquet hall. Chatting with Ms. Garrett reminded Xavier of why he was still single. The twenty-first-century woman was too assertive, had more game than a rap star and didn't have the patience to wait for a man to make the first move. She wanted to be in control. Wanted to run the show. Wanted to be the one to wear the pants in the relationship. *What happened to the good old days when a man used to ask a woman out? Where are all the traditional women hiding?* he wondered. The room was crawling with women. A handful of them were even beautiful enough to strut the runway. But all the ladies who had approached him tonight were of the Ms. Garrett persuasion—pushy, abrasive and eager to engage in carnal pleasures. Sweet, nurturing and modest was more of what Xavier had in mind for a girlfriend. He didn't want to be with a human doormat, but on the other hand, he didn't want to be with a woman who crammed her opinions down his throat and called the shots, either.

His eyes returned to Ms. Garrett. She smelled good, she looked good and she sounded good, but he wasn't going out with her. No matter how hard she pushed. The woman was far too aggressive for his tastes. She had a backside that could rival J-Lo's, but experience told him women who looked like supermodels—primed to perfection and smelling like a cosmetics counter—usually had the diva attitude to match. And besides, he wasn't interested in a one-night stand; he was seeking a meaningful, long-term relationship that would eventually end up at the altar.

"I'm sorry, Ms. Garrett, but I can't." He freed his arm from her grasp.

"Are you sure?"

He thought, *this woman is as persistent as a recurring dream.* "Again, it was nice meeting you." Xavier walked away, without giving her or her offer another thought.

When Ebony retook her seat a minute later, Opal greeted her warmly. "So, how did it go? When are you guys going out?"

"A quarter to never," she said.

Opal broke out into a fit of giggles.

Ebony didn't know what her friend was tittering about. The man had been about as friendly as a bulldog. Draping her napkin over her legs, she reflected on their exchange. The more she thought about it, the angrier she got. Mr. I'm-Too-Good-To-Go-Out-With-You was an arrogant jerk with an unlikable personality.

Her eyes searched the banquet hall. In his tailored suit and designer shoes, Xavier Reed was easily identifiable in the crowd. He was standing near the stage and, to her shock, laughing it up with a plus-size woman with an outrageous weave. *So, he can laugh with her but he can't even give me a smile?* As she scrutinized him from head to toe, her eyes narrowed in distaste.

Xavier Reed wasn't all that. He wasn't even six feet and he had shifty eyes.

What woman in her right mind would want to go out with a short, leery-eyed, sourpuss anyway? she thought, stabbing her fork into a coconut drop. Xavier had done her a favor by turning her down. Going out with him for dinner would undoubtedly have been the longest two hours of her life. Comforted by her thoughts, she told Opal, "He's not all that. He might *look* good from a distance, but up close he's just as cute as the next guy. The man is *no* Taye Diggs." When Opal rolled her eyes, Ebony laughed. "He's not the one to help you get your groove back, girl."

Brushing aside Ebony's fallacious remarks, Opal said, "Who are you trying to fool? 'He's just as cute as the next guy.' *Please.* That man is fine. He'd turn heads in the dark. *You* said so yourself." After a brief pause, she asked, "Did you at least get his name?"

"Xavier Reed," Ebony uttered, as if saying his name made her mouth ache.

"Ooh, he even has a sexy name!"

Ebony said nothing. She sampled her piece of carrot cake, and then washed it down with some sparkling apple cider. "Can we please talk about something else?"

"Oh, you're just bitter because he turned you down. Just goes to show you, girlfriend. You can't always get what you want."

"Says who?"

Ebony checked her program. Eight performances left. She plopped her purse on her lap and fished around for her car keys. It didn't matter if Kirk Franklin & the Family were up next, after this song she was going home. If Ebony had to sit through another hymn or contemporary gospel song, she was going to scream. Holler so loud people would think an evil spirit had possessed her.

When a middle-aged Spanish woman with a beehivelike hairstyle took the microphone a few seconds later and started singing an off-key rendition of Donnie McClurkin's "We Fall Down," Ebony bit down hard on her bottom lip. Most of the performers had an abundance of talent, but they had no stage presence whatsoever. The delivery was always the same. Take the mike, say a few words of encouragement, sing, give the Lord a wave offering or two and wrap it up. The first performance was tolerable, but by the sixth it was akin to slow torture.

Should have left with Opal, Ebony thought, folding her arms across her chest. Opal had departed to pick up her daughters from a birthday party, leaving Ebony to suffer through four more songs. Straightening her shoulders, she inched her chair back and swung her legs out from underneath the table. When Ebony caught her aunt Mae, she gave her a half wave and mouthed "goodbye." One of the church sisters was giving her aunt a ride home, so Ebony was free to go whenever she was ready. She checked her watch again: 10:37. *Time to bounce!*

Ebony was thankful she had had the foresight to pick a table at the back of the hall. Now that she was ready to leave, she didn't have to worry about disrupting the program when she walked out. The same time Ebony slipped her purse over her shoulder and stood, the emcee asked Brother Xavier to join him on the stage. *I guess I can stay a few more minutes,* she decided, lowering herself back onto the chair.

Xavier took the microphone, greeted the audience warmly and thanked everyone for coming. "On May 1 our 'Changing Lives Through Meals' program will kick off again. The last three years of the program have been an enormous success, due largely to our dedicated and selfless volunteers. We're looking for people who can commit to helping out on Wednesday and Friday evenings for the duration of the summer. If you're interested in getting involved in a worthy cause and want to give back to the community, please see me at the end of the program. I would love to discuss…"

No, thanks, Ebony thought, standing and moving briskly out of the banquet hall. *Good night, sourpuss.*

Chapter 3

"Where the *hell* are my thongs? The purchase order I'm clutching has an arrival date of April 28. *That* was three days ago." Taking a deep breath, Ebony drew on every ounce of self-control she had to remain calm. But Mr. Rutherford was goading her, trying her patience like only he could. Tucking a loose curl behind her ear, she half listened as the owner of Logan Warehouse droned on about the latest problems with his business. Two of his best men had quit yesterday. He was understaffed. The warehouse security system was on the blink.

"The truck had mechanical problems while en route to your boutique, Ms. Garrett. You have to understand these things happen from time to time in business. But don't you worry, little lady. I'll have my best driver out there first thing in the morning with the shipment. Now, how's that for service?"

Ebony's eyes narrowed. He was patronizing her. She could almost see the balding man leering on the other end of the line, rubbing a stubby hand over his liver-spotted head. If she had the power to reach through the phone, she'd snatch him up by the collar and shake all two hundred and fifty pounds of him.

"Now, you listen to me, Mr. Rutherford. This is unacceptable and I refuse to tolerate your company's incompetence any longer." He tried to interrupt, but she swiftly cut him off. "This is not the first time I've had to put up with delays and inconveniences. This type of ineptitude has occurred at least a half-dozen times over the last six months. Tomorrow morning is simply not good enough. I want that shipment *today*." Ebony paused, took a deep breath and waited for him to come up with a reasonable solution to the problem.

"Take it easy, little lady. Having a hissy fit isn't going to get the shipment there today. Like I said, it'll be there in the morning. That's the best I can do."

Ebony gripped the body of the receiver, the veins in her neck throbbing uncontrollably. "Let me put it to you in terms you'll understand, Mr. Rutherford. If the shipment is not here by the end of the day, I'll terminate our contract and find another trucking company to do business with." Ebony calmly replaced the receiver. Truth be told, she couldn't afford to do business with another trucking company. The larger companies charged astronomical fees, didn't guarantee shipment arrivals, either, and forced customers to sign long-term contracts. Ebony was bluffing, but Mr. Rutherford didn't need to know that. If he came through for her today, she would renegotiate their contract in a way that would satisfy them both. And if he didn't, she'd kill him with her bare hands.

Ebony inspected her two-week-old manicure. She would call and make an appointment at Total Image Salon. Her French manicure was all but ruined. Chipped paint, dry cuticles and a broken nail needed tending to, and the sooner Ebony could get her nails done, the better.

Ebony buzzed her receptionist.

"Yes, Mrs. Garrett?"

"Please prepare a cancellation request form and fax it over to Logan Warehouse immediately."

"Another late shipment?"

"For the last time." Ebony clicked off the intercom. She moved over to the window and drew open the blinds. From where she was standing, it looked like colorful ants were shuffling down Eighth Avenue. Setting up the Discreet Boutiques headquarters in the Accenture Tower had been the best decision she and Kendall had ever made. The rent far exceeded what they had planned to spend, but on days like this—when Ebony needed tranquility and a moment's peace—the location was worth every cent. Her eyes tracked the sun as it dropped behind the clouds and then faded out of sight. Wrapped up in her observations, she didn't hear the knock on her office door.

"Daydreaming about frolicking on the beaches of Negril again?"

Ebony moaned. This time last year she had been sipping fruity Caribbean cocktails at Beaches Negril Resort, dancing with men of every shade of brown and a few in between and sleeping in hammocks under the shade of overgrown palm trees.

All business in a tweed suit, a few pieces of expensive-looking jewelry and her wavy hair pulled back in a neat bun, Kendall Douglas radiated cool sophistication. The co-owner of Discreet Boutiques sat down on one of the navy-blue padded chairs, crossed her legs and clasped her hands together.

"You'd be daydreaming too if you'd had Caribbean men catering to your every whim." Ebony returned to her desk. Once she was settled in her leather chair, she asked, "So, how did the meeting go? Did Yolanda heed your advice, or do we have to fire her?"

Kendall smoothed a hand over hair, taking a few minutes to gauge her partner's mood. "I got through to her, Ebony. Don't worry."

"Don't tell me not to worry, Kendall. Her unprofessional behavior and complete disregard for the company have caused lost revenue and dissatisfaction among our employees and valued customers." Yolanda Simmons, the store manager for boutique number six, had been showing up late to work, helping herself to unauthorized days off and delegating her duties to other employees for the past month. Yesterday, when Ebony had learned about what was going on, her first inclination had been to fire Yolanda immediately, but Kendall wouldn't hear of it. Her partner liked the single mother and thought she was an asset to the company. She had promised Ebony she would meet with Yolanda as soon as possible and get to the bottom of things.

"Yolanda knows she has a good thing going with Discreet Boutiques and that she'd be a fool to mess it up. Her next raise increase is set for August 1 and I know for a fact she's been eyeing Bridget's position. I told her only serious and committed employees would be considered for the Human Resources post when Bridget goes on maternity leave. I told Yolanda she had two options—either clean up her act or start looking for another job."

Ebony raised an eyebrow. "You said that?"

Kendall nodded.

"What was her response? Was she open to what you had to say?"

"The poor thing burst into tears." Glancing down at her blazer, Kendall brushed aside specks of lint. "Cried all over me. She confided that her live-in boyfriend has been messing around, and she suspects he may have gotten another girl pregnant. You know what the crazy thing is?"

Ebony shrugged a shoulder. "No."

"She doesn't want to leave him! I could sympathize with her because God knows I dated my fair share of *losers* before I married Turner, but I *never, ever* allowed personal problems to impede my work."

Ebony shook her head sharply. Happily unmarried, she enjoyed a rich life, a life more enjoyable and fulfilling than her married counterparts'. No drama. No stress. And most importantly, no heartache. "All relationships start off smelling like roses, and end up reeking like sour milk. When a diamond ring slips on a woman's finger, she becomes a bodyguard, a private investigator, a—"

"Huh?" a completely baffled Kendall asked. "What are you talking about?"

"I've seen it happen a million times before. Confident, self-assured, intelligent women will follow their men around like a Doberman, just to make sure other women don't get too close. They'll take a day off work to investigate whether his business conference at a five-star hotel is a company meeting, or a personal one." Ebony added, "I like my life the way it is. Uncomplicated, stress-free and all the freedom I can stand."

"You're going to be thirty this year, Ebony. In two short months to be exact. You're not a teenager anymore. It's time you found yourself a man, settled down and started working on having a *litter* of your own." Kendall chuckled at her joke. She sobered long enough to say, "You can pretend to be happy, but I know you're miserable sleeping in that big ole house by yourself. Just admit it!"

"Girl, please," Ebony scoffed, her mouth fitting into a smirk. "I'm as happy as a dolphin at Sea World!"

After the security alarm was disabled, Ebony shut the door behind her and kicked off her four-inch heels. There was nothing she loved more than returning home after a grueling day of work. She lived on a quiet street with other impressive homes in Linden Hills, a first tier suburb ten miles southwest of downtown Minneapolis. In the winter, the normally short commute was a killer, but Ebony didn't mind. The privacy and solace that came with living in a respected and valued community outweighed all inconveniences.

Charmed by the elegance of the four-bedroom, three-bathroom home, Ebony had fallen in love with it on sight. It had all the features and amenities she had been searching for: lofty, ten-foot ceilings; colossal picture windows; hardwood maple floors; and a small pool with an adjoining hot tub. Ebony loved the warmth and the light of the sun, and the surplus of oversize windows guaranteed daily doses of sunshine.

Ebony had listened with half an ear, as the rail-thin Realtor lectured about the history of the house, the most recent renovations and the previous owners. After a brief walk-through, she had concluded that this was the house of her dreams. It was four thousand square feet of paradise and she was willing to do anything to call it home.

"A single woman could go mad in a place of this size and magnitude," the Realtor had teased. Ignoring him, she had strolled through the French doors and into the tree-shaded backyard. It was the size of a tiny forest. The Realtor chatted on, and was so unenthusiastic about her buying the Tudor-style house, Ebony started to think he had other clients lined up for it. Making note of his pessimism and mentally slashing his commission, Ebony ordered him to put her offer in. This was the house she wanted, and no one was going to dampen her enthusiasm. By the close of the month she had finalized the deal and moved in five weeks later.

Dragging herself up the stairs, she stripped off clothes as she went. The master bedroom was the size of the apartment Ebony had lived in when she was a freshman in college. The light, open bedroom was an explosion of bright colors. Fuchsia bedding. A maroon area rug. Flower vases overflowing with every color of roses imaginable. The room was boldly decorated, ultrafeminine and perfectly Ebony. A full bathroom, completely outfitted in white; an enormous walk-in-closet; and a balcony wide enough for lounge chairs and a dainty glass table were her favorite aspects of the opulent master bedroom.

Not wanting her sanctuary to be muddled, Ebony had selected a few choice pieces from an antique furniture store. A mahogany dresser, a steel vanity table, an iron-rimmed chair and a pair of glass nightstands framed her elevated sleigh bed. In the adjoining office, alabaster walls were adorned with African art purchased in Manhattan at the legendary Abuja Art Gallery. Her favorite painting was positioned beside the elliptical mirror, and at the peak of day, sunshine bounced off its golden frame and reflected off the opposite wall. A shapely Nigerian woman in traditional dress, balancing a water bucket on her head, and her offspring on her hip, served as a reminder to Ebony that there was nothing she couldn't do. As she reflected on the potency and resiliency of her evocative female ancestors, self-respect stirred within her spirit. She was proud of who she was. Proud of her heritage. Proud of the legacy of her people. And proud of where she had come from.

Ebony turned away from the picture. Clad in nothing but a black silk robe and slippers, she returned to the main floor to get a drink. En route to the kitchen, she passed the family room, which housed a fireplace which she had yet to use— comfy chairs and couches and a fifty-inch plasma screen TV. Ebony entered the kitchen and after opening the window above the sink, poured herself a drink. Ceramic tile counters, stainless steel appliances and a center table that seated eight made it a chef's paradise. Ebony didn't cook, so the less time she spent in the kitchen, the better off she was.

Back in her bedroom, sipping peach-flavored iced tea, Ebony selected CD number three on her stereo. Jill Scott's hypnotic voice filled the room, offering a sweet escape. Closing her eyes, she sang along. She bobbed her head fluently, feelings of tranquility washing over her. But Ebony's peace didn't last long. The telephone interrupted her thoughts and yanked her back into the here and now.

"Hi, suga. Did you just get home?" Not bothering to wait for a response, Mae continued. "I called your office and that precious little receptionist of yours told me you were gone."

"I had a nail appointment."

"Are you okay? You don't sound like yourself, honey."

"I'm tired," Ebony replied. "Wednesdays are typically hectic days and today was no exception. I was about to step into the tub for a soak when you called. Everything all right?"

Mae coughed. "Just fighting off this flu bug that's been going around."

"Do you need me to bring you anything?" Ebony loved aunt Mae with all her heart and she would do anything to put a smile on her face. When her husband died from heart failure, Mae had packed up her load and moved to Minneapolis to be closer to her brother and his family. Out of respect for her husband, she had never remarried or had children of her own. But the seventy-four-year-old woman would tell anyone who listened that her feisty niece was the daughter she had always wanted. Ebony had quickly grown attached to her father's sister. And when her parents had died in a horrific car accident at the hands of a drunk driver, it had been aunt Mae who nursed her through the ordeal and welcomed her into her home.

"I'm all right, suga. I don't need you to bring me anything, but I do need a small favor." She paused, then added, "That is, if you don't mind."

"I don't mind, Auntie. What is it?"

"I hate to have to bother you," she began, her voice growing faint, "but I promised to cook tonight for the Changing Lives Through Meals program at Jubilee."

"What are you asking me to do, aunt Mae? You know I can't cook."

"No, no, chile. Don't be silly." The thought of Ebony in the kitchen, wearing an apron and all, made her laugh. Her shoulders juddered uncontrollably. Once her chuckles subsided, she continued. "I prepared the food this afternoon, suga. Everything is ready to go. All I need for you to do is pick it up and run it over to the church for me."

Ebony didn't want to go back outside. It was hot enough out there to cause a serious case of heatstroke. And tonight was the first time in months she had managed to leave the office at a decent hour. There were only two things on her agenda for the evening: peace and quiet. The season finale of *CSI Miami* was on at eight o'clock and Ebony had been looking forward to it all week. No, there was no room on her schedule to drive halfway across the city to deliver food.

As if she could hear the deliberations going on in her niece's mind, Mae injected her voice with cheer. "It's for a good cause, Ebony, and it won't take more than an hour if you leave the house right now. All you have to do is give the food to Brother Xavier, and then you can be on your merry little way."

Ebony checked the time. Her aunt's town house was a ten-minute drive, the church twenty. If she took a quick shower instead of a lengthy bath, she could drop the food off at the church and make it back home before the theme music for *CSI* started. Ebony didn't want to disappoint her aunt, and on the upside, stopping by the church would give her another crack at Xavier. She had met some stuffy, uptight men before, but no one had ever turned her down twice. *Who knows,* she thought, protecting her hair with a plastic shower cap, *maybe this is one of those blessings in disguise aunt Mae is always talking about.* "I'll be there in half an hour."

Chapter 4

Xavier masked his disappointment with a spurious smile. *Where is everybody?* he wondered hopelessly. Three elderly women and their stern-faced husbands were seated on orange chairs, getting acquainted. Xavier had been counting on twenty volunteers for the program; he'd be lucky if he ended up with ten. He checked his watch and was surprised to see that it was minutes to seven.

At the close of the banquet, scores of people, both young and old, had surrounded him to hear more about the Changing Lives Through Meals program. They praised what the church was doing, and seemed eager to get involved. *Where are those people now?* Xavier didn't know why he was so upset; this happened every year. People gave lip service to helping out and giving back to the community, but when it came time for them to step up, they fell back.

Creak.

Xavier's head snapped up. *Creak. Creak. Creak.* Someone was trying to open the door. Another volunteer! Xavier jumped to his feet, flew down the hall at the speed of light and took the stairs two at a time. He reached the foyer in seconds. But when he saw who was at the door, he came to an abrupt halt. *What is she doing here?* He was desperate for volunteers, but not that desperate. His brief conversation at the banquet with the overtly sexual woman was still fresh in his mind. Xavier didn't allow his thoughts to linger on the past; there was no way of knowing where they would take him and he was in the house of the Lord. Scratching the side of his face, he tried to remember her name. He would feel bad if he had to ask her her name, but for the life of him he couldn't remember. Xavier concentrated for a few seconds. She was named after a color. That much he knew for sure.

Blue? Naw, that's stupid. Nobody names their daughter Blue! Raven? No.

Violet? Definitely not.

Xavier moved forward. The poor woman was wrestling with two gargantuan black pots, several plastic bags bearing the Ralph's Gorcery logo were swinging from her wrists, and here he was standing here watching her like a mannequin.

"Looks like you could use some help," he noted, snapping out of his musings and relieving her of the pots.

Massaging the tenderness out of her wrists, she smiled her thanks.

After a brief pause, Xavier greeted her warmly. "It's nice seeing you again."

Ebony's nose wrinkled. "It's nice seeing me again?" she repeated, the doubtful look on her face carried into her tone. "Funny, I got the distinct impression you didn't like me."

Xavier opened his mouth to dispute her claim but the words didn't come. She was right; he didn't like her. The collar on his striped dress shirt and the accompanying tie were suddenly stifling. Her eyes rolled over his face and he wisely looked away.

Oblivious to his discomfort, Ebony apologized for being late. "I've been driving around this neighbourhood for the last ten minutes trying to find this church. I couldn't remember what side of the block it was on."

"No worries, you're right on time. We haven't even started yet." Then, "Is this everything?"

Ebony nodded.

The aroma seeping out of the pots was tormenting Xavier's empty stomach. Closing his eyes, he inhaled deeply. "Something sure smells good." He motioned with his head to the pots. "What do you have in here?"

Ebony pointed to the pot in his right hand. "Sweet and sour meatballs. The other one has fried chicken. The vegetable casserole, coconut rice and cream and mushroom soup are in these grocery bags." She trailed him downstairs, appreciating the view of his tight butt and muscular legs. *Does the man ever have a body on him!*

Xavier ducked into the kitchen, leaving Ebony in the banquet hall with the others. She blinked rapidly, as her eyes took in their surroundings. Was this the same room she had been in four days ago? The dim lights and oversize paintings had concealed flaky paint, crumbling borders and a stained and tattered carpet. The once elegantly dressed tables were now bare, revealing food stains, pen markings and chipped wood.

A fair-skinned woman, wearing an auburn wig, which looked like it was clinging to her head for dear life, waved her over. "Hello there," she greeted, with a full smile on her plump, collagen-enhanced lips. "I'm Sister Bertha and the man over there in the beige fedora is my husband. Say hello to the pretty lady, Willy."

When the man did as he was told, Ebony said, "It's nice meeting you both."

"Wow! Your hair is just too cute." Sister Bertha touched her nape with clawlike fingernails. "All the big celebrities are wearing their hair like you. I just love the cut. Do you think I should do my hair like that?"

Sister Bertha fluffed her hair and Ebony just about fell out laughing. The sixty-something woman evidently thought she had it going on in her chartreuse A-line dress, multicolored sandals and heavy makeup. The ensemble was hideous, but Ebony couldn't help admiring the old lady's spunk. She didn't know about the others, but she was going to get along just fine with Sister Bertha. "I think it would look great," she lied, averting her gaze. *God, forgive me for lying in church.*

Sister Bertha introduced her to the others. Mr. and Mrs. Hawthorne were the oldest couple, and the introductions seemed to interrupt a heated argument; Maria and Jules Hernandez were a nice-looking Mexican couple, who confessed that they had celebrated their thirtieth wedding anniversary yesterday. After offering her congratulations, Ebony excused herself and set out to find the unbelievably handsome program coordinator. She didn't have to look very far. Xavier stood at the back of the kitchen, with a plate of food in his hand and a fork in his mouth.

"What are you doing?"

The sound of Ebony's voice startled Xavier.

She pointed a finger at the stove, which was topped with plastic bags, casserole dishes and various sizes of pots and containers. Fixing a hand on her lap, she said, "The food you're eating is supposed to be for the homeless."

"I know, but—"

"But nothing. Put down that plate and step away from the stove before I call Sister Bertha in here." The tone of her voice was harsh, but Xavier could tell by the way her mouth was twitching that she was trying hard not to laugh.

Xavier did what he was told, but not before he ate the last three meatballs on his plate. Shamefaced, he threw his hands up in surrender. "Guilty as charged. I was in here tasting the food. But I was starving and the food smelled so good!" He grabbed a napkin from the counter and cleaned his mouth. "You sure can cook! Those are the best sweet and sour meatballs I've ever had." He walked toward her, a smile playing on his lips. "It's true what they say, you know. The fastest way to a man's heart is through his stomach."

That's not the only way, Ebony thought, returning his smile.

He pointed at the stainless steel pot he had carried into the kitchen. "You're going to have to teach me how to make those."

What's the harm in letting him think I cooked the food? It might help him see me in a better light. Deciding she wasn't breaking any of the Ten Commandments by not correcting him, she said, "I'm glad the food is to your liking, Xavier, but keep in mind it's for the less fortunate. I didn't slave over a hot stove for three hours so you can eat it all up before the guests arrive." Ebony ignored the guilt pricking her heart. She waved a hand toward the stove. "It's hard work cooking all that food." *Now you're overdoing it,* said a voice. *Remember, less is always more.*

Xavier cocked his head to the right. He crossed his arms over his chest as he locked eyes with the woman sharing his personal space. Oval-shaped face. Accentuated cheekbones. Small, even teeth flanked by an inviting mouth. A black calf-length body-hugging dress masked her full chest, curvaceous hips and thick thighs.

Black...Black...Black...Ebony! Her name is Ebony! Xavier couldn't hold back his smile. Remembering her name saved him the embarrassment of having to ask. His eyes returned to her face. She was without a doubt his sexiest volunteer to date. He would have to be careful. Very careful. Caution had to be the order of the day whenever she was around. Ebony was a clear and present danger to his emotional and physical well-being, and if he wasn't vigilant he just might yield to her seductive charms. Strikingly beautiful women had the power to turn even the most moral and upright man out, and Xavier didn't want to be the newest member inducted into the Sucker Hall of Fame.

Ebony was just another woman. Albeit, a provocative and amorous one, but a woman nonetheless. He had mixed feelings about her, but decided to reserve judgment until he got to know her better. Xavier plucked at his shirt. *Is it just me or is it hot in here?* he thought, feeling like the walls of the kitchen were shrinking. *Is it her come-hither stare that's got me hot under the collar or did someone turn up the thermostat?*

He watched Ebony walk over to the fridge and pour herself a glass of juice. When she raised the glass to her lips, he wondered what it would be like to kiss her. Sucking her bottom lip. Licking the—Xavier gave his head a good shake. Clearing his throat, he dragged his eyes away from her face. *You're in church for God's sake! Stop lusting after that woman! She's bad news.* But soon, his eyes were back on her. Ebony gave new credence to what made a woman sexy. She definitely had a penchant for fine clothes, but it wasn't her outfit or makeup or diamond rings that made her desirable. It was the way she carried herself. Her lithe movements and sensual grace. She walked like the ground was her runway. Shoulders squared. Chin up. Arms hung loosely at her side. Elegance was integrated in every move. And every step she took was flawless. It was these formidable characteristics that left Xavier wondering why she was here. Volunteers didn't look or act or sound like her.

"Don't take offense to what I'm about to say, but you're the last person I would've expected to volunteer," he said, voicing his thoughts.

"Oh, really? Why's that?"

"Well, with your twelve-hour days and all, I didn't think someone in such high demand would have the time."

Now I have to stay. Ebony stepped toward him, took off her cream-colored trench coat, and flung it over a chair. Xavier had pegged her all wrong, and there was nothing she enjoyed more than proving people wrong. *How hard could it be serving the homeless?* Ebony was a little bummed about missing the season finale of her favorite show but this was more important. Xavier-the-know-it-all Reed would see just how charitable and generous she could be. She would have to catch the season finale of *CSI Miami* some other time, because tonight there was nothing more important than teaching Xavier Reed a lesson.

The doors of Jubilee Christian Center opened an hour later, to a crowd of over a hundred people. Far more than anticipated. Xavier and the male volunteers wasted no time scrounging up more tables and the women had them dressed in no time. After Xavier welcomed everyone and said a short prayer, he saw to it that guests were organized in two orderly lines. Sister Bertha and Maria dished the food, Ebony staffed the drink table and the rest of the volunteers ensured everyone was comfortable and had enough to eat. Aside from the food Ebony had brought, there was macaroni and cheese, fried shrimp, meat loaf, potato salad, baked beans, dinner rolls and an assortment of soups. There was enough food in the kitchen to feed a large army.

When all the guests were taken care of, the volunteers fixed themselves a plate and sat down wherever there was a vacant seat.

"Spend time getting to know the people at your table," Xavier had encouraged, when he was giving last minute instructions. His eyes had circled the room and then lingered on Ebony's face. "The only difference between the people eating here tonight and us is that they fell on hard times and didn't have the necessary support system to survive. Inside, we are all the same. We all want to be loved, supported, cared for and cared about. Make the people who walk—" Xavier had swept a hand toward the hallway "—in here tonight feel special. Talk to them. Ask them questions. Listen earnestly to what they have to say. For a lot of them, it's been months or even years since they had a quality meal and a meaningful conversation."

Xavier's words of encouragement played in Ebony's mind now. He was asking the impossible. She couldn't even look at her tablemates without shuddering, let alone engaging them in conversation. Mariana, the pencil-thin woman to her left, smelled like she had bathed in vodka. And every time she opened her mouth to put food in, some spilled out. Chester, who sat on her far right, was no better. He had a set of utensils, but pretended they weren't there. He scooped up vegetables with his callused hands. Cut meat loaf with his fingers. Slurped his cream of mushroom soup. His shaggy facial hair was soiled with dirt and now remnants of his meal. When he guzzled down his drink, and then belched loud enough to shake the entire church, Ebony pushed away her plate. *I'll eat when I get home.*

She caught Xavier watching her, and managed a weak smile.

"Are you going to eat the rest of your food?"

Ebony redirected her eyes to the beige-skinned man with the fatherly voice. "No, you go ahead." When she handed him her plate, he grinned broadly, revealing badly stained teeth. "Old Man Griffin's the name," he told her. "Thanks."

He tossed a handful of shrimp into his mouth. "Suppa' sure is good, miss. Lady."

Realizing he was referring to her, she said, "Glad you're enjoying it." Sister Bertha had seen to it that all the guests washed their hands and faces with soap, but to remove the grime out from Old Man Griffin's fingertips called for something a little stronger than regular soap. It looked like the man needed some extra-strength bleach.

"We gonna get dessert?"

"I think I saw some chocolate swirl cheesecake around the back."

"Chocolate swirl cheesecake! My old lady used to make that…was good…real good. Haven't had dat in a long while."

"Where is she?"

He shoveled macaroni into his mouth. "Don't know for sure."

"What happened?" Ebony asked in a quiet voice. She was about to withdraw her question, when the older man dropped his fork, propped his elbows up on the table and started to talk.

Ebony, and the other people at the table, listened quietly as Old Man Griffin shared from his past. He recounted how his life had taken a turn for the worse with clear detail and emotion. It was the winter of 2001, three months after September 11th. People were still scared. The economy was crumbling. Jobs were hard to come by. But the construction industry was flourishing. He loathed the cold weather, but he needed a steady paycheck. It was his third day on the job, the coldest day of the year, and he was battling the flu. A gust of bitter wind had rocked his scaffold, and in the blink of an eye, he slid off and landed hard on his back. Neck and facial injuries and a broken back had ended his construction career. He scratched his head. "Da foreman said I wasn't en… entittl…"

"Entitled," Ebony corrected.

"Thank you, miss. Lady. Da foreman said I wasn't entitled to any cump…cumpens—"

"Compensation?"

He smiled his thanks. "Yes, dat's it. He said I wasn't entitled to any compensation because temporary workers aren't covered for disability insurance or health benefits." He fell silent for a few seconds. "Those damn welfare checks weren't enough to feed my pregnant wife and two small kids. It was hell. I couldn't get another job until my back healed and I couldn't send my old lady out to find work, either. When we couldn't pay da rent da second month, our stupid landlord kicked us out."

Old Man Griffin twiddled with the napkin holder. Unshed tears pooled his black-brown eyes. He wiped his nose with the back of his hand, pushed the pain back to its rightful place and said, "We didn't have anywhere to go. My wife's cousin took pity on us and let us stay with her and her family for a month, and then we had to go."

"And you don't know where your family is now?" Ebony asked.

"My old lady took da children to her people down south… I think they're in one of da Carolinas, I'm not sure. I haven't seen or heard from dem in a year. Her family never thought I was good enough for her anyways." He hung his head, but the anguish in his voice was unmistakable when he said, "I miss dem kids, especially the baby. She was just a few weeks old when my wife left. She's three now and don't even know her own daddy."

"At least your ma didn't toss you out on the street so her pimp could move in."

Ebony swung her head to the right. Her gaze landed on the slight adolescent-looking girl with the chalk-white lips sitting next to Amelia. The girl reminded her of Halle Barry in *New*

Jack City. The stringy blond hair. Cheap makeup. Too-short skirt and stretchy blouse. Ebony didn't know what drug she was abusing, but it was obvious she was a slave to something.

"Back in the day, I was the most popular girl in school. All the brothers wanted to get with me. Jocks. Pretty boys. Geeks." She snorted. "Today, those boys wouldn't touch me with a ten-foot pole."

Silence fell over the table. In the silence, Ebony searched for the right thing to say. "There are places you can go and get help. Agencies. Shelters. Community Centers. They'll get you off the street, help you stay clean and give you a fresh start."

"There's no help for me. Ma used to say I'd never amount to anything. Told me I'd end up turning tricks like her. Said it was in my blood." With a flick of her head, she said, "Guess she was right."

Ebony extended a hand. "I'm Ebony. What's your name?"

"Why do you care?" The woman's eyes hardened, and her shoulders arched like she was gearing for a fight. She took in Ebony's perfect hair, flawless complexion and polished nails. "You must feel pretty good about yourself, huh? Serving poor black folk. I bet you think you're better than us. All dressed up in designer clothes and shit."

It took a lot for Ebony to get embarrassed. But when a hush fell over the room and people at surrounding tables gawked at her, she felt her face flush. She didn't dare look over at Xavier; she could feel the heat of his angry stare right where she was. Drinking from her glass didn't loosen her airway. *Keep your cool,* she told herself. *Don't argue with her. If you ignore her, she'll get bored and move on to something else.*

No such luck.

"Is this your good deed for the year, *Ms. Socialite?* Feeding homeless bums? Giving advice? Pretending to care? Trying to make the world a better place, huh?"

For the first time in Ebony's life, she was speechless. Running a shaky hand through her hair, she wished that she were back at home, in bed, figuring out the latest mystery on *CSI*.

"Don't you hear me talking to you?"

Ebony's eyes spread. *Is she talking to me?*

"Yeah, you heard me, Miss I-think-I'm-Better-Than-Everybody-Else. You're too good to answer me now, huh? People like you make me sick. You walk up in here like you know what's going on out there on the streets, but you have no idea. I've been taking care of myself for years—y-e-a-r-s—and I don't need no damn agency making my life worse." Her eyes tapered. "I don't need your advice, either, ya hear? I can take care of my damn self!" She leaped out of her seat and the plastic chair sailed back on the floor and landed with a clunk. Leveling more insults at Ebony, she snatched up her frayed windbreaker and then stormed out of the hall.

Chapter 5

"My dogs ache," Sister Bertha announced, hobbling into the kitchen some three hours later. "I don't know about the rest of you, but my shift is over. Come on, Willy, let's go home. Mama needs to soak her feet."

The other two couples followed suit, leaving Xavier and Ebony alone to finish up. The next forty-five minutes flew by quickly, as they worked to get the church basement back in shape.

Ebony couldn't remember the last time she had worked this hard. She had swept and mopped the kitchen floor while Xavier stacked the tables, collected garbage and vacuumed. Once the dishwasher was loaded, and the cycle set, Ebony was going to bid Xavier good-night and head home. Anything that had been overlooked would be his responsibility. She was beat. So tired she could hardly keep her eyes open.

"Where's the dishwasher?" she asked, checking underneath the sink and along the counter. "Is it in the storage room or something?"

Xavier tapped his chest. "You're looking at it!" The look of disbelief on Ebony's face brought a grin to his mouth. "The church doesn't have the extra money to buy one," he explained. "So for now—" he held up his hands "—these will have to do."

Ebony faced the sink. It was overflowing with crusted plates and utensils and the counter was piled as well. What she really wanted to do was go home, but she didn't feel right leaving Xavier alone when there was still work to be done. The clock on the microwave said it was five minutes to ten. The sooner they got started, the sooner she could go home. Ebony picked up one of the sponges on the counter and flung it his way. "You wash, and I'll rinse."

They worked side by side for the next twenty minutes. Conversation was minimal; the only sound in the kitchen was of clinking dishes and gushing water. Xavier thought of his plans for the weekend while he washed; Ebony thought about work while she rinsed. She would be spending much of the morning behind her desk, proofreading reports on her company's five-year plan. She and Kendall had a follow-up meeting with the senior loan officer at First National Trust Bank in eight weeks and they couldn't afford to be unprepared.

Six Discreet Boutiques stores were scattered throughout Minneapolis, some in high-end malls, others in single standing buildings. The idea of opening her own boutique had been conceived after interning at Victoria's Secret. Ebony had always loved soft things, and in her opinion, nothing made a woman feel prettier or sexier than lace. After she'd shared her aspirations with Kendall, who had an eye for design, they had come up with the idea to host weekly "Silk Parties" in their dorm room. It was new and exciting and before long, all the girls on campus were trying to wrangle an invitation. In the fashion of Avon and Mary Kay, Ebony and Kendall had organized the event to give women of all shapes, colors and sizes the opportunity to sample undergarments, place orders, offer feedback on previously purchased lingerie and make suggestions. The "Silk Parties" had been an instant hit, and after peddling their merchandise on campus for two years, they'd had enough profits to rent a small store.

The present day success of Discreet Boutiques wasn't enough for Ebony. Opening additional stores, expanding the company to neighbouring states and taking it worldwide would be the culmination of all her dreams. These days, lingerie and sensual products were a billion-dollar industry. Ebony was thankful they hadn't thrown in the towel those first few years when business had been rough. Poor quality lingerie, meager sales and slothful and indecorous staff had threatened to do them in when they opened their first boutique, almost ten years ago, but when their marketing director, Sabrina Navarro, had come on board, there had been a dramatic turnaround. The advancement of women in society, and the influx of moms working outside the home, had given "the weaker sex" both confidence and independence. Modern day women knew what they wanted in their careers, their relationships and most importantly—the bedroom.

Ebony was so absorbed in her musings she didn't notice Xavier watching her. Like a well-oiled machine, she took the dish he passed her, rinsed it and placed it on the rack to dry. As she turned to receive the next dish, her hands skimmed his hands and sent a ripple of desire through her body. Recovering quickly from the jolt, she turned to face him. Ebony pointed at the dishes in the sink. "You're supposed to be washing, not watching me."

Xavier gave her a grin. "Looks like someone's head is in

the clouds. He must be very special." Xavier didn't wait for her to deny or confirm. The cheeky expression on her face was answer enough. "So, you have a boyfriend?"

Ebony smiled like she had a secret she was unwilling to share.

Shaking his head in disbelief, he shoved a plate into her hands. Disapproval was in his eyes and in the tone of his voice when he said, "If you have a boyfriend, then why were you all over me at the banquet?"

Ebony rinsed off the dish and dropped it on the dish rack. The other plates shook. "Let's set the record straight. I was *not* all over you last Saturday. I merely introduced myself and asked if you'd be interested in having dinner, that's it." She was quick to add, "And if you must know, I'm single. The last thing a woman like me wants is some man up under her twenty-four-seven. I'm happily dating and that suits me just fine."

Xavier didn't look convinced. "Really?"

She nodded. "My girlfriends think I'm clinically depressed because I'm not sprinting to the altar, but I'm perfectly sane." Ebony found herself laughing when Xavier made a funny face at her. "It's true! I'm just not one of those women in a rush to settle down. I'll be the big three-0 in July but I just don't feel the need to get married. Not one bit," she stressed.

"Your birthday's in July?"

"Uh-huh."

"When?"

"The twenty-ninth."

Xavier stared at her. "You're kidding!"

"Do you want me to show you two pieces of ID?"

He shook his head.

"I was born at 1:22 a.m. on July 29 at the Arthur Hayes Medical Center." Ebony's forehead crinkled. Xavier was staring at her like she'd just confessed she was thirteen rather than thirty. "What's with the wide eyes and slack jaw? Why is it so hard for you to believe I was born on July 29?"

"Because *I* was born on July 29!"

Her stomach flopped. "Really?"

Xavier nodded. "I came into the world three years before you, though." After a minute, a smile flickered across his face. "Crazy, huh?"

"And you said we had nothing in common," she teased. "I guess it's true what they say after all, you can't judge a book by its cover." Then, with her most innocent smile and in a honey-sweet voice, she said, "I'm not as bad as you think, Xavier."

Coughing to hide his embarrassment, he busied himself with washing the last remaining dishes. His mind returned to last Saturday. He hadn't exactly been warm when she came over and introduced herself. In fact, he had been downright rude. He had nothing against her personally, just women like her. She was right of course. *You can't judge a book by its cover. But you can tell what it's about by the packaging,* a small voice said in response. Xavier knew little about Ebony, but he knew her type. She was outrageous and unpredictable—everything he didn't want in a woman. That was reason enough to stay away. Far away.

Xavier looked around the kitchen. It was spotless. The floors had been mopped. Dishes were neatly stacked. Leftover food had been wrapped and stored in the freezer.

He swiped his keys off the counter and turned to Ebony. When she smiled at him, he realized he wasn't ready for their time together to end. The night was still young and he had nothing to do at home except laundry.

"Do you want to go somewhere for coffee?" He pointed to the clock on the microwave. "It's still early."

Is he asking me out? Ebony sure hoped so. She had every intention of saying yes, but decided to make him sweat it out.

"I don't know, Xavier. What would we talk about? We have nothing in common, remember?"

To her astonishment, he guffawed loudly. "Does that mean you're turning down my invitation?" Xavier didn't know why, but he wanted to know more about her. Lots more. Ebony was unlike anyone he had ever met. She intrigued him. There was an openness about her and she was a woman of tremendous charm. *I'm not interested in her on a romantic level,* he told himself, *we're just having a cup of coffee.* Xavier had no intention of falling under her spell. They were going to share a cup of coffee, and then he was going home—alone. "I feel indebted to you for all your help. I'd still be elbow-deep in soapsuds if you hadn't stayed behind. The least I can do is buy you coffee."

Ebony thought for a moment. Xavier's invitation was strictly platonic, but he didn't have to know she had other things in mind. She was attracted to him at the deepest level, and the more he resisted her, the more she wanted him. Her face glowed, radiant with anticipation. She was going to be polite and engaging and flirtatious and her "date" wouldn't know what hit him. Seducing Xavier Reed was going to be fun. "I'm ready when you are," she said, tossing her jacket over her arm and collecting her purse.

A smile warmed Ebony's lips. By the end of the night, Xavier would be on his hands and knees begging to take her out again. She loved challenges, and nothing revved her engine like a healthy dose of competition. Snagging Xavier Reed would be like taking candy from a baby. And Ebony was in the mood for something sweet.

Xavier did another quick sweep of the kitchen. Confident that everything was in place, he flipped off the lights.

When Xavier fixed a hand to her waist and guided her through the kitchen, she had to remind herself to breathe.

Ebony had met hundreds of gorgeous men, everyone from professional athletes to models to actors, but there was something special about the man walking beside her. Xavier Reed was in a class all his own. As far as her eyes could see, he was perfect. Sharp eyes. Long, thin fingers. Thick lips perfect for sucking and kissing. And the spicy, refreshing cologne embracing his skin suggested he had an adventurous side. Just the type of man she was looking for.

I just wish he wasn't so fine, she thought, as they climbed the stairs. *He could turn me out with just one smile!*

While Xavier secured the locks on the doors, Ebony hurried across the church parking lot and climbed into her SUV. Thoughts of their impending date consumed her mind. She would have to keep her loose tongue in check. If she said or did the wrong thing, she might not get another chance.

Xavier jogged over. "Follow me," he told her. "I know the perfect place." When he turned and walked toward a battered gray car, a lusty smile claimed her lips. Ebony shook her head slowly, awe clear in her eyes. *That man is too fine for his own good!*

Dakota's Bar and Grill was not what Ebony had in mind when Xavier asked her out. She was thinking of a fun, happening spot like The Hampton Club, or Sydney's Café, not a mediocre restaurant with second-rate food and poor service. Trailing him into the dining area, she was careful not to touch anything. The customers were a mix of young starry-eyed couples and middle-aged singles who were looking for more than a tasty meal on a Friday night. Ebony took in her unsightly surroundings. Her eyes narrowed in disgust at the hideous neon plastic tablecloths and paint-splashed walls.

"Have you ever been here?" Xavier asked, sliding into one of the booths.

"No. Never." *Thank God* went unsaid.

"Then you're in for a real treat tonight."

Ebony would rather stand than sit down in the flaky vinyl booth, but when Xavier motioned for her to take a seat, she did. It was as cold as a hospital examination table. Inspecting the tablecloth for a second time, she noted that it had bread crumbs and what looked like tomato sauce stains.

"Hungry?" Xavier asked, from behind a laminated menu.

"Starving." Ebony didn't even bother opening her menu. She already knew what she was having. You could never go wrong with soup and salad. But when the frizzy haired waitress with the pierced eyebrow bounced over and described the specials of the day, chicken noodle soup and Caesar salad quickly lost their appeal.

"The snapper is the best thing on the menu, Ebony. Go on. Try it. You'll love it."

She gave the waitress the nod. "And I'll have a glass of red wine."

"And you, sir?"

Xavier closed his menu. "I'll have the Chocolate Supreme Milkshake and a slice of apple pie."

Before Ebony could ask for the table to be wiped, the waitress bent down and gave it a thorough cleaning. Some of the worry lines on Ebony's forehead fell away. When she saw wet wipes lying beside the condiments, she tore open a package and wiped down her hands. *Maybe this place isn't a dive after all.*

The waitress departed, returned a few seconds later with their beverages and then left to check on a trio of black women now seated in her section.

A bowl of peanuts sat on the middle of the table next to a vase of fake flowers. Ebony scooped up a handful and put some into her mouth. When she finished what was in her hand, she took some more. "These are good. I could eat the whole bowl!"

"How can you be hungry after all that food we ate at the church? Where do you put it all?" he joked good-naturedly.

"I didn't eat anything at church," she confessed, double-checking to ensure her napkin was clean. Ebony covered her lap, and then dusted the salt off her hands. When she lifted her head and found Xavier watching her, she asked him what was wrong. "What's with the frown?"

"Why didn't you eat at church?"

"Old Man Griffin was still hungry after he finished his plate, so I gave him mine."

Xavier raised a brow. It was the second time tonight Ebony had surprised him. First she had stayed behind to help him clean, and now this. He had watched her on and off during the night and whenever he glanced her way she looked like she wanted to bolt from her seat. Chester and Mariana were sloppy eaters, and he thought their poor table manners had robbed her of her appetite. But that hadn't been it at all. Xavier was glad his assumptions were wrong. Thinking about dinner reminded him of something he wanted to say. He waited patiently for the waitress to serve Ebony her meal, and then for her to start eating, before he spoke. "I wanted to talk to you about Lydia's—"

"Who?"

"The young girl who stormed out of the church."

"I didn't even know her name." Ebony knew what was coming next. Xavier was going to reprimand her for chasing the girl off. "I don't even know what I did wrong. One minute I'm listening to Old Man Griffin talk about his accident at work and the next thing I know she's yelling at me!"

Xavier reached out and touched her hand.

His warmth spread up her hand and to her heart. It was a dizzying sensation. Ebony stared down at his hands. His fingers were long and thin, his nails neatly trimmed. But it was the size of his hands that made the blood in her body rush to her most intimate parts. She bit down on her bottom lip to keep from blurting out what she was thinking.

"I don't know what she said to you, but don't take it personal. Her mother has a heavy drug habit and she's been arrested for prostitution too many times to count. She kicked Lydia out of the apartment shortly after her seventeenth birthday and she's been hustling ever since. I've been trying to get her into a shelter, but she refuses to go."

When Xavier had been young and idealistic, he had thought he could change the world. He was going to make a difference. Touch lives. Bring change. Under his care, druggies would kick their addictions, dealers would see the errors of their ways and prostitutes would turn away from their corners and head to the church. But he soon realized there was little he could do if the person didn't want to change. And the majority of the homeless people who came through the church doors night after night didn't really want his help. These days Xavier concentrated on providing a place where they could have a hot meal. "Lydia's tough-girl-I-don't-need-anybody persona is a defense mechanism. It's her way of coping with all the crap that's going on around her. You represent everything she's not but would love to be. That's why she lashed out at you. Don't take what she said to heart. They were the words of an angry girl who feels like she's fighting against the world."

In the ensuing silence, Ebony gave more thought to what Xavier said. His words were comforting and made a lot of sense, but she couldn't help feeling guilty. Maybe she had done something to provoke Lydia. Or maybe he was right. Maybe Lydia was a troubled teen trying to find her way. Xavier had given her something to think about.

Ebony sipped her drink. "You're very insightful, Mr. Reed."

He winked at her. "I get that all the time."

They laughed. Ebony looked out the window and marveled at the number of stars in the sky. It was a clear night, flanked by a light breeze. Somewhere between stargazing and finishing her meal, her mind wandered. She would have to go into the office early tomorrow. Piles of paperwork were stacked high on her desk and she had an afternoon meeting with a bank representative. Ebony had realized at a young age that education was key for enrichment, personal and professional growth and most importantly, independence. Starting Discreet Boutiques had been her passport to financial security and its success was a complement to her hard work and dedication. Success came at a price, and Ebony refused to let anything— not even sleep deprivation—stand in her way.

"Who are you daydreaming about now?" Xavier asked, intruding on her private thoughts. He took a bite of his pie.

"Not who, what. I was thinking about work."

"Do you always have work on the brain?"

"Most of the time."

"What do you do for a living?" His right hand flew up before the question was off his lips. "Don't answer that. Let me guess." Cupping his chin and soothing his hand over his jaw, he narrowed his eyes on her face. Admiring her creamy-brown complexion and well-shaped lips wasn't going to give him any clues, but he gawked anyway.

Ebony's heart skipped a beat. And then another one. She tasted her drink, and the rich liquid cooled her body's fire. It wasn't Xavier's steady gaze that made her palms sweat; it was desire. It surged through her body like a hurricane through the state of Florida in the month of June.

"You're a career-minded woman, with great self-confidence," Xavier began, "so I'd guess that you were a stockbroker, a state prosecutor or maybe even a CEO of a Fortune 500 company."

Ebony nodded appreciatively. "Not bad, Xavier. I'm not CEO of a billion-dollar company—*yet,* but I am co-owner of a popular lingerie boutique."

"I knew it!"

"How'd you know?"

"Power's oozing from your pores."

"Am I that easy to read?"

Xavier snapped his fingers. "Like the cover of a book."

Ebony liked the way his smile danced across his face. *I wonder how the rest of his body moves.* "Have you been involved in the program for a long time?" she asked, changing the subject before her lax tongue got her into trouble.

"This is my fourth year as the program coordinator, but I've been going to Jubilee for years. The members have become part of my extended family. Pastor Henderson and his wife, Necee, are my second parents and their teenage sons are the brothers I never had. I don't work too far from the church, so when I need a quiet place to work, I come by and use one of the upstairs offices."

"Where do you work? Oh no, let me guess," she said, imitating him to a tee. Letting her eyes rove over his thick, juicy lips, she wondered if it was possible for him to look anything but delicious. *I bet he'd even look good in a pair of neon pants,* she thought, holding his gaze. "You're a natural born leader, so I'd guess you work in Human Services. You're a firefighter, a medic or maybe even a cop." A picture of Xavier in a blue polyester uniform and handcuffs dangling from his hips flashed in her mind. Then a devilish grin rippled across her face. "Am I right?"

"Not bad. But you're wrong." He chuckled heartily at the exaggerated look of shock on her face. Xavier finished his milkshake. "I'm the guidance counselor and home economics teacher at Christian Academy High. But—" he paused for effect "—when I was a little I used to play cops and robbers."

Xavier's heart warmed at the sound of Ebony's rich, throaty laugh. It was playful, sexy and flirtatious all in one. And he wanted to hear more of it.

For the next forty-five minutes, conversation flowed smoothly between the pair. Flirtatious smiles, shrieks of laughter and amusing tales punctuated the meal. Ebony was shocked at how much they had in common. They shared more than just a birth date. Sushi was their favorite food. Baseball their sport of choice. They both played the piano and were the biggest John Coltrane fans of all time. And they had each seen the movie *Love Jones* about fifty times.

The waitress bounced back over to the table. "How's your meal, ma'am?"

"Terrific."

When the waitress took the plates and asked if they needed anything else, Xavier draped his arms over the back of the booth. "Could you bring us a couple of dessert menus? I think my date is in the mood for something sweet."

Am I ever, Ebony thought, cleaning her lips with a napkin.

"Had you always dreamed about owning your own business?" he asked, returning to the topic they had been discussing before they were interrupted. "Is this what you imagined yourself doing when you were a kid?"

"Nope. When I was seven years old, I wanted to be a firefighter." The words were barely out of her mouth when she felt a sharp stab of pain in her stomach. Ebony's eyes watered. Gripping the side of the table, she took a long, deep breath. It didn't help. She felt like the room was spinning.

Xavier examined her face. "Are you okay? You don't look too good."

"Be right back," was all Ebony could say. Cupping her mouth with one hand, and cradling her stomach with the other, she hurried toward the washrooms.

Once inside the ladies' room, Ebony threw herself over the sink and emptied her stomach. She thought the worst was behind her, but when she tried to stand up, she felt her stomach twist into tight knots. Holding her side, she slumped against the wall and dropped to her knees. Closing her eyes, she prayed that the pain would end.

"Oh my God!" she heard someone yell. She felt a hand on her shoulder. "What's the matter?"

Ebony's eyes flittered open at the sound of the soft and caring voice. The scent of onions permeated the tiny jail-cell-size bathroom. She felt the heat of the woman's breath on her face, but she didn't have the strength to move away. "I'm sick," she said.

"Do you want me to call your husband?" The woman read the question in her eyes. "My sisters and I are sitting in the booth behind you guys. Now, let's get you cleaned up before I go and get him. If he comes in here and sees you slobbering all over yourself, he'll probably pass out."

Xavier! Ebony didn't want him to see her like this, but she couldn't spend the rest of the night on the bathroom floor of Dakota's Bar and Grill, either. She took the toilet paper the brown-skinned woman offered her, cleaned her mouth and dragged herself up off the floor. When Ebony saw her reflection in the mirror, her eyes spread wide in shock. Mascara coursed down her cheeks, the front of her dress was stained and to top it all off, she smelled like spoiled fish.

Chapter 6

Paradise Moore adjusted her denim Lane Bryant dress. She checked her bra, stuck out her chest and drew a deep breath. Sauntering through the dining area, she switched her thick hips to the music playing. She tried on a myriad of smiles as she approached the corner booth, and settled on one that showed every single tooth.

The man with the deep-brown skin and hazel eyes was even better looking up close. He had a straight nose, a pointed jaw and eyes that looked like they could see right through her. When she pulled up in front of his table, his cologne wrapped itself around her and all two hundred pounds of her tingled. It took a half minute for Paradise to remember why she was there. She cleared her throat and once she had his undivided attention, said, "I'm sorry to bother you, but your wife needs your help."

Xavier chewed the pie in his mouth. "Pardon me?"

"She's sick."

"Who?"

"What do you mean, who? Your wife!"

"What wife?"

Paradise wrinkled her nose. Was he for real? His wife was in the bathroom with a sore stomach, a high fever and numbness in her hands and legs and here he was trying to run game. Sure, he wasn't wearing a wedding ring, but that didn't mean anything. He was probably one of those husbands who "forgot" to put it on before he left the house. The man was too handsome for words and his dimples made her want to plop down on his lap and nuzzle up under his chin, but only a fool would mess around with a married man. Karma was no joke and she didn't want to provoke the vicious hand of fate.

Paradise pointed to the other side of the booth. "There was a woman sitting here with you a few minutes ago. About five-eight, kinda bony, exotic features, big butt."

"We're not married. She's a…" What was she? Ebony was certainly friendly enough and he liked talking to her, but he didn't consider her a friend. But for lack of a better word, he said, "She's a friend."

Paradise grinned like she had just won first prize on a TV game show. The man was fair game. He was on the market! She sat down, made herself comfortable and extended a hand. When he squeezed it, she said, "I'm Paradise Moore. What's *your* name?"

"I don't mean to be rude, Ms. Moore, but I believe you came here to tell me about my date. Is she all right? Where is she?"

"In the bathroom throwing up. I'm no doctor or anything, but I am a registered nurse at Hennepin County Medical Center and experience tells me that your friend has more than just an upset stomach. After having three children of my own, I can easily decipher the early signs of pregnancy. Throwing up at any given time of the day and spending hours on end in the bathroom are signs number one and two."

Xavier sat in stunned silence. Ebony was pregnant? Hadn't he just watched her drink a glass of wine? "No, she couldn't be pregnant."

"Oh, yes, she is," Paradise told him, matter-of-factly.

Why would Ebony harm her unborn child by drinking alcohol? Xavier had seen firsthand the effects of fetal alcohol syndrome and other drug and alcohol related learning disabilities. It infuriated him that mothers could be so selfish when it came to the physical and emotional needs of their unborn child.

Xavier rubbed a hand over his forehead, in an attempt to clear his mind. During dinner, Ebony had impressed him greatly. She had a quick smile, a vibrant personality governed with charm and grace, and an abundance of energy. It was exciting to be around a woman who spoke her mind and expressed herself so freely. When their discussion had turned to the present state of politics and government, Ebony had argued her opinion like she was speaking on behalf of the president himself. There hadn't been a dull moment all night.

To his surprise, there was nothing arrogant or egotistical about her. Xavier knew you couldn't really know someone after a few hours, but he had a good idea about who she was. That's why news of her pregnancy took him for a loop. Ebony bordered on being a workaholic and it sounded like she had her personal and professional life all mapped out. Why would she complicate her life by having a child? It wasn't Xavier's place to interfere in people's private matters, but he couldn't sit by and do nothing while she endangered the health of her unborn child. Drinking alcohol while pregnant made about as much sense as smoking a cigarette in church.

"So, where are you going after here?" Paradise asked.

Xavier tested out a smile. "Thanks for your help." He collected his jacket and Ebony's things and slid out of the booth.

A minute later, Xavier stuck his head inside the door of the ladies' room. He found Ebony perched on a wooden stool, sipping a glass of what he surmised was ginger ale. The desire to take her in his arms and kiss the tracks of her tears was overpowering. Xavier didn't know if it was the knowledge of her pregnancy, or the vulnerability in her eyes, but he wanted to hold her. Comfort her. Soothe away the pain lines etched across her face. Tell her she and the baby were going to be just fine. But he didn't. He didn't know her well enough to offer such intimacy.

When Ebony saw Xavier in the doorway, she straightened her clothes and cleaned the corners of her mouth. Embarrassed, she couldn't even bring herself to look him in the eye. Nothing like this had ever happened before. Getting sick all over yourself and then hiding out in the ladies' room was not the way to make a good impression on a man like Xavier. Or any man for that matter. Ebony had rinsed her mouth out with water for a good five minutes, but her breath still smelled like old socks.

Xavier took in her sad eyes and crumpled clothes. Ebony Garrett, a woman of luxurious tastes who prided herself on her impeccable appearance, was a mess. Strands of hair were pasted on her forehead, she had bloodshot eyes and the natural glow of her skin had faded. His sister, Jacqueline, was nearing the end of her first trimester, and complained nonstop about the sudden bouts of dizziness, nausea and vomiting she experienced on almost a daily basis. Maybe there was some truth to what that Paradise woman had said. "What happened?"

After a few quiet seconds, Ebony found the strength to speak. "I just want you to know that I don't make it a habit of crying in front of strangers." Her attempt to diffuse the awkwardness between them brought a smile of understanding to his lips and temporarily put her at ease. "I think I have food poisoning. That, or I suddenly became allergic to snapper. Can you drive me home? I don't think I'm well enough to drive."

"Of course. Do you think you can walk out of here?"

"Yeah, I'm okay."

When Ebony tried to stand, Xavier came over, put a comforting hand around her waist and then guided her out of the washroom. Ignoring the shameless whispers and curious stares of the other patrons, they made their way to the front of the restaurant. People could be so nosy, he thought, noticing Paradise and her band of equally chubby friends eyeing them. *Doesn't anybody mind their own business anymore?*

Xavier stopped at the register to settle their bill, but the white-haired manager took one look at Ebony and said, "The meal's on the house."

The Fairview Southwest Hospital Emergency room was a hive of activity. Doctors and interns bustled down the halls, responding to intercom pages; telephones and pagers buzzed relentlessly and patients—everyone from a man complaining of severe chest pains to a car accident victim—waited intolerantly for their names to be called.

Xavier wiped the sleep from his eyes. He turned to look at Ebony, surprised that she could sleep with all the commotion spinning around her. Stretched out across three chairs, her hands tucked under her head like a pillow, she slept soundly. She murmured in her sleep, and he unconsciously reached out and stroked her hair. It was soft and smooth, felt like silk underneath his fingertips. His hand dropped to her back, where it soothed away any lingering aches. Then he rested it casually on her shoulder.

On the drive to her house, Ebony had asked him to pull over twice. When he pulled over to the shoulder, she had bolted from the car, clutching her stomach. Xavier had never felt so helpless. When she had enough strength to return to the car, tears were streaming down her cheeks and she was shaking uncontrollably. Xavier had tried to comfort her the best way he knew how, but nothing he said or did seemed to help. Ebony insisted that she didn't need to see a doctor, but when her stomach pains got stronger, she relented.

Xavier stared down at her, compassion clear in his eyes. Her face was clammy and deep circles rimmed her eyes. *I wonder who the father of her child is. Does she even know?* Startled by his thoughts, he looked away. Ebony didn't strike him as irresponsible and since she didn't have a boyfriend and was wholly devoted to her career, he couldn't understand why she'd let something like this happen. But it was none of his business. For all he knew, this could have been a planned pregnancy.

When a petite woman with a gash on her forehead staggered into the emergency room mumbling incoherently, one of the nurses jumped up from the front desk. Xavier felt his temper flare as he watched them disappear behind a flowered curtain.

"We've been waiting for two hours," he said, once he reached the front desk, "but a woman just came in from off the street and received immediate medical attention!"

A redheaded nurse jotting notes down on a metal chart glanced up at him. "Patients are categorized into three general categories—immediate, life-threatening, urgent, but not immediately life threatening and less urgent. As usual, we're short on beds so we have to attend to life-threatening conditions first."

"Does she have to die before a doctor will see her?" Xavier didn't realize he had spoken out loud until the nurse said, "Your wife won't die from food poisoning, sir, and there really isn't much Dr. Bellman can do. She'll advise you to buy some over-the-counter medication, and tell you to monitor your wife's condition for the next twenty-four hours."

"Why didn't you tell us that *before* we filled out those stupid insurance forms and wasted two hours of our time?"

The nurse continued writing. "Because I'm not a physician."

Xavier didn't want to disrupt Ebony's sleep, but he didn't want to spend another two hours in the waiting room just to hear the on-duty doctor say, "There's nothing I can do." He wanted to take her home, but he didn't know where home was. As they exited the restaurant parking lot, she said she lived in the Linden Hills area, but she hadn't supplied a street or house number. Xavier could always check her driver's license, but he didn't feel right digging through her personal belongings. That would be intrusive. And besides, the nurse said her condition needed to be monitored for the next twenty-four hours. As far as he knew, Ebony lived alone.

It didn't take Xavier long to realize there was only one thing he could do.

When Ebony woke up, her face felt swollen, and her throat was sore. Swallowing was painful and she could feel a headache coming on. She stretched like a cougar in the wild, yawning loud enough for her neighbors on either side of her to hear. The windows were closed, and the blinds turned up. The room was dark, protecting her from intrusions from the outside world.

Rubbing the sleep from her eyes, she eased out of bed and then shuffled into the bathroom. Only she didn't end up in the bathroom. She ended up in a walk-in closet. Ebony blinked. *Am I still dreaming?* Flipping on the lights, she took in the unfamiliar surroundings. Books and fitness magazines crowded the nightstand, shoes spilled out of the closet, and a flat screen TV that took up a quarter of the room was positioned directly in front of the bed.

Ebony hopped like a jackrabbit when there was a knock

on the door. "Yes?" Her voice was timid and weak. She suddenly felt like she was living out a scene in one of those creepy horror movies she loved to watch.

The door creaked open, and when she saw who was on the other side, both relief and trepidation filled her heart. Ebony was glad it was Xavier at the door and not some masked man brandishing a butcher knife, but his presence left her feeling nervous.

"How is the patient doing this morning?" he asked brightly, walking into the room.

Praying he wouldn't come any closer, she took a step back. One whiff of her morning breath could slay a band of dragons. If she so much as opened her mouth, his eyes would roll in the back of his head and he'd keel over onto the carpet. Ebony gave her head a shake. She was being silly. Her breath didn't smell *that* bad. "I'm okay. I have a slight headache but my stomach doesn't hurt anymore. Why am I here?"

Xavier told her about their trip to the emergency room. "Since I didn't know where you lived, I decided to bring you here." When she lowered her head, and her eyebrows knitted together, he added, "I cleaned you up the best I could. You complained of being cold, so I put some extra clothes on you. Sorry they don't match."

Ebony's shoulders sagged in frustration. She wasn't sulking because her clothes didn't match or because her hair was a mess. It bothered her that he had been forced to take care of her. Ebony started to apologize for seeming unthankful, but his voice drowned her out. "Hungry? I was about to start breakfast." He motioned with his head to the clock hanging behind her. "I guess I'll be making brunch. It's almost eleven-thirty. What would you like to eat, Ebony?"

She waved her hand frantically. "I can't even think about food until I take a shower. I stink! I smell so bad I don't even want to be around me!"

Xavier chuckled. She was right. She did smell bad. He showed Ebony to the full-size bathroom. "There's body wash and soap and extra toothbrushes underneath the sink. Feel free to use whatever you want."

"Looks like you've entertained women here before," she teased, holding up a bottle of sensual body oil. She took a whiff. "Smells good."

Xavier shoved his hands into the pocket of his jeans. "Those things belong to my sister. She moved in with me when she found out her ex-husband was cheating."

"Sure, sure. That's what they all say."

"Seriously, it's been months since I had a woman in my house. I don't let just anybody in here."

Ebony recognized the edge in his voice, and wiped the smirk off her face. The man who had chatted freely with her last night was not the same man standing in front of her now. Xavier had done a Dr. Jekyll and Mr. Hyde switch. But Ebony didn't hold his present temperament against him. If she were in his shoes, she would be sour, too. He was an incredibly private person, and she didn't doubt for a second the truth of what he had just revealed. His house was his castle, and in his mind, she was an intruder. "I'm going to take a quick shower, get dressed and be on my way," she told him, as she closed the door.

Chapter 7

The aroma of freshly squeezed lemons wafted under the bathroom door, and a thunderous rumble ripped from Ebony's stomach. Rubbing a hand across her midsection, she examined herself in the mirror. She might look pale and sickly, but she felt like a new woman. The hot shower—though short—had revived her mind and body. When Ebony emerged from the bathroom, the only thing on her mind was feeding her empty stomach. But not at Xavier's house. She didn't want him to do anything else for her, except drop her back at Dakota's Bar and Grill so she could pick up her car.

"Ready to eat?" Xavier asked, when he saw Ebony. He had found some of his sister's old clothes in the storage room and had left some outside the bathroom door. The blue sleeveless cotton dress had never looked so good. "I didn't know what you were in the mood for so I made a bit of everything. We have eggs, toast, grits, pancakes and I thought you might like to start with something light like oatmeal."

"Thanks, but I'm not hungry."

Ebony saw the pained expression in his eyes, and turned away. To cover the silence, she pretended to be looking around the kitchen. Maple cupboards, a generous island, stainless steel appliances, hardwood flooring and thick granite cupboards fixed with decorative accents made his kitchen both cozy and modern. A sliding glass door led to a wide patio area that overlooked a small pond. Ebony wanted to ask for a tour of the rest of the house, but she didn't want to wear out her welcome.

"Ebony, don't tell me you're not hungry. You must be starving."

She was poised to repeat herself, but he pressed her further. "You have to eat something. You lost a lot of fluid last night."

Don't remind me, she thought, her cheeks flushing with humiliation. Everything on the table looked appetizing and smelled delicious. The banana pancakes were thick and fluffy, just like she liked them; the bacon was light and crispy and the omelets were seasoned with green and red peppers. But Ebony didn't want to have breakfast with him. It wasn't Xavier's job to take care of her, and if she was honest with herself, she didn't feel comfortable being around him anymore. He had seen her at her worst, and that bothered her. Her parents had hammered it into her from the time she could crawl that the only person she could depend on during times of crises was herself. "You want it, go out there and get it," she remembered her father saying regularly. It took a lot for Ebony to trust someone, especially members of the opposite sex.

"Is there something you wanted to eat that I didn't make?"

"No. I just don't have much of an appetite," she lied, averting her eyes. Ebony wondered if he could see her nose growing.

Xavier didn't believe her, but if she didn't want to eat, there was nothing he could do. She was pregnant, and on top of drinking alcohol and doing God knows what else, she was starving the baby. He was trying not to pass judgment, but it was hard to do. "It's a shame to see good food go to waste, especially when there are homeless people scrounging through garbage right now to find something to eat." He shook his head sadly. "Sometimes we don't know how good we have it."

Ebony checked her temper. She knew what Xavier was doing, and she didn't like it one bit. That reverse psychology trick might work on his students, but it wasn't going to work on her.

Xavier tried to lighten the mood. "Ebony, if your bottom lip gets any lower, it will be sitting on your chest."

"Can we go? I've been gone all night and my friends and family are probably worried sick."

The silence was loud. Xavier studied her for several seconds. Ebony Garrett was something else. Ungrateful. Ill-mannered. Self-absorbed. *Me, me, me must be her favorite expression.* He snatched up his keys from the counter. His words came out like a direct order, "Get your stuff and let's go."

Somber, slate-gray clouds blanketed the afternoon sky. Ebony peered outside the window, watching houses, cars and people whiz by. The silence that had started in the house had followed them into the car and engulfed the tight space. Apologizing for her behavior back at the house would be the proper thing to do, but Ebony couldn't find the words. And the way Xavier was carrying on only made it more difficult to seek his forgiveness. He was ignoring her. He hummed along with the radio, and when there was a break in the music, he fiddled with the dial. Ebony was surprised the radio even worked. His car was a shack on wheels. She couldn't believe a man with Xavier's looks would drive around in a rusted '81 Chevy Lumina that had ripped seats, broken door handles and a cracked windshield. But he did.

Ebony gasped when Xavier swerved into the far right lane, narrowly missing the guardrail. The car driving behind him honked, but instead of slowing down, Xavier sped up and switched lanes.

Shifting in her seat, she gripped the door handle with all her might. Ebony couldn't believe what she was seeing. This respectable, churchgoing man had a serious case of road rage. He ranted about every slow-moving grandma on the road and smacked his horn every few seconds. He tailgated, switched lanes without signaling and drove twenty miles an hour over the speed limit. Ebony opened her mouth to tell Xavier to take it easy, but remembered that they weren't talking to each other.

When he pulled into the parking lot of the Dakota Bar and Grill, Ebony sighed in relief. She had driven with speed demons before, but Xavier was the worst of the worst. He might be soft-spoken and gentlemanly, but when he got behind the wheel, all his admirable characteristics flew out the window.

"Thanks," she said, when he pulled up beside her car.

Her gaze brushed across his face, and Xavier's anger abated under their warmth.

"Are you sure you're all right?"

She nodded. Ebony felt awful about the way she had acted back at his house, but for the first time in a long time, she didn't know how to articulate what she was feeling inside. She was a confident, ambitious woman who took great pride in her appearance. Weekly manicures and pedicures, deep tissue massages and yoga helped keep her mind and body in top shape. Alcohol was limited to social events and special occasions, and since the smell of cigarettes and cigars made her head spin, she avoided smoke-filled areas at all costs. Her look could be summed up in three words: fashionable, sexy and unique. She shopped at the best stores, wore designer clothes and spared no expense when it came to achieving the perfect look.

But today, she looked less like a woman who shopped at high-end boutiques and more like a woman who bought clothes from Goodwill. Vacillating between sharing her feelings with Xavier and keeping them to herself, she considered his response. *Will he understand where I'm coming from or will he think I'm shallow?* Fidgeting with the zipper on her purse, she explored her heart for the right words. Nothing. But Ebony knew she had to explain her bizarre and confusing behavior. "Thanks, Xavier. I appreciate everything you did last night. I don't know what I would have done if you weren't there."

Xavier smiled softly. "I'm surprised you don't hate me." His tone was equally gentle. "And I definitely don't deserve your thanks. You wouldn't have gotten sick if you hadn't ordered the snapper entrée."

"It's not your fault. You weren't the idiot who cooked it."

He thought about what she said. She was right, but her estimation didn't lessen his guilt. Examining her face, he noticed the light freckles on the bump of her nose. Ebony wasn't wearing any makeup and her hair wasn't curled, but she looked prettier than when she was all dolled up. "You shouldn't wear all that gunk on your face. It takes away from your natural beauty."

Ebony didn't know what to say, so she said nothing at all. An awkward silence followed. When it became too much for her to stand, she secured her purse over her shoulder and grabbed the plastic bag holding her dirty clothes. When she turned to say goodbye, his lips grazed her cheek.

She touched the spot where his mouth had been. "What was that for?"

"Just seemed like the right thing to do."

The heat of his kiss warmed her cheeks, and a southern region, as well. If she didn't feel like a bum sitting in used clothes, she would have pursued the kiss further. "Thanks again." She exited the car, but turned back when he captured her arm.

"See you on Wednesday?" Xavier hoped she didn't pick up on the excitement in his voice. It was weird but he was kind of disappointed to see her go. The thought of returning to an empty house to eat breakfast alone was depressing. Ebony hadn't been at his house long, but he had liked her being there.

Ebony had no intention of going to the program ever again, but instead of telling him the truth, she said, "Of course," and hurried to her car. When she got behind the wheel, she gave Xavier an obligatory wave.

Ebony strode through the receptionist area of Discreet Boutique headquarters at six o'clock on Monday morning. She flicked on lights, rearranged chairs and turned on the fax machine. Since Ebony arrived to the office first every day, she saw to it that the coffee was made and the phone messages checked. The earlier Ebony started the day, the better. Unlike her partner, she did her best work first thing in the morning. Kendall's workday didn't start until nine-thirty and whenever Ebony suggested an early morning meeting, Kendall would protest that leaving the house before sunrise was unhealthy. Her partner strolled into the office at nine o'clock, sometimes later, and refused to work past three o'clock.

Ebony didn't let her partner's work habits bother her. Discreet Boutique was her baby. Her brainchild. She'd shared her dream with Kendall, and over time her best friend had bought into it. In the beginning, they had toiled day and night, shoulder to shoulder trying to get the business off the ground. But now that Discreet Boutiques had achieved financial success, Kendall didn't feel the need to put in as many hours. She had a husband to take care of, and he was priority number one now.

"We've done it, Ebony! Every year our sales surpass our projected revenue figures and our customers are more than satisfied with our merchandise. We shouldn't be working more, we should be working less!" she proclaimed.

Ebony begged to differ. She wasn't going to let anyone prevent her from achieving her goals. And as for "slowing down," she'd slow down when they had boutiques in all fifty states. Rest and relaxation would come when she was a multimillionaire. Then she would have the luxury of choosing her workdays or working from home. Until then, she had a plethora of work to do and no time to waste.

Generally Kendall's lackadaisical attitude didn't ruffle her, but when her partner ambled into the conference room a few minutes past ten o'clock, chattering into her cell phone, Ebony couldn't hold back her tongue. "How nice of you to join us, *Kendall.*"

"You're welcome," she replied casually. She ended her call, placed her cell phone on the table and checked her watch. Smiling ruefully at Ebony, she undid the lone button on her tangerine-colored blazer and took a seat. Her teakwood-brown complexion shimmered against the sun streaking through the conference room window. Kendall's soft and movable hair was flipped at the ends in a sassy style, and grazed the back of her neck. After opening her leather briefcase, she did a quick sweep of the agenda. "What have I missed?"

"Everything," Ebony mumbled. Disregarding the contrite expression on Kendall's face, she took a drink of her vanilla-flavored coffee. "I faxed a revised version of our existing contract to Mr. Rutherford for him to review. I am expecting to hear back from him today. If he doesn't agree to the specified terms, we'll have to shop around for a new trucking company." Ebony motioned with her hands. "Sabrina was about to fill us in on her new marketing proposal when you joined us. Go ahead, Sabrina. We're listening." She helped herself to another low-fat bran muffin and chased it down with coffee.

Sabrina clasped her hands in front of her. The bronze-skinned woman, who was all of five feet, might have resembled a sixth-grader but when she opened her mouth, people listened. She was feisty and outspoken and what she lacked in stature, she more than made up for in personality. "The Women of Sensuality products should elicit confidence, glamour and a sense of magic in our clients." The more animated Sabrina became, the more visible her accent was. After receiving a full academic scholarship from the University of Minneapolis, the Brazilian-raised woman had traveled to the United States to pursue a degree in business and marketing.

Sabrina picked up the red perfume bottle on the table and sprayed the scent around the room. She closed her eyes as if she was meditating. "When I smell Seduction perfume, I'm transported to another time and place. I see glorious sunsets, sandy beaches and can feel a gentle breeze whipping my hair around my face." Her eyes fluttered open. "To sum up all in one word, Women of Sensuality products should make our clients feel *irresistible*."

Ebony could barely contain her excitement. As usual, Sabrina was dead-on. She didn't know where her marketing director was going with this or how much it was going to set them back, but she was sold. She pressed her hands on the table, a smile dominating the corners of her mouth. "What do you think we should do to launch the product?"

"I'm glad you asked. The first thing we need to do is find a face. A name. An image. I contacted Beyoncé's people to see if she wanted to be the face of the Women of Sensuality line. Her assistant said Beyoncé's flattered that we considered her, but she has too many commitments to sign on with us right now. The woman suggested we try again in six months."

"Six months!" Kendall scoffed. She took a mouthful of herbal tea. "We can't wait around for the rest of the year.

Beyoncé is fabulous and all, but she's not the only celebrity woman synonymous with glamour and sensuality. I vote we move on to somebody else. What about Jada Pinkett Smith? Or Layla Ali? Or Kelly Rowland?"

Sabrina read from her notepad. "On tour with her band *Wicked Wisdom*. Training for an upcoming fight. And shooting a VH1 special about life after Destiny's Child." When Kendall sighed, Sabrina patted her hand. "No worries. I promise we'll get someone spectacular. There are some other ideas I'm flirting with, but I need another week or two to iron them out. I'll let you know what I come up with at the next meeting."

The next hour and a half was devoted to discussing company revenue, employee relations and how to increase sales. When Jocelyn poked her head inside the conference room and told Ebony she had an urgent call on line two, Ebony returned to her office. It was probably Mr. Rutherford. It wouldn't surprise her if she picked up the phone and he lashed out at her. The contract she had faxed over to his office was more than reasonable, but she had a feeling he wouldn't see it that way.

Ebony took a deep breath. She would need an extra dose of strength to get through this conversation with the officious warehouse manager. "This is Ms. Garrett," she greeted, in her friendliest voice.

A brief silence followed. "Hi, Ebony. How are you?"

Ebony didn't recognize the voice. "Fine, but I would be even better if I knew who was calling."

Another pause, this one considerably longer. "Xavier."

This was the urgent call? Ebony gripped the receiver. When she got off the phone, Jocelyn was going to get an earful. Ebony had given her secretary very strict orders not to put through personal calls while she was in meetings, and what did Jocelyn go ahead and do? Pull her out of the meeting to take an "urgent" call from a man she didn't want to talk to.

She wondered how he had gotten her number. "Hello. How did you get this number?" she asked, keeping her tone light.

"I have my sources. We missed you last week at Changing Lives Through Meals. What happened? You promised you'd be there."

Ebony didn't have the time to get into this. She was at work and if there was one thing she hated, it was when people brought their personal lives with them to the office. "There was an emergency at one of my boutiques last week." Before he could question her further about the problem she had just invented, she said, "I have to get back to work, but thanks for calling."

Kendall stuck her head inside Ebony's office. "The meeting just wrapped. We're going to lunch. You coming?"

She tilted the receiver away from her mouth. "If you're buying the drinks."

"Meet us down in the lobby in fifteen minutes."

Ebony nodded, then put the phone back to her lips. "Sorry about that."

"Do you think it's wise to be drinking in your condition?"

"I feel fine, Xavier. It only takes a couple days for food poisoning to—"

"I'm not talking about that," he cut in. It wasn't his place to tell Ebony how to live her life, but somebody had to educate her on the dangers of drinking alcohol while pregnant. Xavier had seen firsthand the challenges children with FAS had to face. Not to mention those kids born with facial abnormalities, heart defects, mental retardation or learning disabilities. "I know, Ebony." He paused long enough to push the rest of the words out of his mouth. "I know about the baby." The line was so quiet you could hear a pin drop miles away. "What you're doing to your unborn child is—"

"What child? I'm not pregnant!"

"You're not?"

"No! Why did you think I was?" She anticipated his response and added, "Just because I got sick doesn't mean that I'm pregnant. I had food poisoning, Xavier. That's all it was."

Xavier didn't know whether or not to tell Ebony what Ms. Certified Nurse had said. Some things were better left unsaid, he thought. And besides, he didn't want to risk sounding any more idiotic than she already thought he was. "Ebony, I'm really sorry. I guess I should learn to check my facts before I go off and start accusing people of things."

Ebony discounted his apology. She didn't care how handsome he was, or how scrumptious he smelled, or how her body tingled when he said her name. The man had some *serious* issues and his predisposition to judge people, namely her, was infuriating. Ebony couldn't abide any more accusations and there was no telling what would come out of his mouth next. "Goodbye, Xavier." With that, she clicked off the phone.

Taking a seat behind her desk, she leaned back in her chair. The man had some nerve. If there was one thing Ebony hated, it was people pointing fingers. Even if she was pregnant, it wasn't any of his business what she was doing with her body. He wasn't God; he couldn't part the sea or walk on water or turn water into wine. Xavier Reed apparently thought he was something special. Shaking her head, she wished she had taken the time to set him straight.

Ebony took a few minutes to calm herself. She didn't want to show up to lunch in a funk. When she felt better, she stood and grabbed her trench coat from the back of her chair. Discarding all thoughts of Xavier "Nosy" Reed, she slammed her office door behind her and told Jocelyn to hold her calls. As she was boarding the elevator, she heard Jocelyn ask Mr. Reed if he would like to leave a message.

Chapter 8

Xavier slumped back in his armchair, stunned. Dragging a hand down the length of his face, he wondered what had just happened. The lunch bell sounded but Xavier didn't move. He wasn't hungry. And besides, going to the staff room and listening to fellow teachers whine about how this student was that or the other would only aggravate him further. He was better off in his office.

Lockers squeaked, the rapid-fire talk of teenagers polluted the air, basketballs bounced on the tile floors and high-pitched giggles drowned it all out. Then the halls were quiet. The bird outside his window chirped merrily, but it did nothing to squelch the heaviness in his heart. *How could I have been such a jerk? And not once, but twice?*

Xavier had to find a way to rectify this situation. Something told him flowers and candy wouldn't be enough to soothe her bruised feelings. He had to come correct. Had to do something big. Huge. No, enormous. Something that would knock her off her feet. Just as he was about to pick up the phone and call his sister for some suggestions, bits and pieces of past conversations with Ebony came back to him. A slow smile stretched across his lips. Xavier knew exactly what he had to do. When he was finished with Ebony, she wouldn't know what hit her.

Somebody was going to lose an eye when Ebony got downstairs. Couldn't a woman sleep in anymore? If it wasn't aunt Mae calling at the first light of day, it was some jerk trying to sell her something she didn't need. Belting her silk robe, she stomped down the stairs, mumbling under her breath. Ebony worked like a dog during the week, and all she wanted on the weekends was to sleep in. *Just wait until I get down there,* she thought, growing more agitated with each shrill of the doorbell.

Ebony yanked open the door with such force, the long-limbed teenager in the white delivery uniform almost teetered off the steps.

The tail of her robe flapped in the wind, giving the pimpled adolescent a glimpse of her bare thigh. His eyes glistened like a puppy's, about to get its first meal of the day. Warm sunrays kissed her face; the cool morning breeze whipped her hair to and fro. She propped herself against the door, waiting impatiently for the teenager to speak.

"I have a package for a Ms. Garrett," he said in a shaky voice. When he spoke again, his sentence had more cracks in it than a sidewalk. "Sorry to disturb you, but my manager told me I had to deliver this—" he tipped his head toward the package in his hand "—before ten o'clock. Are you Ms. Garrett?"

She nodded and scribbled her name on the invoice. "Let me get you something for your trouble," she said as he turned away.

"No worries, ma'am. It's already been taken care of."

The teen jogged down the steps and climbed into a navy truck with the logo Spanky's Delivery Services on the side. When he waved, Ebony returned the gesture. She shut the door and thoroughly inspected the package. There was no card, no note and no hint as to who might have sent it. Not unusual. She hadn't expected to find one. None of the previous packages had had a card or a note, either. Anonymous gifts had been showing up for the last week. The first, two dozen helium balloons with the words Thinking About You, had arrived Monday afternoon while she was at lunch, and on Tuesday, it was a bottle of her favorite wine. A seafood lunch had been delivered on Wednesday and when she arrived home later that evening, an enormous box of edible chocolate roses was waiting for her on her welcome mat.

Thursday morning, Ebony had more than enough work to keep her occupied, but every five minutes she checked the clock. She was anxious to receive gift number four and jumped out of her chair every time there was a knock on her office door.

Over lunch, Ebony had listened to Sabrina and Jocelyn discuss who they thought her secret admirer was. Her receptionist thought it was one of the corporate attorneys who worked on the first floor; Sabrina was convinced it was an old flame who had finally come to his senses. Ebony pretended she didn't care who it was, but she did. Deep down, she was touched. What woman wouldn't be? Someone was going to great lengths to impress her. Romantic gestures of this magnitude were restricted to romance novels, Hollywood movies and dreamy love songs. Things like this just didn't happen to her. The man behind the gifts was sharp and Ebony found herself intrigued by the creative workings of his mind. Mr. Secret Admirer had taken the time to study her. He had investigated what her favorite things were, found unique ways to surprise her and kept her guessing. And even if it turned out that they were all wrong for each other, she would never forget him.

Thursday afternoon crawled by. No peculiar packages arrived. No deliveryman showed up. Nothing out of the ordinary happened. By the time Ebony left her office that evening, she was feeling low. She was so consumed with her thoughts, she didn't notice the card stuck in her windshield, until she unlocked the driver's side door. Inside the card was a list of twenty-five ways to beat stress. Ebony laughed until her stomach ached. Her mystery man had a rich sense of humor and she liked that.

Gift number five was propped up against the office door when Ebony arrived at work the next morning. A gift certificate for the ultraexclusive Serendipity Spa and Hair Salon in downtown Minneapolis suggested her secret admirer knew how to treat a woman right.

Ebony sat down on the couch. She shook the box. No rattle. No tinkle. No jangle. Not even a thump. When the last slither of wrapping paper was ripped off the box, a hand flew to Ebony's mouth. Inside the box was a five-disc CD set, entitled Jazz Vocal Greats.

A hundred thoughts whizzed through her head.

There was only one person who could have sent this.

One man.

One unbelievably handsome man.

Ebony sighed softly, an impish smile curling the corners of her mouth. Xavier Reed was something else. It had never crossed her mind that he could be the man behind all the gifts. Xavier just didn't strike her as the type who would go all out to impress a woman. But he had.

Ebony studied the cover of the CD set. An extended version of "Come Rain or Come Shine" by Art Bailey and George Benson's "Kisses in the Moonlight" would inevitably become her favorites. She turned the box over, anxious to see what other artists she could look forward to hearing. A single slice of paper was taped to the back of the case. It read, "I'll be there at four to pick you up."

Ebony combed over the nine words to ensure she had read it correctly. Xavier was taking her out? If someone had told her yesterday that not only was Xavier the man behind the presents but he would cap off the week by taking her out, Ebony would have laughed in their face. *Why did he go through all this trouble?* she wondered, rising to her feet. Xavier didn't want a woman like her. He was a good old-fashioned church boy. Soft-spoken. Decorous. And as hard as it was for her to believe, chaste. He rarely drank, he didn't smoke, he didn't do drugs and his last relationship had ended six months earlier. When Ebony asked Xavier how he managed to control his urges in a society inundated with sex-sex-sex, he had credited his pastor and his parents for keeping him on the straight and narrow. Gloria and Theodore Reed had been married for thirty-plus years and according to their son, still fawned over each other like a couple of teenagers. That's what Xavier said he wanted. He wanted a woman who would love him unconditionally. He was searching for a type of love that came around only once in a person's lifetime, and if he was lucky enough to recognize it, he'd embrace it.

Ebony was unsure of what to make of all this. Xavier had something up his sleeve. But what? Flashbacks of their last conversation came back to mind. *Maybe this is his way of saying sorry.* Ebony stood up. She had much to do between now and four o'clock and not a moment to waste. Closing the doors to her thoughts, she raced back upstairs to her bedroom.

"Wrong. Wrong. Wrong," Ebony said, as outfit number three sailed to the floor. She combed through her closet, decided on a skintight apple-green dress and was in the process of putting it on when she heard the doorbell. *Oh no! He's early!* Ebony couldn't let Xavier see her like this. No makeup. Half dressed. Hair uncombed. He would take one look at her and sprint down the walkway faster than Carl Lewis.

The doorbell rang again.

Ebony checked her options. Go downstairs looking like a mess, or risk him leaving because he thought she wasn't home. The latter was a far worse fate. Dinner at Dakota's Bar and Grill had been a disaster, but Ebony wasn't going to start date number two on the wrong foot. She dashed down the staircase. Displaying her most seductive smile, she opened the front door. "You're early."

Kendall smirked. "No, I'm not. You didn't even know I was stopping by."

"I thought you were someone else."

"And I thought we were supposed to meet at the office. What happened? Everything okay?"

"Couldn't be better. Sorry, I should have called. I had every intention of coming in, but things changed. I have a date with my secret admirer." She couldn't resist asking, "You remember what a date is, don't you, Ken?"

Kendall stuck out her tongue, and Ebony laughed.

"So, did Mr. Romantic turn out to be Gavin, or Michael?"

"Neither."

"Well?" she prompted. "Don't leave me hanging, who is it?"

"Xavier."

"Hum… That's the church guy, right?"

Ebony shot her friend a look. "Don't call him that. He's the fine guy, *not* the church guy. Get it straight, girlfriend." She returned upstairs to her bedroom, her best friend hot on her heels.

Kendall made herself at home on the bed. "Fill me in. Start from the beginning and don't skim over the juicy parts."

Ebony told Kendall everything. By the time she was finished, they were both laughing. "It was bad, Kendall."

"I hear you. Sounds like the two of you had the date from hell!"

"We did, that's why it is so hard for me to believe that Xavier was behind all those gifts. Most men would fall off the face of the earth if their date had gotten sick like a dog on the first date. Having him carry me out of the restaurant was the single most humiliating experience in my life." Ebony dragged the curling iron down her hair and sprayed the ends with hair spray.

"At least he cared enough about you to make sure you were okay. *Not* like that bone-headed husband of mine, who only cares about himself."

Ebony took a close look at Kendall. Her bottom lip was quivering, her shoulders were hunched and she looked as if she was about to cry. "Uh-oh. What did Turner do now?"

Ebony had never seen a woman love a man the way Kendall loved her husband. In some ways it was touching, in other ways it was disturbing. Ebony had never taken a psychology course, but she knew it wasn't healthy for a woman to worship a man the way Kendall did Turner. Turner was the be-all and end-all. His opinion was the *only* opinion. Ebony wouldn't be surprised if one day Kendall opened her mouth and said, "Thus saith Turner Douglas…" Kendall punctuated her sentences with "Turner says," and "Turner thinks," and when she wasn't yammering about what a delight he was, she was gazing off into the sunset, thoughts of him clearly on her mind.

Ebony would never admit it, but she inwardly rejoiced when the couple had a fight. Because when the couple argued, Kendall shut up about how wonderful Turner was. She excluded him from all conversations and didn't want anyone around her to mention his name, either. Ebony, and the rest of their employees, got a much-needed break from Juliet nattering on about Romeo. A Kendall and Turner blowout usually lasted for a few days. The reprieve wasn't long enough, but it was better than nothing. For two full days, Ebony didn't have to hear about how great Turner was or how he did this or that wonderfully.

"Before Turner left for the hospital this morning, he pointed out that I was due for my next Depo shot. I reminded him that we agreed *we* would try getting pregnant this year, and therefore I didn't need to make another appointment. You know what he said?"

Ebony shrugged.

"He said '*we* did? Well, I think we should wait another year.' I was so angry I started crying. He stormed out of the kitchen and I haven't heard from him since."

"Why is he so dead set against this? You've been married long enough, you're financially stable and the two of you have a solid relationship. What more does he want?" Turner treated Kendall fabulously and had been spoiling her silly since they met on a singles' cruise, six years ago. He was devoted, responsible and sensitive to his wife's needs, but when it came to getting pregnant, he kept stalling.

"Every year it's the same story, 'we'll try next year. We'll try next year,'" Kendall ranted, mimicking her husband's voice. "But we're no closer to getting pregnant than a ninety-year-old woman with a hot stud and a bottle full of fertility drugs."

Ebony laughed so hard, she had to put the curling iron down to keep from burning herself.

Unable to share in her friend's laughter, Kendall stared sadly out of the bedroom window. "I just don't know what to do anymore. Turner just doesn't seem to get it. I'm thirty-three. *Thirty-three,*" she stressed, "but he keeps saying, 'We're young, we're young. Don't worry, don't worry. We've got plenty of time.' *Right.* My biological clock is ticking so loud it's keeping me up at night!"

Ebony knew her best friend was being serious, but she couldn't ignore the hilarity of it all. When Kendall was upset, she was as funny as a stand-up comedian. Applying mascara generously to her eyelashes to create a sultry look, Ebony watched her friend through the three-way mirror. "Don't you think you're being a tad dramatic, Ken? Turner's right, you're only—" She broke off when she saw Kendall's eyes fill with tears. "Go on, Kendall, I'm listening."

When she spoke again, her voice was full of emotion. "I want to get pregnant more than anything in this world."

Ebony wanted to ask Kendall if that included the dreams they shared for the business, but didn't. Great question, wrong time.

"I want to wear cute maternity clothes from Two Peas in a Pod, send Turner out in the middle of the night to satisfy my cravings and decorate the baby's room in shades of pink or blue. I want to be a young mom. I don't want to be pushing a stroller when I'm in my forties."

"What are you going to do about it?"

Kendall's shoulders sagged. "Don't know."

"That's the problem with love," Ebony announced, as if she was a trained therapist and Kendall was one of her clients. "Women compromise to make their partners happy and when it's all said and done, they end up losing out. In every relationship, there is one who gives and one who takes. Kendall, I hate to say this, but you're the giver and Turner's the taker."

Kendall fingered the tassels on the Egyptian-style pillow-case. "You're not helping, Ebony. I need advice about what to do about this baby issue. I don't want to hear your opinion about what's wrong with relationships."

"The solution is actually quite simple, Ken. Tell that hus-band of yours that you're ready to start a family and if he doesn't get with the program, you're going to have to look into other alternatives."

"I can't do that! I don't have any other alternatives," she said.

Maybe I need to take another approach, Ebony thought, turning around to face Kendall. Her best friend looked utterly pitiful. Long face, sad eyes, hunched shoulders. Ebony sat down on the bed and wrapped an arm around Kendall. "Tell Turner exactly what you just told me. Your husband's a stand-up guy. He'll come around, I'm sure of it. And if he doesn't, implement the 'no baby, no nooky' rule."

"The what?"

"You heard me, the 'no baby, no nooky' rule. If Turner doesn't get his act together, then cut him off."

A small smile formed on Kendall's lips. "I like that." She giggled to herself. "'No baby, no nooky.' That could be my new slogan."

"Now you're talking!"

Ebony was set to give more advice when she heard the doorbell chime. She sprang to her feet like a racehorse out of the gate. Hauling Kendall off the bed, she pushed her toward the bedroom door and said, "Go and let Xavier in. Tell him I'll be down in two shakes of a lamb's tail."

Kendall planted a hand on her hip. "Well, how about that? Ms. Ebony has gone off and found herself a man!"

Chapter 9

Oh, mercy, mercy, me, Xavier thought, repeating the infamous words of R&B crooner Marvin Gaye. His eyes raked over Ebony's mouthwatering physique and lingered on her hips. *Nothing is more aesthetically beautiful than a black woman's body.*

Sauntering down the stairs as if she had all the time in the world, Ebony shot him an award-winning smile. Her electric-blue, off-the-shoulder top outlined the mold of her breasts, and her short black skirt, which grazed her thighs, highlighted the definition in her long legs. Bouncy curls framed her face and the sumptuous smile she was wearing suggested she was ready for more than just an afternoon in the park.

Xavier ran a hand over his hair. He would need an extra dose of discipline and self-control today. Ebony was sensual and erotic and had the bodacious personality to match. Her hip-swinging walk, the way she ran her tongue over her bee-stung lips, and her throaty laugh were mesmerizing. Xavier found himself wanting to touch her, and the twinkle in her eyes told him she was reading his thoughts.

When Ebony reached the foot of the stairs, she bent down and adjusted the straps on her sandals. Her shirt dipped, exposing the soft curves of her cleavage. Xavier gulped. Yeah, Ebony Garrett knew exactly what to do to make a man sweat. It was bad enough he was nervous, now he had to worry about gawking at her every time she moved. Xavier felt like it was prom night—minus the overpriced limo, frilly corsage and awkward meeting with her parents, but he was just as tense. He had the sweaty palms and ragging pulse to prove it.

Xavier didn't hear her friend say goodbye, but he did hear the front door close behind her. His eyes brushed over her body approvingly. Her fine hips and well-rounded thighs were nice and firm. "Blue is definitely your color," he heard himself say out loud.

Ebony inclined her head to the right. Had she heard him right? Was he actually complimenting her? She resisted the urge to shake her head.

Xavier took a lungful of her floral-scented perfume, feeling no shame for what he was about to say. "If I had to sum up your look in one word, it would be sexy. You look amazing and you smell good, too."

Desire shone brightly in his eyes and there was an unmistakable bulge in the front of his shorts. Ebony smiled sweetly, impeding the laughter rising up her throat.

"Thanks," she told him. Her hungry eyes worked their way over his six-foot frame. "You don't look too bad yourself, Xavier. Nice legs." A short sleeve camel-brown T-shirt had been paired with black shorts and sandals. He resembled a Scout leader in his casual attire, but his quiet confidence was definitely a turn-on.

They smiled at each other, neither one sure of what to say. Xavier felt a powerful desire to kiss her, but he didn't. As tempting as it was, he didn't want to start off their time together by making out.

"I *love* the CD set, Xavier," Ebony confessed, "and all the other gifts, as well. Thanks for brightening up my week."

"I felt bad about…well, everything and I just wanted to make it up to you."

A seductive smile fashioned itself to her lips. "You didn't have to go out and buy me anything," she said moving closer. "You could have given me something else. Something more… um, personal."

Xavier reached out and slipped a hand around her waist. A great tenderness washed over him as she curled herself into his body. All he wanted was one kiss. That would satisfy his curiosity. Her sultry sex appeal was hypnotic: the depths of her nut-brown eyes, her delicate button nose and her soft, luscious hair. And the more time he spent with her the more he felt his self-control and common sense recede. Now was a perfect example. The desire to kiss her was suddenly an all-consuming need.

Ebony waited. She wanted to kiss him, but didn't want to risk driving him away. Xavier had to be the one to set the pace. He had to be the one who called the shots. An old-fashioned guy like Xavier wouldn't take well to a woman putting the moves on him. Acquiescence was a new role for Ebony, but it was one she was willing to try. Something told her Xavier was worth it.

"So," he began, unsure of what to say.

There's nothing wrong with giving him a little push, Ebony thought, angling her head to the right. "The ball is in your court, Xavier. What's your next move?" Parting her lips to receive his kiss, she closed her eyes tight, and waited.

He responded to her query by grazing his lips across hers. When that failed to mollify his desire, he captured her lips with his mouth. Xavier had never tasted a mouth so sweet. So willing. So open. *Ebony Garrett sure knows how to kiss,* he thought, as her tongue probed his. *She's kissing me like she's making love to my mouth!*

Ebony's passions were kindled by Xavier's light intimate touches, but then he sucked on her bottom lip like it was a cinnamon-flavored lollipop. All hell broke loose. Pressing herself to his chest, she slipped a hand under his shirt. She threw her head back as if she was being tormented and Xavier granted her unspoken wish. He planted kisses down her neck, touching and teasing her breasts through her shirt. Lost as he was in the moment and the feel of her caress, his mouth slowly adjusted to her speed and intensity.

The shrill of the telephone jarred Xavier back to the present. His eyes flapped open. He was in Ebony's living room, not back in his bedroom like he'd envisioned. *This is the first date for God's sake! Get it together, man.* Xavier released his hold.

Ebony stared up at him, her face lined with confusion. Kissing Xavier Reed was a truly sensual experience, one that she wasn't ready to end just yet. God, he can kiss, she thought. *I bet that's not all he can do.* She liked his technique. Lots of tongue. Lots of passion. Her kind of kisser.

"The phone's ringing." When she made no moves to answer it, he said, "Aren't you going to answer it?"

She stepped back into his space. "That's what answering machines are for." But when Ebony heard Gavin's sleepy voice beg her to pick up the phone, she almost knocked Xavier out of the way to answer the call. Not because she was anxious to talk to her ex, but because Gavin was notorious for leaving lengthy messages. Once, when she was away for the weekend, she returned home to find ten messages on her machine. He had blathered on and on about how much he missed her, but she never returned his call.

Ebony snatched up the receiver. "Gavin, I can't talk to you right now. No, I won't be home." She agreed to call him later and expeditiously ended the phone call. A smile was on her face when she turned back to Xavier. Ebony didn't know why, but she suddenly felt the need to explain. "That was an old friend."

"An old friend, huh? What kind of friend?"

Ebony sidestepped his question by asking one of her own. "Ready to go?"

Xavier looked around the living room. The sun streamed in from the windows and bounced around. Everything, from the furniture to the antique picture frames to the vibrant, oriental-themed rugs, looked ridiculously expensive. The room was as wide as it was long, and housed an enormous cantilever that held the biggest big-screen TV he had ever seen. Ebony obviously attached a lot of importance to material possessions and had spared no expense in outfitting her home. "What? Trying to get rid of me already? I was hoping you'd give me a tour of your *palace,*" Xavier teased, a wide smirk on his lips. "I've been dying to see how the other side lives."

"The other side?"

"The rich."

"I'm not rich."

"I beg to differ, Ms. Garrett."

Ebony didn't appreciate being teased. She had worked hard to buy this house and she didn't like Xavier poking fun at her. Her face took on an ugly look, as she crossed her arms under her chest. Ebony had dated enough to know that most men were intimidated by women who made more money than they did. She didn't care what a man did as long as he treated her well. Diamonds and furs didn't mean anything to Ebony;

it was confidence and intelligence that won her over each time. "Does it bother you that I make more money than you?"

"Of course not!" Xavier touched a hand to her shoulder. "I didn't mean to upset you, Ebony. I was just joking around. This place looks fabulous. Really." He turned the corners of his mouth down and stuck out his bottom lip. "Forgive me?"

Ebony cracked up. Xavier looked like a puppy dog with his droopy lips and sad eyes. She told him all was forgiven and laughed some more when he pulled her back into his arms for a bear hug.

"I still want a tour."

Thankful she had taken a few minutes to straighten up that morning, she took him by the hand and led him into the kitchen. Ebony didn't want Xavier to think she was a slob, so she wisely sped past the main floor laundry room. Upstairs, she gave him a quick tour of her office, the spare bedroom and the game room.

When they reached the master bedroom, Xavier's eyes spread wide in shock. It was hard to believe that an outspoken, business-minded woman like Ebony Garrett could be so feminine. The room had pink walls, enough flowers to beautify a church and red heart-shaped pillows sat on the middle of the king-size sleigh bed.

The next stop on the tour was the fully developed basement. Xavier paused to examine the graduation pictures hanging on the wall. "Are these your parents?"

"Simeon and Ingrid Garrett," she said, in a flat tone of voice. Ebony loathed the photograph, but it was the only picture taken with her parents at graduation. Her father was scowling as if he had stubbed his toe and her mother didn't look much better in an unsightly, black and white polka dot dress that should have been tossed out years before. Ebony remembered how Simeon had raised hell when Ingrid asked him for money to buy a new dress. "Money doesn't grow on trees," he'd barked, cutting his eyes in her direction. "Just wear some ole thing in your closet. Nobody's going to be looking at you anyway."

Ebony would never understand why a grown woman, who worked full-time and earned twice as much money as her husband, had to ask *him* for money. Not wanting Xavier to ask any more questions about her family, she shepherded him back upstairs and out the front door.

Chapter 10

Ebony motioned toward the entrance of Martin Luther King Jr. Park with her index finger. "Wow! Look at all the people lined up to get into the park."

Xavier directed his gaze to where she was pointing. A mischievous grin settled over his mouth. "With a crowd that thick I'm going to have to keep *both* eyes on you."

I wish you would, Ebony thought.

Marveling at how perfect she looked, Xavier stole a glance at her. His smile grew, as he listened to her sing along with the Aretha Franklin song playing on the radio. Ebony wasn't musically inclined, but her enthusiasm made up for what she lacked in talent. Her face had a soft shimmer to it, like she had been sitting underneath the sun. Not a hair was out of place and her outfit was wrinkle-free. Returning his eyes to the road, he searched for a parking space. Circling the lot for the third time, he stole another quick peek at his passenger.

He didn't know why, but he felt like this was going to be a special day. Maybe it was something in the air. Or maybe it was that body-tingling kiss they had shared in her living room.

Once the car was parked and the engine was off, Xavier slid out of the driver's seat.

"You are quite the quintessential gentleman," Ebony commented, when he opened her door. Taking the hand he so graciously offered, she stepped out of the car. Well aware that the heat passing between them had little to do with the sunshine and everything to do with chemistry, she squeezed his hand. "It's refreshing to be out with a man who opens doors and pulls out chairs."

He joked, "What can I say? Some brothers just have it like that."

Ebony laughed.

"I can't take all the credit. My mom had something to do with it."

"Tell Mrs. Reed I said she did an exceptional job."

Touched by the compliment, he draped an arm casually around her waist. The sights and sounds of spring welcomed the couple as they strolled toward the park and, after a short wait, through its open gates.

Music lovers, eager to take advantage of the pleasant May afternoon, descended on Martin Luther King Jr. Park for the International Jazz Festival like bees to a honeycomb. The stomach-grumbling aroma of hot dogs, ice cream and fried doughnuts pervaded the air, and lines at the refreshment stands clogged the walkway.

"Hey, here comes Palmer, Conway and Slaughter."

Three taller-than-average men, with thick bodies and broad grins, were heading their way. "Hey, guys. What's up?" Ebony looked on as Xavier greeted each man with a high-five and a manly hug.

Xavier put a hand on her back. "Ebony, this is Darius, Juan and Nathan. We play on the same recreational football team."

Ebony exchanged hellos and nice-to-meet-yous with the men. The group talked about the musical guests slated to appear that afternoon, and the guys chuckled heartily when Ebony glanced up at the sky and said, "It better not rain 'cause I just got my hair done."

While the quartet discussed their next game, Ebony scanned the park. Martin Luther King Jr. Park had never looked so clean. The grass was trimmed, an assortment of spring flowers lined the pavement and there wasn't a stitch of garbage anywhere. Couples strolled hand in hand, families reclined on the lawn under monstrous trees and die-hard fans bordered the stage, waiting anxiously for the musicians to appear.

Spotting a street vendor pushing a cart filled with everything from water to dried fruit, Ebony popped open her purse and pulled out some money. When there was an interlude in the conversation, she politely excused herself. "Xavier, I'm going to go and get a snack. Do you want anything?"

"A bottle of water would be great."

She nodded. "It was nice meeting you guys."

Bug-eyed, the four men watched her sashay over to one of the street vendor carts.

Darius wiped the sweat away from his forehead. Xavier's date was a woman of indescribable beauty. She was sophisticated and everything about her was sexy. Her smile. Her walk. Even her laugh. Nudging Xavier with his elbow, he asked, "Where in the world did you find baby girl?" He shook his head wistfully. "I'm not trying to knock you down or anything but Ms. Thang is *way* out of your league. Honey needs a man with my charm and expertise, so why don't you slide me her number?"

Xavier chuckled.

"A young pup like you can't handle all that woman, X," Nathan chimed in.

Juan couldn't resist. "Careful, boy, girlfriend looks like she could put a hurtin' on you."

"Back to my original question," Darius cut in impatiently, "where did you meet her and where can I get one just like her?"

"I met Ebony at the church banquet I invited *you* three knuckleheads to." When Darius's mouth cracked open, Xavier jabbed a finger at his chest. "I think your exact words were 'church is for suckers.'" In a mocking tone of voice, he said, "See, that's what you get for not listening to me. The food was delicious, the entertainment was incredible and there was a roomful of gorgeous, professional women."

Darius released a slow whistle. "If there are sisters at your church who look like *that,* sign me up, X. I'm there!"

After two hours of fighting the crowds and contending with the heat and humidity, Ebony and Xavier were starving. While she hunted for a secluded space at the park, he set off in search of lunch.

A frown formed between her eyebrows when she spotted Xavier. He was headed straight for her, but he didn't have hot dogs or hamburgers or chilli cheese fries. "What's that?" she asked as he approached.

"A cooler."

"What's in it?"

Xavier had an amused glint in his eyes. "You'll see." He spread a white blanket on the grass and unloaded the cooler. Bacon and lettuce sandwiches, a fruit platter laced with watermelon, pineapple and cantaloupe, homemade fruit punch, and cinnamon buns covered the width of the blanket in mere seconds. Jazz music playing softly in the background, supplied a romantic scene. The delightful shrieks of children far off in the distance made Ebony suddenly feel youthful and free.

Ebony looked down at the blanket. Xavier had thought of everything. No paper plates for them, either; he had brought along dishes, cutlery and even wineglasses. "Did you make all this?" she asked, once he was finished blessing the food.

"Everything but the fruit."

Ebony laughed. While they ate, they spoke freely about their backgrounds. In the next hour, she learned that he had had a fleeting basketball career overseas, had been to all seven continents, and spoke French and Spanish fluently.

"French and Spanish? Wow! That's impressive. I had the hardest time just trying to master English!"

Xavier chuckled. "My great-great-grandparents' immigrated to America from French Guiana, back in the early fifties. My mother wanted us to retain as much of the culture as possible so she forced us to take French classes at the local YMCA. Jackie and I joined the Guianese Association and there we learned how to make traditional foods like cumin chicken, tomato rice and my specialty, callaloo soup. Every other year, my parents took us to Guiana for summer vacation. Jackie and I had the time of our lives. We swam in the ocean, played with our cousins and even climbed coconut trees."

"I envy you, Xavier. You have such a rich background." What she didn't say was that she wished her parents had taken that kind of interest in her. Ebony helped herself to another piece of fruit. "Say something to me in French."

"La prochaine fois que nous dinons, vous allez être le... cuisiner."

Ebony fanned herself with her hands. "Ooh! I don't know what you said or what it means, but it sounded good! What did you say?"

"I said, 'the next time we have dinner, you're going to cook!'"

They shared a laugh.

"I know you probably get asked this all the time, but what's it like being a twin? Do you and Jacqueline get along?"

"Do black people like chicken?" Xavier chortled at his own joke, and Ebony couldn't help laughing, too. She was high on fresh air and conversation and Xavier could do no wrong. "It's true what they say about twins. We share the same thoughts, finish each other's sentences, and I know this is going to be hard to believe, but when something's wrong with Jackie, I can sense it. It sounds spooky, but it's just a part of who we are. She got remarried last year and she and her husband are expecting their first child."

Xavier stared at the family of four meandering past, a contemplative expression on his face.

"How many kids do you want?" Ebony could see Xavier with a whole bunch of kids. His warm nature would make him an excellent father.

"I don't know, but five sounds like a good number."

"That's five too many for me."

"You don't want to have kids? Why?"

Ebony took another piece of watermelon from the bowl and bit into it. Watermelon juice dribbled down her chin. She patted her mouth with a napkin and wiped her hands. "I couldn't imagine balancing a family with my hectic career. I love what I do and I've worked hard to get where I am. The way I see it is, some women are destined to achieve greatness in the business world and some are destined to be incredible wives and mothers. I think I fall into the first category."

As Ebony shielded her eyes from the sun, her mind wandered back to her childhood days. She had never had dolls or played house when she was a little girl; firecrackers, trucks and action figures had been her favorite toys. Her dreams had never revolved around being a wife or a mother. All she had ever dreamed about was being a firefighter. At twelve, she had shelved the idea of running into burning buildings and instead, spent hours combing teen magazines for the latest trends in clothes, hair and makeup.

Ebony had never been wedding-obsessed. Not even in college, when her closest friends were getting engaged and all she heard about was designer gowns, guest lists and honeymoon destinations. When she thought about marriage, there was only one word that came to mind: misery. And she had her parents to thank for that.

"Marriage is hard work," Xavier was saying when Ebony returned to the conversation. "But nothing worth having in life is easy." He studied her for a few seconds. "I'm surprised you think you can't balance having a family and a career. You strike me as the type of woman who can accomplish anything she puts her mind to."

She acknowledged his compliment with a smile. "A few years ago I bought the cutest brown terrier. I bought all the pet supplies the clerk recommended and took her home. I had the dog bed, the fancy combs, all the grooming supplies and the most expensive dog food, but you know what? After three weeks I had to return Lace to the pet store. She ended up being too much responsibility and I couldn't handle it all. Pathetic, huh?"

Xavier smiled softly. "Not at all."

"Could you imagine me taking care of a baby?" Ebony shuddered at the thought.

"Are there other reasons why you don't want to have children?"

This time when Ebony spoke, she did from her heart. "I didn't have much of a relationship with my parents. My dad was a city bus driver and my mom was a supervisor at a convalescent home. They spent their entire day serving other people and by the time they got home, they didn't have anything left to give to me. My dad, Simeon, was a bully and my mother buckled under his domineering personality. Most of the time, I just stayed in my room reading and doing crossword puzzles. I found ways to keep myself busy, but I always envied the close relationships my classmates had with their parents."

Xavier didn't want to pry, but he wanted to know more. The loneliness and pain she had endured as a child were evident in her voice, and outlined in her eyes. He ached to take her in his arms and stoke away the hurtful words and neglect she had faced. "What's your relationship with your parents like now?" he queried, after a notable pause. "Are you on better terms?"

"They died in a car accident eight years ago."

Xavier reached out and covered her hands with his own.

The welcomed gesture made Ebony yearn for more. Much more. It had been months since she had felt the soothing touch of a man's hands. Three months to be exact. She found herself fantasizing about what it would be like to make love to Xavier. He was generous and polite, and if his personality was any indication of what he was like in bed, he was probably a tender, patient lover. Ebony could do tender and patient. She would do anything he wanted her to. The sound of his voice snapped her mind into focus.

"I'm sorry about your parents." Xavier shook his head sadly, his eyes communicating that he understood what Ebony must have gone through. "I don't know what I would do if I lost one of my parents, let alone both. That must have been a difficult time for you."

Ebony could only nod. He had no idea.

Xavier wanted to know how she had survived losing her parents. Maybe hearing about that time in her life might give him insight into why she was so fiercely independent. He was starting to understand why Ebony felt the need to be in control all the time. She had been taking care of herself for years. "Do you feel uncomfortable talking about what happened?"

"No." Ebony was uncomfortable, but not because they were talking about the death of her parents. She didn't want Xavier to think less of her than he already did. If she bared her soul to him, told him she didn't shed a single tear during the ordeal and didn't miss them, Xavier would label her heartless.

Ebony had tried for years to win her parents' affection with no success. She survived her high school years on a meager five hours of sleep a night, and studied relentlessly in the hopes of having the highest grades in her class. She'd succeeded. But when Ebony told her father she was going to be valedictorian, he mumbled congratulations and continued watching the nightly news.

That was the day Ebony had given up trying to impress him. She had surrounded herself with friends, and spent more time with her aunt Mae. In her mind, Simeon and Ingrid Garrett had died long before Officer Huntington stood in the dimly lit foyer and told her the tragic news. Ebony remembered that bitter winter day as if it were yesterday, rather than almost a decade ago.

Her entire body had gone numb and then her legs had slipped out from underneath her. Aunt Mae said she had passed out, but to this day Ebony couldn't remember what happened. The days following were a blur. Flowers arrived in what seemed like hundreds, visitors came by to offer their sympathies and funeral arrangements were made. Food was cooked, desserts were baked and when the day of the burial finally arrived, all eyes were on her. But Ebony held it together. She cried, but not for her parents. She wept for what could have been. The missed hugs. The words of encouragement. Their unwavering love and support.

There is no fear in love; perfect love casts out all fear, the minister had said, his gentle eyes searching her face. His message of hope was simple and touched her deeply. An overwhelming sense of peace had washed over her as she listened to him speak. And when the last guest had left her parents' house five hours later, Ebony had a plan and a purpose for her life.

"How did your parents meet?" Xavier wanted Ebony to open up to him. Trust was the foundation for every relationship, regardless of the degree, and he wanted her to know he could be trusted with her secrets.

The silver bangles on Ebony's hand clanked together when she dusted bread crumbs off her skirt. As her eyes drifted around the park grounds, she thought about the answers. Simeon and Ingrid's eighteen-year marriage had been one of convenience, not love. When Ingrid had discovered she was three months pregnant, Simeon had done the right thing by proposing. There was no elaborate wedding with family and friends. The occasion hadn't been commemorated with wine toasts, photographs and wedding cake. A civil court ceremony on a frosty Tuesday afternoon, an office receptionist and security guard the only witnesses, had been sufficient for the penniless couple.

Ebony didn't know how to answer Xavier's question. Vacillating between sharing her most vivid childhood memories and changing the topic altogether, she said, "You have a lot of personal questions, Xavier. Are you trying to figure out why I don't want to have children, or convince me that the past has little bearing on one's future?"

"You may not have had a picture-perfect childhood, Ebony, but that doesn't mean you wouldn't make a good mother. I think you'd be a kind and loving parent." Xavier winked. "What child wouldn't be thrilled to call you Momma?"

A smile found its way on to Ebony's lips. *Me a mother?* A comfortable silence hovered over them, allowing enough time for her to digest her thoughts. Ebony watched as people packed up their supplies and strolled leisurely toward the park entrance. The park was virtually empty but the musicians kept right on playing.

Xavier felt something stir within him. He didn't know if it was the way Ebony looked, so feminine and pretty, or learning about her troubled upbringing, but he wanted her in his arms. Something about being with her felt right. The space between them suddenly seemed restrictive. Xavier reached out and caressed her cheek. In response she nuzzled her face against his hand.

Ebony knew that if they were ever going to get anywhere, Xavier had to be the one to make the first move, so she waited patiently. She leaned into him, and he took it from there. He glided his tongue into her mouth, tasting and teasing. The scent of her skin was intoxicating. It enveloped him like a hug. Lost as they were in their own escape, the distant chatter whirling around them ceased to exist. Wanting, needing, aching, Xavier palmed and stroked her breasts through her flimsy shirt. He fondled and plucked. Ebony was the type of woman a man could never get enough of. She was so sensual and utterly erotic, it hurt.

Ebony was hot. Her skin was tingling, her nipples were hard, and she could feel moisture building between her legs. Apt fingers brushed back and forth across his crotch. Then, in one fluid motion, her hands were inside his shorts and she was stroking his shaft.

Xavier moaned. Returning the favor, he unhooked her bra and took her breasts into his hands. Soon, the feel of her nipples under his fingertips was not enough. He wanted to capture a nipple in his mouth, and suck it until his tongue was sore.

Ebony wanted him in the worst possible way. Well aware that they were in a public place, she forced herself to maintain an element of control. But as their kisses and touches intensified, Ebony found it an impossible task. She wanted to rip off Xavier's shirt and taste every inch of him. Love him like he had never been loved before. Brand him with the heat of her lips. Stroke him to ecstasy with the work of her hands. Show him a kind of pleasure he had never known before.

"I…should take you…home," Xavier stammered, ending the kiss. He checked the zipper on his pants, his eyes flittering nervously around the park. *Thank God no one's watching.* They were the only couple left on the east side of the field, and as far as he could see, the once thriving crowd of music lovers had thinned. Darkness had swallowed up the day, the glow of the stars the only light.

Xavier didn't know what had gotten into him. He had been one second away from hoisting up her skirt, plunging deep inside her and satisfying his craving. Never mind that they were in a public place or that they were on their first "official" date or that he had promised himself he wouldn't go there with her. Xavier knew things had gotten out of hand but he had felt powerless to resist.

Xavier averted his gaze from her eyes. One deep breath followed another. He poured himself some juice and gulped it down. Within seconds, his head had cleared and he was back in control. "It's getting late," he stated, checking his watch. The sun was sinking behind the clouds and the temperature had dropped considerably. "We should go. We're the last ones here."

Good, she thought, her lips curving into a sinuous smile. Ebony didn't want to leave. She wanted more. They were in a deserted park and the possibilities were endless. Ready to finish what Xavier had started, she kissed him again.

When they broke away, she could see his resolve was faltering. His eyes were heavy with lust and his breathing was quick and ragged. "I think we should stay," she told him, putting a hand to his cheek.

Xavier stood to his feet.

"I don't get it…we were on the verge of…I thought you wanted to—" Ebony stopped. There was no point in going on. Xavier wasn't listening. He was busying himself with gathering up the empty food containers. Garbage was thrown out, plates and utensils were returned to the cooler and the blanket was folded and tucked under his arm.

"Ready?"

Ebony nodded and followed him through the park.

"Are you free tomorrow?" he asked, once they were back inside his car. Xavier wanted to see her again, but he didn't want to appear eager. Women didn't respond well to being smothered, especially independent ones like Ebony. She didn't have to verbalize her feelings, but he knew she didn't want anyone getting too close.

"What do you have in mind?" Ebony hoped it was more of what they had left behind in the park. She had expected the day to end on a high note, not with her sexually frustrated and entertaining thoughts of breaking out her little black book. Xavier had dangled explosive, toe-curling sex in front of her and then snatched it away. Ebony wanted to make love tonight, but it wouldn't do any good to call up one of her old loves. Xavier Reed was the only man she wanted.

Ebony looked over at Xavier. He was clearly Mr. self-control. She didn't know anybody who had that type of discipline. It was a commendable trait. Not one that could be fully appreciated or admired at the present moment, but maybe after an ice-cold shower she would reflect on all of his formidable qualities.

"I'd like you to come with me to church."

He can't be serious. Church as a second date? Ebony wanted to see him again, but she didn't want to go to church. They couldn't talk in church. Or laugh at each other's jokes.

Or kiss. And besides, churches were filled with imperfect, hypocritical people, who wagged their crooked fingers at others. Ebony would rather stay home and watch Bishop T.D. Jakes from the comfort of her sofa than go to a real life church any day. Mock smiles, insincere welcomes and stilted conversation would greet her at the front door and finger pointing and hushed voices would guide her down the aisles.

"My sister and her husband will be there and I'd love for you to meet them." Xavier pulled out of the parking space, and followed the trail of cars leaving the park grounds. "Afterward, we can all go for lunch." He put a hand on her lap. "I promise not to take you to Dakota's."

Ebony laughed. "Why don't you call me in the morning? I'll let you know how I'm feeling and we'll go from there."

Xavier nodded. The rest of the twenty-minute drive was a quiet one. The driver wrestled with feelings of guilt over what had happened in the park and the passenger wondered how much longer it would take to get him into bed.

Chapter 11

"People of God, get it together!" bellowed Pastor B.J. Henderson, striking his fists vehemently against the pulpit. His voice boomed across the church, amplified by the mini microphone clipped to his suit jacket. "It's time we *stop* playing church and *start* being a church! Is anyone in here listening?"

A chorus of amens and hallelujahs rang out from the congregation.

Pastor Henderson peeled off his pea-green suit jacket. The slim-faced deacon standing off to the side took it and draped it behind the reverend's oversize chair. The shiny pews, glass pulpit and decorated altar complimented the simple elegance of the church.

"We need to get real with ourselves and get real with our God! Don't waste your time and—" he pointed to the ceiling with his index finger "—His time *playing church*. If you're not going to give the Lord your all, don't bother." Pastor Henderson dragged a hand down his face, his large, owl-like eyes penetrating the audience. "God doesn't want our sloppy seconds, church. He wants your heart, your soul, your mind and your body. He wants everything you have and everything you are. It's all or nothing, saints. Can I get an amen up in here?"

"Amen!" Ebony didn't realize she had shouted until Xavier smiled over at her.

He whispered, "Looks like somebody is enjoying herself."

She cast him a sideways glance, and when he broke out into a cheesy grin, she did, too. Pastor Henderson asked the assembly to open their Bibles to Psalm 51 and Ebony dutifully obeyed.

"Everything you have and will ever have in this life is a gift from God," he told them, after reading the scripture. "If you have food on your table and clothes on your back and shoes on your feet, you ought to give the Lord some praise. Stop puffing out your chest and swaggering around the neighborhood like you're something special. You're not! Don't look down at others because you have an Ivy League education, a six-figure salary, an expensive car and a four-bedroom house with a *pool.* How do you think you got all of those things? You didn't get them by yourself! God gave them to you! He blessed you with the intelligence to graduate from a college or university. Blessed you with the necessary skills to secure that prestigious job. Helped you to buy that fancy house. Don't take what God has done in your life for granted, people of God." Pastor Henderson paused long enough to wipe the sweat trickling down his face. He warned, "Don't play with God, saints, because as quickly as he blessed you with that *job,* that *car,* and that *house,* it can all be gone!"

Heads nodded and hands clapped. Pastor Henderson had evidently struck a nerve. "Before I close, I want to have a word with my sisters in Christ." His mouth was set into a deep scowl. "Stop being so hard on the brothers!"

The women in the congregation chuckled.

"Trust me, sisters, they are doing their very best. So what if the brother looks more like Derrick from up the block than *Denzel Washington?* Give the man a chance!" Worshippers erupted in laughter. Women of all ages shook their heads furiously; men nodded and exchanged high fives. Pastor Henderson guffawed. A full minute passed before the parishioners quieted down. "Now, bow your heads in prayer."

Xavier took Ebony's hand.

The pastor instructed the congregation, "Pray for someone who you know could use a touch from the Lord."

Ebony couldn't remember the last time she'd prayed and didn't know who to pray for. But when she closed her eyes, she saw Lydia Miller's angry face. She prayed for the young girl and soon she was crying.

Pastor Henderson's soul-stirring message had her name written all over it. Ebony had replaced God with work and in the process had lost her way. She had given up on faith and stopped believing in miracles. But her past didn't have to be her future. Right where Ebony sat, she made a promise to God. She would attend church on a regular basis and try to pray every day. The church choir was phenomenal and she responded to Pastor Henderson's tell-it-like-it-is approach, but Ebony didn't know if she was going to make Jubilee Christian Center her home church. This was Xavier's church. And she didn't want him to think she was attending church to win him over. Ebony was doing this for herself and not because she wanted him to like her.

When the service came to a close, Ebony carried herself confidently through the church doors and stopped only when Xavier introduced her to the pastor and his wife. Parishioners waited in line to have a word with their pastor, but Pastor Henderson took the time to greet his "son's" pretty friend. He thanked Ebony for all her help in the Changing Lives Through Meals program and his wife, Necee, promised to have them over for dinner one day soon. By the time Ebony left the church foyer and followed Xavier outside, her heart was full. She felt different, renewed, changed.

"What did you think?" Xavier asked, weaving his car around a shiny SUV and merging into midday traffic. "I heard you hooting and hollering, but what do you really think of what you heard this morning?"

"The choir was amazing and the African woman who stood up and testified about being healed from throat cancer is incredibly brave. I don't know what I'd do if I was in her shoes."

Xavier agreed. "Me, neither, but thank God her cancer is in remission. If anyone can survive throat cancer, it's Sister Mobuto. The woman is a fighter."

Ebony was happy to hear that. "It's too bad your sister couldn't come to church this morning. I was really looking forward to meeting her."

"I know, but morning sickness is kicking her butt." Xavier made a point of adding, "But don't worry, there'll be lots of other opportunities for you to meet her."

Ebony didn't ask him to elaborate. They were still testing the waters, as she liked to call it, and she didn't want to read too much into what he said. When the time was right, they would discuss where things were going. Until then, she would keep things as simple as possible. "Her husband seems nice."

"Yeah, Andrew's a cool guy. Not like that jerk she married the first time around." Ebony picked up on the resentment in his voice, but when she opened her mouth to ask what happened, he changed the subject.

"I'm glad you came with me to church, Ebony. It means a lot to me."

Ebony smiled softly. The more time she spent with Xavier,

the more she liked him. Beneath his serious nature was a supersensitive romantic who was witty and sincere. He was warm and sweet and kind and although they would probably never be anything more than lovers, Ebony was thankful that they had met. Knowing a man of Xavier's caliber and character would undoubtedly change her forever. From now on, she refused to settle. No more self-centered, scheming, two-faced, no-good brothers. If she couldn't have the best, then she didn't want anyone at all. Ebony stared outside the window. *It's like the song says,* she thought with a chuckle, *I can do bad all by myself.*

Ebony leaped to her feet. She hoped it was Xavier on the phone. That night at dinner, they had discussed their favorite vacation spots, argued about the best players in the major leagues and flirted shamelessly. Things had been going great until the waiter brought the bill.

Ebony had expected Xavier to be relived when she pulled out her credit card and handed it to the pale-skinned waiter. A teacher's salary was barely enough to keep body and soul together, let alone pay for expensive meals. Ebony didn't mind paying; she could afford it. Most men would be over the moon if their date offered to pay for dinner. Not Xavier. He had argued with her for ten minutes. In the end, she had reluctantly agreed to let him pay, but had insisted on leaving the tip. The drive back to her place was a quiet one, and when Xavier pulled up in front of her house, he was still sulking. Ebony invited him inside, but he politely declined. "Call me later, okay?" Xavier had promised to call her in a couple of hours, but it was going on ten o'clock, and she still hadn't heard from him.

"Hello?"

"Hey, girl. Long time no talk."

Ebony pushed aside her disappointment and greeted Opal warmly. She went to the fridge, poured herself a glass of chocolate milk and grabbed a handful of cookies.

"Where have you been? Have you forgotten about your family?"

"Don't be like that," Ebony said sternly. "Kendall and I have been working crazy hours trying to get the business proposal finished before our next meeting with the bank." She dunked a cookie in the glass of milk and popped it into her mouth. "You of all people should know what it's like trying to meet a deadline."

"I hear you. Things are just as busy on my end, but that doesn't mean I can't find the time to check on my friends. Unlike you, my job isn't my life. There are more important things, like—"

"Okay, okay, save the rest of your speech for someone who cares," Ebony said with a laugh. "You made your point, Opal. I'm a horrible friend."

"Admitting it is the first step."

More laughter passed between the two friends.

"How are my goddaughters doing?" Milk spewed out of Ebony's mouth when Opal said she was thinking about checking herself into a psychiatric ward. "That bad, huh?"

"Worse! I can't handle Iyesha anymore. She's only thirteen, but her scrawny little butt is wearing me out! Whenever I tell her she can't do something, she hems and haws and then spends the rest of the evening pouting. I feel like pulling my hair out from the roots every time she whines about wanting this or that. And this morning when I told her she needed to put a T-shirt over her tank top, she had the nerve to roll her eyes. You know what that fresh-mouthed girl said when I told her she was one eye-roll away from being grounded? She said, 'Mom, you're such a drainer!'" Opal imitated her daughter's voice, which elicited chuckles from her best friend. "What does that mean?"

Ebony dabbed the tears at the corner of her eyes. Every woman needed a friend as funny as Opal. She always had a story to tell. Between the characters she counseled at the group home she worked at, her crafty ex-husband and her two spunky daughters, there was always something exciting happening in her life.

"We should get together one day this week," Opal said.

"Just pick the time and place and I'm there."

"Good, 'cause if I don't get away from Iyesha and Tessa for a few hours, I'm going to lose it!"

Ebony did a mental check of her week. She was booked solid until next Friday. "Q's Joint is celebrating their three-year anniversary next weekend. Interested?"

"Sure, count me in."

"Do you mind if I bring Xavier? When I mentioned it to him this afternoon he said he wanted to go."

"You two kids have been spending an awful lot of time together," Opal noted. "When you aren't burning up the phone lines, you're off having dinner and who knows what else. Is there something you want to tell me?"

"Nope. Nothing at all."

There was a ruffling sound on the phone and then Opal said, "I seriously doubt I'll be able to keep it together until Friday."

"Then come over tomorrow night and we'll order in some Chinese food."

"Deal, but no Chinese. I started Atkins today."

Ebony frowned into the phone. "Again?"

"Yup. The first time around was just a trial run."

"And this time is…" She left Opal to finish the rest of the sentence.

"The real thing."

"All right, I got it. No Chinese food. We'll have salad and tofu and watch my girl Fantasia tear it up on *American Idol*."

"Deal."

"Okay. See you then."

After Ebony replaced the receiver, she washed the dishes, dried them and then stacked them in the cupboard. Outside the kitchen window, an angry wind scattered leaves back and forth and murky clouds sailed across the dark gray sky. Though the sun had set, the neighborhood was still very much awake. The Addisons, the Trinidadian family to her left, had their sprinklers going; a lawn mower roared in the distance; children laughed merrily and dogs barked.

Why hasn't he called? Ebony stared at the receiver for a moment, then picked it up and punched in Xavier's number. But she hung up before the call could connect. No, she wasn't going to call. Xavier was being petty and if he couldn't handle being with a woman who made more money than him she was better off without him.

Ebony returned to the master bedroom. A long, luxurious soak in the tub quieted her thoughts and soothed her mind. Clad in a red lace teddy, she shut off her bedside lamp and slipped underneath the silk sheets. She spent the next twenty minutes rehashing what happened at dinner and when Ebony finally dozed off, it was with a heavy heart.

Chapter 12

Summer was in full bloom by the first week in June. Rain showers had come and gone, the scent of fragrant flowers over-shadowed the city and birds twittered the melody of the season.

Ebony had started the week off with bright, enthusiastic energy, but by midweek, she was an exhausted executive running on empty. Ebony hated Wednesdays with a passion and it was the one day she struggled to wake up. By midweek, customers and employees were irritable and more times than not Ebony staggered through the day.

On this particular afternoon, her sinuses were acting up and the humidity only added to her foul mood. Ebony was angry, and not even the soft soothing voice of Roberta Flack could bring her out of her funk. She had butted heads with Kendall during the morning meeting and she was still smarting over the groundless accusations her partner had made. It had all started when Ebony suggested they work overtime to fine-tune the Women of Sensuality promotion. Kendall had quickly rejected the idea. She had plans with Turner and she wasn't staying a minute past four o'clock, she'd said.

Ebony had lost it. After labeling Kendall lazy and unmotivated, she accused her of neglecting the business.

Kendall had fired back, "You're a control freak who has no life. You can work all day and night if you want to, but I'm not going to. *I* have a life. *I* have a husband waiting for me at home."

Three hours later, the insults were still playing in Ebony's mind. *Am I really that bad? Do I push my co-workers and employees too hard?* From time to time she struggled to control her temper, but everyone had flaws in their personality. Ebony had made her fair share of mistakes but she hadn't built a lucrative business by being a quitter. Or shunning her responsibilities. Her greatest characteristic was her tenacity and she wouldn't let anyone knock her down because she aspired to be at the top of her game. It didn't matter if Ebony was dealing with an insubordinate employee, or a disgruntled customer, she handled every challenge head-on.

Ebony wondered what Xavier was doing. It was six o'clock so he was probably at church getting things ready for tonight. Thoughts of Xavier had been sneaking up on her all week. He invaded her thoughts while she was driving to work, when she was soaking in the tub, and even in the privacy of her dreams.

Her eyes strayed to the window. Ebony wished she could look inside that handsome head of his. Maybe that would give her some insight. A week had passed since their argument at Oysters, but Xavier was still holding a grudge. He was carrying on as if she had hopped up on their table, hiked up her skirt, and given the patrons an impromptu strip show. She hadn't willfully embarrassed him, so why was he still upset? Was offering to pay for dinner a sin? Xavier was acting like a two-year-old on a self-inflicted time-out and Ebony was tired of feeling guilty. She hadn't done anything wrong! Part of her wanted to forget him but she couldn't stand the thought of him being mad at her. So when Ebony arrived at church that evening, she pulled Xavier aside.

"Can we go somewhere to talk?"

He led her into a dingy storage room with weak lights.

"Why are you avoiding me? If you're still angry about what happened last Saturday at dinner, then just say so." When he didn't respond right away, she prompted, "Well, are you?"

Xavier hesitated. She was putting him on the spot and he didn't have an answer. Dinner at Oysters had left a bad taste in his mouth for more than one reason. Ebony had made a big production out of paying for the meal. She had acted like he lived on the streets and therefore couldn't possibly afford to take her to a nice restaurant. Xavier didn't know what type of men Ebony was used to dating, but based on the way she acted, he concurred they were parsimonious in nature. Men who would rather keep their money in their wallets than spend it on a woman. Xavier grew up seeing his father spoil his mom. His pops opened doors, pulled out chairs, paid for meals and bought flowers for no reason. In his father's eyes, his mother was the most beautiful woman to walk the face of the earth and that's how Xavier treated the women in his life. He loved to spoil. Loved seeing a woman's face light up when she opened an unexpected gift. He put time and effort into planning elaborate dates. Went the extra mile to let his girl know she was special.

Xavier didn't want Ebony paying for meals. Or reminding him that she could afford it. She insisted on making the decisions and it bothered him greatly. Ebony had to learn to back off.

"I'm not mad at you, but I…"

Ebony smiled and Xavier lost his train of thought.

There was no denying it: he was hooked. He liked her a

lot. More than his last three girlfriends combined. They had been great in their own right, but none of them had Ebony's energy. Or confidence. Or sassiness.

The electricity that passed between them whenever they kissed had the potential to turn his life upside down. But Xavier welcomed the chaos. The woman standing before him in the off-the-shoulder top and fitted bell-bottom jeans, which hugged her full, very round bum like no other, was a tremendous woman. She had a personality and a way of thinking all her own. Ebony Garrett lived life by her own rules and played the game any way she saw fit. Xavier was drawn to her, and utterly helpless to resist her. But no matter how much he wanted her, he had to proceed with caution.

"Ebony, I think you're a fantastic woman who I'd love to get to know better. But we need to straighten out a few things first. I don't drive an expensive car. I don't live in a six-bedroom palatial home, and I don't have a six-figure salary." Xavier locked eyes with her. "But I'm determined to reach the goals that I've set for myself. Everything I have I paid for with my *own* money. Ebony, I don't need anyone taking care of me. If I invite you out for dinner, or take you to a show, I'll pay for it. That's what a man is supposed to do. If you think I'm not good enough for you because I'm not a wealthy executive—"

Ebony didn't let Xavier finish. "I never said you weren't good enough for me!" Her hands dropped to her sides, her face marred with frustration. One deep breath helped to clear her mind. "Don't speak about what you don't know, Xavier. I've never said, or insinuated, that I was better than you. Offering to pay for dinner wasn't to embarrass you," she reiterated for the fourth time in days. "If I had known my generosity would incite an all-out war, I would have kept my big mouth shut. Like I said that afternoon, picking up the check is no big deal. I do it all the time."

Xavier was primed with a rebuttal, but the sound of chairs scraping across the floor and lively chatter coming from the kitchen forced him to hold his tongue. Now was not the time to be arguing with Ebony; the program was set to begin. "Let's forget about this for now."

Ebony would let it go for now, but this matter was far from over. "Are you coming with me to Q's Joint on Friday night or have you changed your mind about that, too?"

Xavier had promised to be her date and he had a feeling things would get ugly if he attempted to back out now. "No, I haven't changed my mind."

"We'll talk then," she said turning away. Ebony flung open the storage room door, rattling the small eight-by-ten space, and walked down the hall.

At one time, Q's Joint had been a dilapidated-looking bar that served cheap food, entertained unsavory customers and enjoyed frequent visits by the local police. But all that changed when Kale Washington bought out the existing owner and poured a considerable sum of money into renovating the bar. The former professional baseball player had put Q's Joint on the map. Now, almost three years later, it was the hottest place in town. The sensual lighting, polished decor, formal attire policy and twenty-five-dollar cover charge set the establishment apart from all the other nightspots.

Reclining in her buckskin chair, Ebony surveyed the crowd. Q's Joint was a world all itself. College-aged women clad in slinky cranberry red cocktail dresses served drinks and appetizers; young athletes, who had tasted their first bit of fame, swaggered through the club with ten-men entourages; and scantily dressed women bounced from man to man like kangaroos. Simone T, a local pop singer with a number one hit single, pranced around the bar, her see-through lace one-piece outfit attracting attention from all four corners of the room.

Ebony returned her eyes to Xavier. He sat to her immediate left, discussing the nature of the NHL lockout with Opal's friend Spencer Daniels. The pair had been engaged in an animated discussion for three-quarters of an hour, and although their topic of choice bored her to the point of falling asleep, she was stimulated by the rise and fall of Xavier's voice. It was rich and strong. And turning her on in the worst way. She closed her eyes, and imagined his mouth on her lips. His hands on her breasts. His tongue working its way down the slope of her neck, then capturing a nipple in his mouth.

"Good evening. I'm Bliss. I'll be your server for the rest of the night."

Ebony opened her eyes, just as the waitress handed her a cocktail menu. The brunette rattled off a list of the night's specials, her piercing blue eyes shifting casually around the room. Opal had excused herself to make a phone call, and the men were still arguing, so Ebony took the liberty of ordering a round of cocktails for the group. Handing the waitress her credit card, she said, "Charge everything to my account."

The brunette nodded.

When she departed, Ebony took out her compact and discreetly checked her makeup. In the reflection of the mirror, she found Kale Washington watching her. His almond-shaped eyes glimmered under the bright lights of the bar, and he was wearing a wide smile. Vainglorious and overconfident, the multimillionaire thought he was God's gift to women. The tabloids said he cheated on his wife and engaged in kinky sex with females half his age, but Ebony knew better than to believe rumors. She wasn't keen on the man, but that didn't mean she believed everything she read.

The show was set to start, but if Ebony didn't go over and

greet Kale, he would hold it against her. His wife, Amelia, was a regular at the boutique and the Hispanic beauty was one of Ebony's favorite clients. She didn't want to leave Xavier's side, but she didn't have much of a choice. This was business. Networking was the key to the game; it put her name out in the business world, and the more people she knew, the more opportunities would be afforded to her. Ebony wasn't fond of Kale Washington, but he was somebody she had to be on friendly terms with.

Ebony found a smile as she made her way over to the bar. Watching Kale watch her was enough to make her laugh. His eyes were wide and his lips moist. It had been three months since she last saw the club owner, and there was no doubt in her mind that he wanted to catch up. Ebony cast a glance back at her table, relieved that Xavier and Spencer were still talking. Xavier was so busy arguing his point, he probably didn't even notice that she had left the table.

"What do you think, Ebony?" Xavier turned to his right and was surprised to find her seat empty. His eyes moved carefully around the room. Befuddled, he watched as Ebony embraced a broad-shouldered man and then planted a kiss on his cheek. Xavier instantly recognized her companion. It was Kale "lady-killer" Washington.

Everyone knew who Kale Washington was. The former Twins pitcher smiled down from billboards, hawking everything from sneakers to medicine to cologne, and was a regular fixture around the city of Minneapolis. Visits to children's hospitals, generous donations to inner city schools and hosting a baseball summer camp kept him in the newspapers and on the evening news on a weekly basis.

The ex-bad boy of the American Baseball League was living the American dream. Happily married to an ex-model, he had three cute kids, million-dollar homes on the East and

West Coasts, commercial investments and a staggering net worth of 125 million dollars. The media said he had it all. Money. Fame. Power. And last month he had been named one of *People* magazine's Sexiest Men Alive.

Xavier suddenly felt insignificant. He told himself it had nothing to do with Ebony rubbing up against Kale Washington, but his heart knew differently.

Spencer pointed in the direction of the bar. "Is Ebony talking to Kale Washington? *The* Kale Washington?"

Xavier nodded absently.

"Damn! Ebony knows everyone!" Spencer smacked his hand on the table. He spoke with pure admiration. "The last time we were here she introduced me to Kevin Garnett. I almost passed out when he approached our table. He gave me a pound and everything. Cool guy." Spencer nudged Xavier with his elbow. "Must be nice dating a woman who rubs elbows with stars and celebrities." He dug around in his pocket, removed a wrinkled ATM receipt, then held it up for Xavier to see. "Think Washington will autograph this? Maybe I can send Opal over there when she gets back."

Xavier inclined his head to the right, in the hopes of getting a better view of the attractive twosome. They were standing as close as Siamese twins, Ebony's full breasts only a few inches from Kale's chest. Chasing away feelings of jealousy, he leveled a hand over his shirt. He had no claims on Ebony. She was free to do as she pleased. Xavier thought for a moment. They weren't a couple, but that didn't mean he was comfortable with her flirting with other men. He wasn't.

Xavier kept a nervous eye on his date. He didn't like seeing Ebony with Kale Washington. Or anyone else for that matter. He resented her popularity and the interest she received from other men.

A buxom waitress who would make Dolly Parton look flat

chested bent down and set a cocktail glass before him. "Enjoy," she said cheerfully, her breasts jiggling in his face.

Xavier shifted his eyes away from Ebony and Kale. "I didn't order this."

She flicked her head in the direction of the bar. "She did."

Ebony knew he didn't like to drink, but what did she do? Go ahead and order him a cocktail. He pulled out his wallet, took out a ten-dollar bill and handed it to the waitress. "Can you take this back and bring me a glass of iced tea?"

"Keep your money. She prepaid for the drinks." The waitress returned the cocktail to her tray and promised to return in a few minutes with his drink.

An ugly scowl worked its way onto Xavier's mouth. Ebony was taking over again. She had taken the liberty of ordering for him, and if that wasn't enough, she had paid the check—again. Xavier rubbed the side of his face. This was all too much. His life hadn't been the same since he met her, and that bothered him. He wasn't comfortable with change. Wasn't comfortable being with a woman who garnered attention wherever she went.

Xavier checked his watch. Kale and Ebony had been talking for…for twelve minutes. Seven hundred and twenty seconds. Watching her from across the room stirred all sorts of desires within him. Her white sleeveless dress displayed her toned arms and slender legs. Xavier longed to have Ebony in his arms, and craved her touch in return. His mind lingered back to the afternoon they spent at the jazz festival. Just as he was about to revisit their impromptu make-out session, he turned away from his thoughts. Xavier faced the facts. Wherever Ebony Garrett was, trouble would soon follow. She used her sexy ways to entice as many men as possible and got a kick out of turning heads. Not his type of woman. Xavier wanted a good girl. A truthful, respectable woman who was ready to settle down and start a family. Ebony didn't fit that description. She was dangerous and wild and a slice of temptation too captivating to resist. Like Eve and that damn apple.

The waitress returned with his drink. Xavier downed it in three gulps. After tonight, there would be no more dates with Ebony Garrett. She was bad news. Mind made up, he turned back to Spencer and asked him who he liked in the NBA finals. He gave Spencer his full attention, but every few seconds his eyes strayed to the bar. It was going to be hard severing ties with Ebony. They hadn't known each other long, but he liked her immensely. No, he couldn't second-guess himself now. It was over.

But at the end of the night when Xavier led Ebony through the lounge area, and caught the envious I-wish-she-was-my-woman stares the men fired his way, the last thing he was thinking about was severing ties with her. Her must-have body made her the desire of every man in the room. And when Ebony slipped her hand around his waist, Xavier's chest puffed out like a hot air balloon. It felt good to have the best-looking woman in the bar on his arm. So what if she was a flirt? Did it matter that she craved attention? Xavier found Kale Washington through the crowd. Surprised to find the athlete watching them, he held Ebony a little tighter and guided her out of the bar.

Chapter 13

Ebony stepped inside the foyer, shut off the alarm and slipped off her high heels. She beckoned Xavier to follow her inside.

The image of Ebony in Kale Washington's arms flashed in Xavier's mind.

He hovered on the porch, wavering between the prodding of his heart and the deliberations going on in his mind. If he went inside, he'd probably fall back under her spell, but if he left without giving her the room to explain, he'd be judging her again. "Ebony, what kind of games are you playing?"

"I'm not playing any games. Like I told you before, what you see is what you get." Ebony flicked on the hallway light to get a better look at Xavier. He didn't look angry but there was no mistaking the harshness of his words.

"What I see is what I get, huh?"

Feeling the heat rise up the back of her neck, she unzipped

her jacket and hung it up in the closet. "Out with it, Xavier. What's your problem?"

He leveled the irritation in his voice; he didn't want to come across as being hypersensitive or jealous. "You slink over to the bar, without bothering to say where you're going, spend twenty minutes flirting with Kale Washington and then return to the table like nothing happened! Why did you bother inviting me tonight if you were going to spend most of night hanging out with other guys?" He added, "You know what your problem is, Ebony? You're an insatiable flirt! Every time I turn my head, you're batting your eyelashes at someone."

Ebony's first inclination was to tell Xavier to get out of her house. She didn't like his tone and he had no right talking to her like that. She wasn't a child and he wasn't her father. What she did, where she went and who she spoke to was none of his business. He wasn't her man. Or her husband. And since she didn't remember them taking a trip down a rose-scattered aisle, exchanging vows or being pronounced as husband and wife in front of a roomful of family and friends, he had no say in who she spent her time with.

But instead of giving in to her temper, she held her tongue. Counting to ten calmed her nerves and cleared her head. In the painfully long silence, Ebony revisited his accusations and thought back over the night. Ebony couldn't take issue over what Xavier had said; he was right.

Visiting with Kale had been inconsiderate. She hadn't even realized that her quick hello had lasted almost a half hour. But when Kale got to making jokes, it was hard to leave. He plied her with compliments, shared humorous tales about his days in the major leagues and had a way of making her feel like he was really listening to her. She enjoyed his company, and the more time that ticked off the clock, the more she thought the rumors about him were just that—rumors. He nattered nonstop about his wife and children and had mellowed out considerably since the last time she'd come by the club.

Ebony closed the space keeping her from Xavier. Licking her lips, but managing to do it with just the right amount of sensuality, she smoothed her hands over his chest. Ebony wished Xavier would put them both out of their misery. He wanted her. She wanted him. It was as simple as that. "Are you attracted to me?" she asked, her eyes flitting over his lips. "Do I turn you on?"

Xavier swallowed. *Where did that come from?* he thought, clearing his throat. He paused, unsure of what to say. He wanted to say no, wanted to deny his true feelings, but Ebony would see right through him.

"I think you're charming and—"

"That's not what I asked you." Ebony reached up and traced a finger gently over his lips. "Answer the question," she ordered.

Xavier shut his eyes, reveling in her touch. Before he gave in to his desires, he recognized the attack for what it was: another one of her tricks. She had been touchy-feely all night and her ever-changing erotic arsenal had kept his head spinning. Ebony was always misbehaving. When she wasn't rubbing her perky D-cup breasts against his forearm, she was stealing kisses or "accidentally" grazing a hand across his crotch. Now this.

Disobeying his flesh, which was screaming out for some kind of sexual release, he stepped out of her reach.

Permitting her eyes to wander over his perfectly formed physique, she dropped her voice to a sexy whisper. "Do you think I'm sexy, Xavier? Do I turn you on? Do you want to make love to me tonight?"

"Enough!" he said, holding up his hands to silence her. He sounded defeated when he spoke, as if he had already lost the battle. "Who wouldn't be attracted to you, Ebony? You're stunning. Your honesty is refreshing and you're fun to be with, but that doesn't mean we're right for each other. I think—"

Ebony had Xavier up against the door before he could finish his thought. She circled her arms around his neck, parted her lips and then smothered his mouth with her lips. Pressing herself against him, she lightly caressed the back of his head. Ebony reveled in the moment. The heat of his mouth, the feel of his chest against her breasts and his hands gliding up her back only intensified her need. Encouraged by his muffled moans, she dipped her tongue further into his mouth.

Mouth-to-mouth, chest to chest, they pleased each other with their hands and lips. Xavier dug his hands into her hair, drawing her closer.

Ebony nibbled on his bottom lip like it was a piece of fruit. Her nipples strained against her dress, aching for his touch. Xavier stroked Ebony through her clothes, eliciting a grunt from her mouth.

"Let's…go…upstairs," she managed. "We'll be more… much more comfortable…in my…bedroom."

Xavier was tempted, like Adam had been in the Garden of Eden that fateful day, but he couldn't follow Ebony upstairs. Not tonight. Making love to someone you loved and respected was one of God's greatest gifts. He was wildly attracted to her—the plump lips, dark exotic eyes, tight curves—but he wanted to know her on a deeper level. There was no doubt in his mind that when the time was right, the sex would be great. He desired every inch of her delectable frame, but he didn't love her. Xavier was waist-deep in lust, and although he'd acted on those feelings in the past, he wouldn't tonight. Freeing himself, he used his fingers to erase all traces of her lipstick from his mouth.

"We can't do this, Ebony."

Her face fell. "Are you still angry about what happened at

Q's?" When he hesitated to answer, she said, "Just so you know, I was *not* flirting with Kale. I have no control over what men say or do, but I don't encourage their advances. And about me being a flirt…" Her eyes rolling upward, she smiled naively. "It's a gift. Take it up with God, not me."

Xavier couldn't contain his laughter. "You're something else."

"Something good or something bad?"

"What do you think?" he asked, enjoying their playful banter.

"I like you, Xavier." Ebony giggled when he raised an eyebrow sky-high. "I want to get to know you better. *A lot better.*" With that, she kissed him again. "Sorry about the whole drink thing. That was my fault. I wasn't thinking."

Xavier believed her. Something about her was endearing. He didn't know if it was her blatant honesty or the way she held his gaze when they spoke, but whatever it was touched him deeply. He was chivalrous by nature and loved to make the woman in his life feel special, but he felt compelled to go the extra mile for Ebony. He sensed that she had some trust issues, and wanted to prove to her that she could count on him.

Giving in to his need, he drew her back into his arms. His hold was tight. His eyes showcased his feelings, and his words came from the heart. "We have to trust each other, Ebony. No games. No lies. No half-truths."

"I hear you."

"Are you seeing anybody else?"

"No."

"Good." It came out like a sigh of relief. "'Cause I'm a one-woman man and I expect the same from my girl. I don't want to share you, Ebony."

"You won't. You'll be the only one," she promised. Long-term relationships terrified Ebony and the thought of marriage made her break out in hives, but when she was dating someone she remained faithful. Trust was important to her, too. Just because she wasn't out shopping for a husband didn't mean she was jumping from man to man. Ebony had a past like everybody else, but she was older and wiser now. She wisely grilled lovers about their sexual history, practiced safe sex, and got tested regularly for STDs. A woman couldn't be too careful these days. With brothers living on the down low, and playboys sleeping with two or three women at a time, the twentieth-century female had to be militant about who she let into her life. And her bed. But Ebony had a feeling she didn't have to worry about Xavier. He wasn't going to sit her down Maury Povich-style and tell her that he'd been living a secret life. No loud, out-of-control woman was going to show up on her doorstep in the middle of the night claiming he had fathered her child. Xavier might look, but he wouldn't be foolish enough to touch. The man was practically a saint. He was compassionate, responsible, sincere and brimming with a host of other venerable traits. So, when he suggested they go into the living room and "talk," Ebony knew that was all he wanted to do.

Rain dotted Xavier's face as he dashed from his car to his house. Once he was inside, he propped his briefcase up against the door, kicked off his shoes and after hanging up his jacket, set off for the kitchen. A minute later, he entered the living room with an apple between his teeth and a stack of mail in his hands. He hit the playback button on his answering machine, before stretching out on the couch and making himself at home between two fluffy pillows.

"It's me, E-b-o-n-y. Just wanted to confirm that you're still taking me to the movies tonight. Don't forget, Xavier, you promised. Bye, sexy, see you later!"

Xavier tossed the mail on the coffee table. He cupped his hands behind a cushion, thoughts of his budding relationship with Ebony at the front of his mind. Somehow, she had managed to turn his life upside down in just a matter of weeks. But Xavier wouldn't dare complain; he loved his new life.

Three weeks had passed since the night at Q's Joint. Despite Ebony's hectic schedule and all the demands on her time, they managed to get together two or three evenings a week and spoke on the phone at least once a day. It was easy to be around her, and the more they talked, the more he liked her. Ebony had a knack for making people feel comfortable and no matter where they went or what they did, they always had a great time together. They played at video arcades, went shopping and ate together. On Sundays they attended services at Jubilee and last weekend Xavier had accompanied Ebony to her aunt Mae's house. The elderly woman shrieked with joy when she opened her front door and saw them. Dinner had been filled with laughter and amusing tales from Ebony's childhood, and there hadn't been a dull moment during the two hours they were there. When Ebony stepped out of the room to make a phone call, Mae Murdock had given him some pertinent advice.

"Be patient with my girl. She's a tad rough round the edges, but stick with her. She's one of the good ones. Hardworking, trustworthy and she can do for herself." Mae added proudly, "She gave that fancy speech at her high school graduation, you know."

Xavier nodded appreciatively.

Mae handed him a plate of leftovers wrapped in aluminum foil. "You're just the kind of man my Ebony needs. Someone who wouldn't shrink under her confidence and strength. A man. A real man." She patted his cheek lovingly. "Remember what I said, son. Be patient."

It turned out Mae Murdock was right. Ebony *was* one of the special ones. She made him feel like a king and when she was around he felt more alive than he had ever been. They went out for dinner, spent nights at the movies, and hung out with their friends. Xavier just loved to show her off. When Ebony was on his arm, he felt like a teenage boy with the most popular girl in school. There was never a shortage of laughs or smiles or kisses when they were together.

Xavier didn't know when or how it had happened, but his feelings for Ebony had veered from a tender affection to something deeper. He wasn't ready to say the L word, but what he felt for her couldn't be described any other way. She added to his life, both emotionally and spiritually, and if he had things his way, she would be with him twenty-four-seven. Being with her felt right, but Xavier knew he had to proceed with caution. Ebony was starting to open up to him and the last thing he wanted to do was scare her off with some mushy declaration, especially after what he'd disclosed last Saturday.

While playing a round of miniature golf, Ebony had revealed that she had never been in love. Ever. Xavier's golf club had flown out of his hand and landed in the pond. Then she had dropped another bombshell: she didn't ever want to get married. After he retrieved his club and dried it off, he led her over to a nearby bench and questioned her further. Xavier wasn't surprised when she got defensive and the usual smoothness in her voice fell away, but he was bowled over when she confided that her parents had turned her against the idea of marriage.

"When my father snapped his fingers, my mother went running. He barked at her nonstop. I don't know why she stayed. My parents were miserable every single day of their marriage and I refuse to follow in their footsteps. Besides, I'm happily married to my work."

"You make marriage sound like a death sentence."

"It was for my parents."

"Lots of couples manage to maintain strong, healthy relationships, Ebony. Look at Pastor and his wife. They're pushing twenty years! Don't they look happy?"

She shrugged. "Yeah, I guess."

"Ebony, you don't know what the future holds. Who's to say you won't meet Mr. Right somewhere down the road and change your mind?" Xavier didn't want her to read what was in his eyes, so he looked away. "Remember what Pastor said last week? 'You can plan all you want, but *God* has the last say.'"

"If marriage means so much to you, then where is your red minivan and five kids?"

His silence spoke volumes.

Ebony stepped in front of him, obscuring his view of the twelve-hole golf course. "Time to fess up, Xavier."

"There's nothing to say."

"Come on," she urged, donning a grin. "I've been wondering why you're still single. What's your story? Are you one of those commitment-shy brothers or do you have some crazy fetish like wearing women's underwear?"

Xavier laughed until his eyes watered. "You don't pull any punches, do you?"

"I believe in speaking my mind. Now quit stalling and answer the question."

"I don't have any serious hang-ups or quirks that I'm aware of. But my mother told me that when I was four years old I used to drink out of the toilet bowl."

"Now, that's just nasty," Ebony said, giving his shoulder a playful shove.

Xavier took in some air, and then reopened a painful chapter from his past. "I was engaged four years ago, but it didn't work out."

"What happened?"

Xavier told her everything. How Nathan had dragged

him along to be the fourth member of a double date and at the end of the night he had asked Patrice Weaverly out. It hadn't been love at first sight, but over time he had come to care about her.

"She was terrific. Sweet, quiet, modest."

"Sounds like your kind of girl," Ebony interjected.

"So I thought. After graduation, I went to Europe to play ball, and she took a full-time job at an ad agency. At first, things were great. We talked every night, wrote letters, she even sent me care packages. But after a few months, the calls and letters grew less frequent, and the packages stopped coming. When I finally returned home after being on the road for a six-month stretch, she didn't have time for me. She canceled dates, insisting she had work to do, and when she did manage to tear herself away from her office, her mind was always on work. When she showed up halfway through Jacqueline and Andrew's wedding ceremony, claiming she had been at the office and lost track of time, I broke things off."

"Did you expect her to quit her job for you?"

"No. I'd like my wife to stay home with the kids, but I'm a flexible guy. I'd be supportive if she wanted to work part-time."

"I can't cook," Ebony blurted out, looking contrite.

Xavier chuckled.

"What's so funny? Did you hear what I just said? I can't cook."

He patted her leg and then gave her a peck on the cheek. "I know." When her eyebrows creased, Xavier revealed how he had discovered her secret. "I put two and two together a long time ago. I kind of figured it out when Sister Bertha asked you to make some more gravy for the turkey, and you almost burned down the kitchen. And when we went over to your aunt Mae's house for dinner, she told me not to hold your noncooking skills against you." With a grin and a wink, he added, "But it's cool. I'm not dating you for your culinary skills."

Xavier could still hear Ebony's throaty laugh. She had given him a kiss, asked him if he could give her some cooking lessons, and laughed some more when he said, "Only *God* can perform miracles."

Xavier could easily spend the rest of the night thinking about Ebony, had it not been for the sound of the doorbell. Rising from the couch, he tossed his apple core in the wastebasket and then made his way down the hall. "Who is it?"

"Your bloated, puffy-faced sister. Now open up! The baby and I are getting soaked!"

Chuckling, Xavier opened the door for Jacqueline and ushered her inside. His sister was positively glowing. Her heart-shaped face couldn't be any brighter, her gray eyes were highlighted by the smile on her face and aside from her protruding stomach, she didn't look any different to him. From the neck up, you couldn't even tell that she was five and a half months pregnant.

Xavier closed the door. "What brings you all the way over here in this kind of weather?"

"Boredom," Jacqueline drawled, "and I had to get away from that husband of mine. He's driving me crazy!" She deepened her voice. "'Need anything, babe? Comfortable? Want me to get you anything? Should I rub your feet?' Augh! The man is taking this whole pregnancy thing *way* too seriously."

Shaking his head, he helped take off her coat.

"Don't look at me like that, Xavier. You couldn't possibly understand what I'm going through."

"Oh, I do," he replied. "Some women are just never satisfied. They moan and groan about not being able to find a good man, but when they do they complain that he's 'too nice' or 'too sweet' or 'too kind.' Should I remind you of how miserable you were when you were married to Malcolm? How you cried yourself to sleep because you didn't know where he was or whose bed he was in?"

Jacqueline cast her eyes down at the floor. "You're right. I shouldn't be bad-mouthing Andrew." A tear dribbled down her cheek.

Xavier wiped it away, and then embraced her. "Is this one of those hormone things?" he asked, trying to make her feel better.

Jacqueline looked up at him and stuck out her tongue. Just like that the tension lifted. She followed him into the kitchen, glancing around the room as if it were her first time there. With some effort, she sat down on one of the stools. Observing the fresh cream paint, assortment of flowerpots on the shelf above the sink and African-inspired pictures, she said, "Did some redecorating around here, huh?"

"A little."

Xavier set a plate of fresh fruit on the counter and handed his sister a glass of orange juice. Noting the diamond-studded wristwatch on his left hand, Jacqueline took a good hard look at her baby brother. Xavier normally wore khakis and a casual shirt to work, but today he had on an aquamarine-blue dress shirt and black wrinkle-free dress pants. His hair was cut, his nails were trimmed and he was wearing new cologne. Jacqueline smiled to herself. Either her brother had been the lucky recipient of an Oprah Winfrey makeover or he had a new woman in his life who had an eye for design. "Looks like *someone* went on a shopping spree. Pick anything up for me and the baby?"

"Nobody went on a shopping spree. I'm just taking better care of myself." Xavier took a mouthful of orange juice. He wasn't going to tell Jacqueline about his last outing with Ebony. He had walked into Mall of America with the intention of picking up a couple of pairs of socks and the new Air

Jordans. But at the end of the day, he'd left with six shopping bags overflowing with everything from underwear to cologne and ties. Arguing with Ebony over the purchases had been futile; he couldn't dissuade her from buying them no matter how hard he tried. Their shopping expedition had been over a week ago, but he still had mixed feelings about the whole thing. Xavier felt like she had bought all those things to impress him. He hadn't asked for the watch or the clothes or the shoes, but he felt guilty nonetheless. To placate his conscience, he'd taken Ebony out to dinner and sent her a gigantic bouquet of tulips the following day.

Jacqueline grabbed his hand. She inspected the watch, her eyebrows rising with each blink. "So, when does the family get to meet Ms. Moneybags?"

"Don't call her that."

She put on her most innocent expression and pointed at his wrist. "That's at least a five-hundred-dollar watch, you're wearing new clothes and I remember you telling me she insists on paying for everything. I think 'Ms. Moneybags' is an appropriate nickname for your ladylove, don't you?"

"Her name is Ebony, if you must know."

Jacqueline waited for more information. When he didn't supply any, she said, "Is that all you're going to give me? I need more. I want details. I already know she's beautiful—" she broke off when Xavier's eyes crinkled. "Okay, okay, so I grilled Andrew about her. It's not my fault I've been too sick to go to church."

"What else did Andrew say?" Xavier tried to sound indifferent, but there was no fooling his twin sister.

"He said she speaks in an elegant, almost queenly manner, and that she's the best-looking woman he's ever seen in the flesh." She grinned. "Aside from me, of course."

Now it was Xavier's turn to smile. Andrew was right. And

so were Daruis, Juan and Nathan. Ebony was gorgeous and everything about her was stunning—her skin, her face, her body. And she was smart, too. *Jeopardy!* wasn't much of a challenge for her, she did the Saturday crossword in no time and read her old university textbooks to keep her mind sharp. They had many similarities but it was their differences that kept them together. Ebony was spontaneous. He wasn't. But every now and then, she could persuade him to try something new. She was a risk-taker, an envelope pusher, a daredevil, a modern day Marilyn Monroe. Xavier was terribly meticulous. Ebony wasn't. But when she needed help assembling a new bookshelf for her home office, he had showed her how. Xavier had learned a lot from Ebony since they started dating and he valued her opinion greatly.

"Are you bringing her to the barbecue?"

Xavier had forgotten all about it. His parents were having a barbecue to celebrate their birthday. It was a family tradition. Xavier had never done anything else to celebrate his birthday, but he'd been so busy with Ebony it had slipped his mind. In honor of her birthday, he had booked two nights at a hotel, and after scouring the entire city for the perfect gift, had found something he was sure she would love. Dinner at his parents' house with his relatives just didn't hold its usual appeal. But there was no getting out of it. His mom would lose her natural mind if he told her he had made other plans. It would take some effort on his part, but Xavier would convince Ebony to come to the party. A small detour to his parents' house didn't have to ruin their plans. He would introduce Ebony to his family and then they would leave. He had been planning her birthday for weeks now and he didn't want anything to spoil her day.

When Xavier told Ebony he thought they should put off making love until they knew each other better, she had surprised him. He had expected her to disagree. Or pout. Or beg. But she hadn't done any of those things. She had kissed him softly on the lips and said, "I'm fine with that, Xavier. I think waiting is a good idea." She didn't pressure him. Never asked him when he'd be ready. Didn't label him old-fashioned or weird. Just waited. And Xavier loved her for that. More than he had ever thought possible.

Chapter 14

"Sorry about the movie," Xavier said, "but I'm sure we can find something to watch here." Twenty-five newcomers had turned out for the Changing Lives Through Meals program, which meant there was a bigger mess to clean up at the end of the night. Xavier had sped to Golden Globe Theatres, but the movie Ebony wanted to see was sold out. Since they didn't want to wait around for the next showing, Xavier had suggested they watch a movie at his place.

Ebony pulled her lips in, feigning anger. "I know it was all part of your plan, Xavier. You probably paid all those people to show up so you wouldn't have to take me to see *Jeepers Creepers.*"

Xavier looked to the ceiling. "Most women like romantic comedies, tear-jerkers, movies that make them cry, but not my girl. No, my woman likes to watch people get chased through the woods and hacked up like meat."

His girl? If that isn't the cutest thing I've ever heard, Ebony thought, wearing a wide, toothy smile. Standing up on her tiptoes, she planted a kiss on his lips. Pulling away she donned her naughtiest smile. "I never actually said I wanted to *watch* the movie, Xavier. I had other things in mind."

"What am I going to do with you?"

"I'll let you do anything you want," Ebony said, with a smirk.

Xavier swatted her bottom playfully. "You go pick out a movie, and I'll go get the snacks."

An hour later, they were curled up on the couch, munching on buttered popcorn, midway through watching *The Best Man.* The living room was dark, except for the light coming from the TV, and the Surround Sound was at full pitch.

Staring intently at the screen, Ebony wondered how Morris Chestnut's character could live with himself. He had sowed his royal oats for years but the knowledge of his fiancée's past indiscretion made him want to call off the wedding. *Some men have no conscience.* Ebony snuggled closer to Xavier, confident that she would never have to worry about him stepping out on her. He didn't have a disloyal bone in his body. They weren't superserious, but she knew he'd be true to her for as long as they were together.

Later, when Ebony thought about the night, she wouldn't be able to remember how it happened. She would struggle to put her finger on what it was that had brought them together. All she knew for certain was that when Xavier kissed her, everything she had been holding inside came gushing out. Her words were a jumbled mess, but somewhere between kissing and undressing, she told him how much he meant to her.

Xavier's hand slipped inside her bra, eliciting a groan from Ebony's mouth. Stroking a breast with one hand, he pressed his lips against her earlobe and then twirled the tip of his tongue in circles.

Ebony's heart had danced with excitement at the prospect of making love. It had been so long. Too long. And it was time. Time for the two to become one.

A frisson of pleasure rippled through her when his hands slipped inside her jeans. Cupping her breasts through her black lace bra sent her pulse careening into overdrive. Ebony wanted him to remove the physical barriers between them, but she didn't want to spoil the mood with words. As if reading her mind, he unhooked her bra, allowing her breasts to spill out in his hands. Xavier lavished attention on each breast. First, circling each one with his tongue, and then capturing the nipple in his mouth.

Ebony didn't trust herself to speak, but she wanted Xavier to know how she felt under the care of his expert hands. "Baby…you make me feel…so good."

Xavier pulled away and abruptly got up from the couch.

Staring up at him, she sighed deeply. She should have kept her trap shut. Knowing what was coming next, Ebony shrugged back on her shirt and started to do up the buttons. They had been at this junction many times before, and as frustrating as it was to get this far and turn back, she wasn't going to make an issue out of it. When Xavier was ready for them to be lovers, he would let her know. Ebony only hoped it was soon. A girl could only wait so long.

"Things are getting out of hand," Xavier would say in a guttural tone. "It's getting late. I should take you home." Whenever they rounded second base, he stopped. Ebony opened her mouth to tell Xavier she wanted to finish watching the movie, but he bent down and kissed her before she could get the words out.

Xavier touched a hand to Ebony's face. He had been planning for their first time to be on her birthday, on a bed of roses, under dim lights and romantic music, but he couldn't wait a second longer to make love to her. Love was conveyed in actions, not words, and tonight he was going to show Ebony just how much he cared for her.

Xavier took Ebony by the hand and led her down the hall. When they reached his bedroom, he flicked on the bedside lamp, laid Ebony down like she was a piece of porcelain and stretched out on top of her.

Ebony loved being naked. Liked the feel of air on her skin. The freedom. The sexiness of it all. She pranced around the house naked, blinds open, not the least bit self-conscious about her body. A perpetrator would need high-powered binoculars or X-ray vision to see her from the street, she would reason to herself. She implored her girlfriends and clients to get in touch with their bodies. Wear silk, sleep naked, get a bikini wax, take belly-dancing lessons. Ebony was as uninhibited as a woman could be, but when Xavier finished undressing her, she drew the blanket up to her neck. Ebony had "problem" areas that she didn't want him to see. Her breasts weren't as perky as they used to be, a thin pad of fat obscured her abs, and her knee was tarnished with a childhood scar. And just the thought of Xavier looking at her thick, ham hock thighs made Ebony cringe. She knew where her flaws were, and if he continued studying her body the way he was, he would, too.

"What's the matter?"

"Nothing."

"Come on, Ebony, tell me what's up."

Self-conscious about her tummy, or rather the fat around it, she turned onto her side. "I have flaws, you know."

Xavier stared down at Ebony. She was perfect. Full breasts, flat stomach, curvaceous hips, toned legs he couldn't wait to feel circling around his waist. "You're perfect, babe."

Ebony licked her slightly swollen lips. Though it wasn't her intention, the move was unbelievably erotic.

A thousand thoughts crowded his mind. No one had ever stirred or enticed him the way Ebony did. Not even his first love, and he had loved Mia with all that he had. His feelings for Ebony weren't some high school puppy love thing. This was real. He was sprung and proud of it. In the corner of his mind, he could see a future with her. He saw a sprawling white house, picket fence and all; a minivan in the driveway; a kiddie pool in the backyard; and a gang of kids at his feet. And when their lips reunited for a wickedly sexy kiss, Xavier almost dropped down to his knees and proposed.

They kissed and teased and kissed some more and when he discarded his T-shirt, jeans and boxer shorts, Ebony waited anxiously for him to rejoin her. Xavier had refused to admit the obvious, but from the moment he first saw her, he knew she was special. He had known instinctively that she had the power to change his life. And he had suspected if they ever hooked up, she would rock his world. He was right. They hadn't even done the deed yet, but here he was, panting like a dog in heat.

Xavier positioned himself on top of Ebony. He took in the rise and fall of her chest and the sudden wariness on her face. If he questioned her, she would deny it, but her eyes never lied. In all the time they had been dating, Xavier had never seen Ebony look anything but self-possessed. She typified poise and grace at all times. But tonight, in his bedroom, under the muted lights, she looked vulnerable.

Xavier dropped his mouth to her ear. "You're beautiful, Ebony." He pecked her cheek. "Like a rose." More kisses. "Like a sunset." They locked eyes. "Like a John Coltrane song."

Ebony felt tears in her eyes. Now she knew she was losing it. Crying because he called her beautiful? That was silly. Sudden bouts of self-consciousness? Crazy. And wavering between sleeping with him and waiting a little bit longer was even more ludicrous. In past relationships she had never felt the need to hold off, but for some reason, completely unknown to her, she wanted to with Xavier. She didn't want to ruin what they had, what they were building on, didn't want to wake up tomorrow morning to discover he resented her.

While Ebony struggled with her emotions, Xavier loved her. Tenderly and slowly and with as much love as a man could give. He paused only once, just long enough to protect them both, then resumed touching her, kissing her and soothing her heart with sweet words. And when he finally entered her, after driving her to delirium with his hands and mouth, a single tear spilled down her cheek. Not because she was in pain, but because she felt loved. Ebony had never, ever been loved like this. Had never been worshipped. Or treasured. She had always believed that "making love" was just a fancy, sophisticated term for sex; in her mind they were one and the same. Both produced the same result. But with each thrust, each touch, each kiss, each spoken word, Ebony discovered how different the two were. One was wine, the other beer. Sex was good in its own right, but making love was exceedingly better. It was a whole-body experience. Mind, body and soul came together and filled the heart with love. And for Ebony, there was no greater feeling.

Xavier did things to her she didn't even know she wanted. And after a body-numbing orgasm, his body enveloped her to create a warm and cozy cocoon. Ebony had been loved, thoroughly, completely and without reservation. For as long as she lived, she would remember the magic and passion of their first time.

Ebony's eyes slowly flickered open. Sunlight trickled in through the open window. The air smelled fresh and the sky was bright. Her eyes adjusted to the light as she struggled to roll over onto her side. A few seconds passed before she remembered where she was. Ebony's eyebrows furrowed when she reached across the bed and didn't find Xavier beside her. *Where is he?* Thoughts of last night wiped the frown from her face and brought a smile to her lips. *Did we really make love all night long?* she asked herself, swinging her wobbly legs over the side of the bed. *It feels like it was all a dream. A very naughty dream.*

Concealing her nakedness with one of the oversize T-shirts in the closet, she thought back to last night's events. Xavier had rocked her world. Not once, but twice. He had introduced her to a style of loving she had never known. He was gentle, but urgent. Tender, but physical. Wild, but controlled. And just the thought of where his lips and tongue had been made her shiver. Ebony had kissed her fair share of handsome men. A couple of them had known a thing or two about sex, but no one came close to making her feel the way Xavier had. He had put it on her, *big time.* He had done everything right, said all the right things and touched her the right way without having to be coached. It was as if he could read her innermost thoughts.

Her eyes strained to the mirror. She was so hungry she could eat Xavier out of house and home, but she wasn't going anywhere until she got herself together. Her face had to be washed, her teeth brushed and her hair combed. Dragging her hands through the tangled ends of her hair, she set off down the hall for the bathroom.

When it came to sex, Ebony had three very strict rules. Rule number one was the easiest to follow: no condom, no loving. In all the years she had been sexually active, she had never had unprotected sex. And whenever she talked to her girlfriend Cassandra, who said she didn't like the feel of them and enjoyed the spontaneity of "going with the flow," she lectured her about the dangers of "going with the flow." No sleepovers, under any circumstances, was rule number two. When the deed was done, Ebony went home. It could be the dead of night, and she would still crawl out of bed, say her goodbyes and drive back to her place. Rule number three had been revised several times, but it had never been broken. She loved her house. It was her sanctuary. Her sacred place. Dates could come over, they could even stay for dinner, but they couldn't spend the night. Couldn't even sit down on her bed. Memories lingered. Played with your mind when you least expected it. Ebony was smart enough to know that nothing lasted forever, and when a relationship ended, she wanted to be able to move on without painful reminiscences about what used to be.

Last night, Ebony had broken rule number one and two, and she knew it was just a matter of time before she broke rule number three. Fortunately pregnancy wasn't a fear because she was on the pill. Funny, but Ebony didn't feel guilty for "going with the flow" or for allowing herself to fall asleep in Xavier's arms, either. If anything, she felt lucky. For the first time in her life, she had found a man who truly cared about her. His number one priority was pleasing her, not fulfilling his own sexual needs. Xavier wasn't satisfied until *she* was satisfied and there was nothing sweeter than being with such a selfless man.

After freshening up, Ebony set out in search of Xavier. The corners of her mouth turned down when she entered the kitchen. The air was saturated with the aroma of eggs, bacon, and freshly brewed coffee, but there was no food anywhere. However, as she turned toward the dining room, she caught sight of a pink envelope in the middle of the pear-shaped glass table. Ebony ripped it open. It read: *Breakfast is waiting for you on the patio, Beautiful.*

Ebony rushed outside. Xavier was reclining on a chair, his

face masked by the front page of the *Minneapolis Tribune*. Plates of bacon, omelets, pancakes and blintzes covered the table and pitchers of fruit juice sat on a nearby cart.

Xavier put down the paper. "Sleep well?"

Her face came alive when he stood and dropped a kiss on her lips.

"Yes, thanks to you."

"I hope you don't mind me cooking you breakfast."

"Why would I mind?"

"Because the last time I tried to feed you you refused to eat!"

"Xavier, I was a mess! What did you expect me to do? Sit across from you with puke breath?"

"I thought you looked good."

"Liar."

"Okay, you did smell a little funky."

She pinched his arm playfully. "Thanks a lot. You really know how to make a girl feel special."

He chuckled. "I'm just playing."

"I know," she conceded, looping her arms around his waist.

Xavier loved that Ebony was so quick to laugh. "Is that why you didn't want to stay for breakfast that morning, because you thought you looked bad?"

Ebony nodded.

He wished Ebony had told him the truth instead of demanding he take her home. Xavier had thought she was acting like a spoiled brat. When he thought about the fifteen-minute drive from his house to Dakota's Bar and Grill, he laughed out loud. When she raised her eyebrows in disdain, he filled her in on the joke and she laughed, too.

"I thought you were trying to kill me!" she confessed.

"I was!"

More laughter.

They sat down at the table and when Ebony took a bite of

the blueberry pancakes and said they were the best she had ever tasted, he smiled proudly.

"Is there anything else I can get you?"

Ebony glanced up from her plate, a seductive smile on her lips. She had been dying for some good lovin', and now that she had found the right man, she wanted to make up for lost time. The pancakes could be reheated, the orange juice could be iced and the cantaloupe would taste just as good warm as it did cold. Putting down her fork, she eased out of her chair and stood. "Well, since you're in such a giving mood…" Sitting down on his lap, Ebony linked her arms around his neck.

Xavier felt his throat constrict. Her touch tickled the hairs on the back of his neck and when she trailed her tongue over his ear, an intense rush of pleasure settled in his groin. The feel of her mouth on one of the most sensitive parts of his body left him speechless. His whole body was alive now. It was as if he had an uncontrollable craving for her that couldn't be quenched.

His mouth reached hungrily for her. The kiss was full of heat and love. Worried that his neighbors might hear them, Xavier took Ebony by the hand and led her back inside. He pulled her down on the couch and bathed her lips with kisses that sent shivers from her head to her feet. His touch was light and soft; hers was impatient and rough. Xavier decided to follow Ebony's lead. He let his mouth stray from her lips. It wandered down her neck to her breasts. The slow circular pattern of his tongue traced along her skin.

Ebony and Xavier licked and sucked and stroked like they had all the time in the world. Her smooth, velvety skin was warm and her body responsive when he parted her legs and positioned himself inside her.

Ebony wished she could freeze this moment. She was with a man who treated her with tenderness, a man who respected her, a man who made love to her like no one had before.

Closing her eyes, she gave in to her thoughts. Xavier listened to her, comforted her and spoiled her. Ebony didn't want to get ahead of herself, didn't want to read too much into his actions, but she couldn't help wondering if this could be love. Promising to explore these exciting, new feelings later, she lifted her chin higher and embraced his kiss.

Chapter 15

Dark storm clouds hovering over the sky did little to dissuade Iyesha and Tessa from an afternoon swim. The trees shielding the yard leaned in the wind, carrying the scent of barbecue from the house next door. *So much for basking in the sun,* Ebony thought as she watched her goddaughters put on life preservers and scurry off in the direction of the pool.

Iyesha and Tessa jumped into the pool, shrieking with glee as the ice-cold water swallowed them up in one big gulp. Like a game of peekaboo, the sun inched away from the clouds and hung high in the sky. Rays of sunshine cascaded off the pure blue water. Ebony sat back in her lounge chair and hid her eyes behind an oversize pair of sunglasses, before turning to the report on her lap.

"Aren't you going to swim with us?" Iyesha asked.

"Come on, Auntie!" Tessa waved her over, her broad smile

revealing three missing front teeth. "I promise not to splash you like last time."

Ebony shook her head wildly and both girls dissolved into giggles. She held up the file and said, "Auntie has to finish her homework before she can play."

Her answer seemed to appease them, at least momentarily. The girls swam a few laps, and then played a round of Marco Polo. Eight-year-old Tessa struggled to get away from her sister, but with the floatation device weighing her down, Iyesha was able to tag her easily. At thirteen, Iyesha was the spitting image of her dad. Periods of lassitude and inactivity made it impossible for Jamal Sheppard to hold down a job, and that had caused a heavy strain in his marriage. But it wasn't his inability to work that had caused the split. After twelve years of marriage, Jamal had walked out on his wife and daughters for a much younger woman. Opal and the girls were used to not getting much of his time, so there were no tears when he finally packed up his things and moved out of the family home.

Ebony laughed when Tessa unintentionally smacked Iyesha in the face with her swimming tube. She marveled at how different the sisters were. Tessa was a rough-and-tumble kind of girl who liked to keep up with the boys, her sister a girly-girl who liked to stay abreast of the latest fashion and celebrity gossip.

Opal had dropped the girls off Friday after school and they had followed Ebony to church. When she had introduced the girls to Old Man Griffin, his face had lit up like the New York skyline. Lovable and chatty Tessa had easily captured the old man's heart. The offensive odor and the contemptible appearance of their tablemates didn't seem to faze the girls and when Tessa shared a story about how she had forgotten the class rabbit on the playground and almost *died* when he came scurrying into the classroom, even Lydia had cracked a small smile

Midway through the meal, Lydia had made eye contact with Ebony and after stuffing a bun into her mouth, mumbled, "Sorry 'bout the other day."

Ebony had assured her that all was forgiven. Lydia must have wanted someone to talk to, because she opened up to Ebony. At one point, she even admitted that living on the streets was starting to take its toll on her. She was getting migraines, she had the flu every other week, and she had to sleep with one eye open to protect herself.

"Sounds like you need to get off the streets." Ebony checked on Iyesha and Tessa, who were helping to serve dessert. Sister Bertha had them in arm's reach. "The New Hope Women's Shelter takes in homeless women between the ages of sixteen and twenty-five. You should check it out."

"I hate those places. They stink. And the staff looks down at—"

"You'd only be there a short time," Ebony pointed out. "A women's shelter isn't the best place to be, but it's a lot better than living on the street and having to look over your shoulder every two seconds. You wouldn't be there long. Just until you get back on your feet. You're looking at a month, two tops." She took a bite of her carrot cake, trying to think of something else she could say to persuade the young teen to get off the streets. "I know what it's like to feel unwanted, Lydia. There was a time when I was in your shoes."

Curiosity shone in Lydia's dark brown eyes.

"You know what saved me from a life of crime or prostitution?" After a short and profound pause, she said, "My aunt Mae. She was the only person who believed in me. She encouraged me to go to school, cheered when I graduated and told me I could do and be anything I wanted as long as I believed in myself." Ebony caught Xavier watching her and sent him a smile. There was nothing more important to her than getting Lydia into a safe and stable environment, so she focused on the teen. "Sometimes you have to be willing to take a risk, Lydia. The shelter may very well be filthy, the food disgusting and the staff a bunch of jerks, and then again, it might not be. It may end up being better than what you expected. But what do you have to lose by giving it a shot?"

Lydia finished her pecan pie. "I'll think about entering the shelter, but don't get your hopes up."

"I won't." But Ebony did. She could tell by the way Lydia was watching her that she had taken what she said to heart. And for now, that was enough.

Ebony wanted to stay behind at the end of the night to help Xavier clean, but she'd promised the girls ice cream and their favorite store closed at nine. Xavier had walked them outside, pecked her on the cheek and promised to call when he got home. After the girls fell asleep, she had called and invited him over to watch a movie.

Xavier refused. "That wouldn't be right," he'd said, his voice firm. When she accused him of not wanting to see her, he had laughed. "Ebony, you know that's not true. I want to see you, but we both know if I come by, there'll be a lot more going on than watching a movie. And besides, you know how loud you are! You're liable to wake up not only the girls, but the family living next door!"

Laughing, Ebony had snuggled between the pillows, wishing Xavier was lying in bed beside her. They had talked a while longer, but when they hung up and she turned off the lights, she couldn't help feeling alone.

Ebony watched the girls. Xavier loved to swim. He swam like a fish and he loved children. Maybe she could convince him to come over for the afternoon? Yes, inviting him over was a great idea. And it would give her an excuse to change out of her house clothes and into the new orange and lavender bikini she had picked up at Macy's. With a white silk scarf and a pair of low-heeled shoes, Xavier wouldn't be able to resist her. Ebony put aside the file and reached for the phone.

"Mommy!" Tessa ran up the steps of the pool and threw her arms around her mother's waist.

"How are my girls doing?" Opal asked, kissing her youngest daughter. "I hope you aren't causing your auntie Ebony any trouble."

"Not me, Mommy," Tessa promised, "but Iyesha spilled a glass of chocolate milk all over the table and Auntie's papers were ruined." She added, "Auntie had to throw them out."

Iyesha pushed Tessa out of the way. "Tattletale. It was an accident," she told her mom, "and I cleaned it up right away."

Kendall rounded the corner and entered the backyard. "Anyone want a slushie?"

"Me! Me!" Tessa hopped up and down like a kangaroo in the wild.

Drinks in hand and wide smiles on their lips, Iyesha and Tessa returned to the pool.

Kendall put the tray down on the patio table. "Be right back. Nature's calling."

"Again? You stopped twice on the way over here!"

"When you gotta go, you gotta go." Smiling sheepishly, she entered the house through the French doors.

Opal made herself comfortable on one of the chairs. Waving when Tessa called her name, she said, "Ready to pull your hair out yet?"

"Please, you know I love those girls like they're my own. They've been terrific. We just got back from aunt Mae's. She didn't want us to leave, but I promised the girls a swim before I dropped them off. I thought we agreed I'd bring them back at eight?"

"I know, but I missed my babies. The house has been

eerily quiet since I dropped them off on Friday. Thanks again for watching them, Ebony. Things were crazy-busy this weekend at work." Opal worked as a youth care worker at Evergreen Woods, a residential treatment center for teenage girls. She had been the one to suggest the New Hope Women's Shelter as a suitable residence for Lydia. Last week, she'd even arranged for Ebony to meet with the program director, Ms. Donaldson. The kindhearted older woman had assured her that while in care, Lydia would receive nutritious meals, full medical attention and individual as well as group counseling.

"Did you end up going out with Charles last night, or did you stand him up again?" Ebony asked.

Charles was the head psychotherapist at Evergreen Woods. The man had a monster-size crush on Opal, and when the two women had run into him at the mall a few weeks back, Ebony had encouraged her friend to give him a chance. He was a decent-looking brother, had a respectable job and was obviously smitten with her. Opal had promised to give it some thought. When he asked her out again the following week, she had agreed. But just as she was about to leave the house for their scheduled date, Tessa had come down with a fever, and like any good mother would do, she had canceled her plans.

"We went out for drinks last night after my shift. We had a nice time. He asked me out again but I don't know. We'll see what happens." Opal crossed her legs and shifted in her chair so she and Ebony were now face-to-face. "Speaking of men, what's going on with you and Church Boy?"

Ebony turned, and found Kendall staring down at her, too. Her girlfriends had descended on her lounge chair like hungry vultures.

In recent weeks, Ebony had been happier and more fulfilled than she had ever seen her and Opal had a theory as to why.

"It's too late to be shy, girlfriend, 'cause we already know you've been spending nights at his house—"

"And vice versa," Kendall chimed in. "*And* I happened to notice an extra toothbrush and a host of men's grooming products on the counter in the bathroom. What happened to rule number two and three, Ebony?"

Ebony didn't feel like sharing, but if she didn't give them something, they would interrogate her for the rest of the afternoon. To buy some time, she picked up one of the slushies, and sipped slowly.

"Last Monday, I stopped by with the girls but you weren't home. After I put Tessa to bed, I tried calling you but your cell phone was turned off." Opal motioned with her head to Kendall. "On the drive over here, we were comparing notes and Kendall told me you've been ducking her at work all week. You've been leaving work early, canceling our girls' nights out and you're rarely home anymore. So, either you and Xavier have something hot and heavy going on, or you're moonlighting as a stripper."

Ebony tossed her head back and laughed from the pit of her stomach. Several seconds passed before she was composed enough to speak. "There's nothing to tell. We've been hanging out a lot but that's what people do when they're dating. That's all I'm going to say about it, so you two heifers get off my back."

"Girl, please." Kendall pursed her lips together. "When Turner and I ran into the two of you at Valley Fair last Saturday it looked like you could use a hotel room. Y'all were wrapped up so tight you'd need a crowbar to separate you."

Ebony found herself smiling.

Opal lowered her voice to an almost inaudible tone. "What's Church Boy like in the sack? Is he good in bed or could he use some instruction?"

Ebony was not about to divulge the intimate details of her relationship and told her friend just that. "That's private, Opal. I'm not going to—"

"Come on," she begged shamelessly. "You know I live vicariously through you. It's your steamy sex life that gives me hope. What's the big deal? You've never had a problem sharing before."

"That was then and this is now," Ebony snapped. Discussing her sex life with Opal and Kendall wouldn't be fair to Xavier. And if he learned that she had given her friends a rundown of the intimate things they did together, he would never speak to her again. Ebony loved Kendall and Opal like sisters. They were the best friends she had ever had, but what she did with Xavier was nobody's business.

"What makes this Xavier guy so special?" Kendall wanted to know.

Cracking a playful grin, she said, "You mean besides the fact that he's gorgeous, kind and incredibly thoughtful?"

"Yeah, besides that."

All three women laughed.

Opal crossed her legs again and gave Ebony a smile of reassurance. "Come on, quit stalling. We want to hear everything, and I *do* mean everything. I for one am dying to know what Xavier did to put that goofy smile on your face."

The sound of his name was like a gentle caress on Ebony's face. She'd run the risk of sounding like a lovesick fool if she repeated what was going through her mind, but she couldn't ignore the truth of her feelings. Her life had become an endless stream of board meetings, conference calls and late night business dinners without her even realizing it. Beneath her vaulting ambition to be a successful entrepreneur lurked a desperately lonely woman searching for someone to share her life with.

Enter Xavier Reed.

In the last two and a half months, he had come to be much more than just a lover; he was a friend. Her best friend. When they were together, time drifted by and Ebony felt like she was living in another world. A world filled with soft kisses, tender touches and deep and meaningful conversation. She cherished those quiet moments they spent together. Waking up beside him, inhaling the scent of his skin and sharing her thoughts with him brightened each and every day.

Ebony's ears perked up at the mention of her name. "Huh?"

Kendall's eyebrows came together in a frown. "We're waiting," she sang. "Waiting to hear what Xavier did to make you break all of those rules."

Sighing wistfully, she shook her head in wonder. Since it was impossible to clear the smile from her face, Ebony didn't even try. Her voice was full of emotion when she spoke. "When I'm with Xavier, it's as if everything's right in the world. I don't think about meetings, or late shipments or business proposals. Just us. I've been so consumed with making Discreet Boutiques a success that somewhere along the line I forgot how to live. He calls me in the middle of the day just to hear my voice, he surprises me with little gifts and the man can cook his pants off!"

"Does he have any brothers?" Opal asked, in all seriousness.

"Sorry, girl."

Kendall shrugged a shoulder. "So, he's sweet. Big deal, a lot of guys are."

"No, it's more than that, Kendall. Xavier is a gentleman through and through. He opens doors, pulls out chairs and we can't go anywhere without him taking my hand or wrapping his arms around me." Ebony paused. Xavier also knew what turned her on both mentally and physically, but she decided to keep that pertinent piece of information to herself.

"I've never met a man as generous and as passionate as he is. He leaves notes on my pillow, listens to what I have to say—even if he doesn't agree—and can make me laugh like no one else." Ebony's face glowed as the memory of last Saturday washed over her. "We were watching TV late one night when I went into the kitchen to grab us some ice cream. On my way back down the hall, I caught sight of the calendar hanging near the storage room." Ebony got choked up every time she thought about how lucky she was to have Xavier in her life. "He had penciled in the day we met and every single date we went on. I flipped ahead to next month, and was shocked to see he had almost every day filled in with places he wanted to take me and gifts he thought I'd like." Astonished at how emotional she got talking about their relationship, she took a long sip of her drink. It seemed like minutes but it was only seconds before she said, "Xavier's unlike anyone I've ever met and I truly feel blessed knowing him."

Opal and Kendall exchanged invidious looks. Before Kendall could respond, her cell phone rang. Excusing herself to take the call, she walked to the other end of the yard.

"Girl, you're sprung! Your eyes are open so wide I can see your heart!" Opal patted Ebony's hand. "I say go for it. Hold on to that brother with both hands and don't let your career get in the way. Discreet Boutiques can't pull you in its arms when you've had a bad day, or make you soup when you're sick or love you all night long the way I'm *sure* Xavier can."

Ebony chuckled. As usual, her best friend was right.

"Who knows," she said, with a casual shrug of her shoulders, "maybe we'll be planning a wedding before the year's end."

"Now you're just talking crazy. We've graduated from seeing each other to being a couple, but that's where the road ends. I'm not the type of woman Xavier would consider settling down with. He wants his wife barefoot and pregnant and you and I both know that's not me."

Opal could tell Ebony was holding something back. Maybe she *was* thinking about marriage. "Don't worry too much about the future. Just enjoy the present. I'm happy that you've finally found someone who puts a smile on your face."

"Me, too," she confessed.

"Where is Xavier taking you for your birthday?"

"I have no idea. He mentioned something about his parents having a barbecue at their house, but I reminded him that I don't do family functions."

"No, you didn't!"

"I did." She was about to explain, when Kendall returned. Bad news was written all over her face. "What's the matter?"

"It's the first day of the summer clearance sale and stores two, five and six are stuck with sales associates who haven't been properly trained. Yolanda gave employees a half day of orientation instead of the standard three days, and then put them on the schedule." Kendall pushed a hand through her hair. "You were right about her all along, Ebony, but don't worry, I'll take care of it. I'm going to fire Yolanda first thing tomorrow morning. We'll promote Cynthia Baines to the district manager position and hire—"

"Not so fast, Kendall. You said yourself that Yolanda was having problems at home. We'll meet with her and give her the chance to explain. Then we'll decide what course of action to take."

Kendall looked at her narrowly. "A chance to explain what? This has been going on for months! *Months.* Her behavior has been completely unprofessional and I'm tired of her crap. Consider her gone, Ebony, because there's nothing you can say to change my mind."

"That's not your decision to make, Kendall. *We* own the company, remember?"

Tension hung in the air like the Goodyear blimp.

Opal had to act fast. This had the potential to turn ugly and she didn't want her best friends duking it out in front of the kids. "Why don't we all take a deep breath and—"

"Damn, Church Boy must have put it on you good!" Kendall's voice was dripping with contempt. "What happened to the don't-take-no-crap-from-nobody woman we've all grown to love and fear?"

"Nothing's changed, Kendall. I just think Yolanda deserves another chance."

"Love's made you soft," she spat out. "You know what, Ebony? I don't really care what happens between you and Xavier, just don't let your newfound outlook on life interfere with *our* business. Okay?"

"And don't let your problems at home impede your good judgment, *okay?*" Ebony shot back, trying to maintain her cool. Kendall had been short-tempered and irritable all week and Ebony didn't know how much more of her attitude she could take. She felt bad that Kendall and Turner were having problems, but she didn't appreciate her partner taking her anger out on her.

"I'll meet with Yolanda tomorrow. I'm sure you have more important things to do with Xavier, so don't worry about it. I'll handle it."

Instead of arguing back, Ebony turned to Opal and said, "Let's go inside and have some tea. I feel a *bitter* wind sweeping through the backyard."

Chapter 16

Giddy excitement coursed through Ebony as she reentered the kitchen and turned off the oven. Working at a torrid pace to put dinner together, she hummed along with the Earth, Wind & Fire song playing on the radio. She transferred a plastic container of chicken Parmesan to an enormous china bowl, then prepared a garden salad with all the fixings. When Xavier suggested they celebrate their birthday the day before the actual date, Ebony had agreed. Since they would be apart tomorrow—he with his family and she with her girlfriends—it was the perfect compromise.

Ebony had offered to "cook" for the occasion, which meant she'd be ordering in from her favorite restaurants. But minutes before Xavier was due to arrive, she was running around the kitchen as if she had been the one to prepare the five-course meal. French onion soup, roasted eggplant, Cajun seafood, and brown rice were on the dining room table, bordered by flowers and candles.

Ebony switched off the radio and then turned on the stereo. The emotional fire and heartfelt lyrics of the Freddie Jackson classic, "You Are My Lady," made her eyes water. The balladeer's melodious voice and deft range sent chills down her spine and resonated through her soul. It was as if the lyrics were squeezing her heart. She thought of Xavier, and how much he had come to mean to her. Ebony had opened her heart to him in a way she hadn't been able to with anybody else. Secrets and hurts she had planned to take with her to the grave had come tumbling out during one of their many intimate talks, and to her joy, Xavier hadn't judged her or looked down at her.

"Simeon's dead and gone and I know he can't hurt me anymore, but I still hate him. The only reason I wish he was still alive was so I could tell him how insignificant and worthless he used to make me feel," she had confessed, thankful the darkness concealed the hurt on her face. Xavier had gathered in his arms, and under his loving embrace, she had drifted off to sleep.

After the lights were dimmed and the room sprayed with a rose-scented mist, Ebony double-checked to ensure everything was in place. Pleased with what she saw, she exited the kitchen and headed down the hallway. Her hair and makeup needed a quick touch-up. The ceiling fan was on, cool air gushed through the kitchen window, but it didn't help diffuse the heat from the stove. As she rounded the corner to the hallway, she felt strong arms curl around her waist.

"And where do you think you're going?"

The sound of Xavier's voice brought a wide smile to her lips. She turned to receive his kiss. "What are you doing sneaking up on me?"

"No one's sneaking. I have keys, remember?"

Ebony gave him another kiss, this one much longer. Giving Xavier his own set of keys had been the best thing she had ever done. Sometimes she woke up in the middle of the night to find him in bed holding her, other times he was undressing her. Both were pleasant surprises. "I didn't hear you come in."

"How could you when you have the stereo on full blast?" Xavier reluctantly let her go. He went into the living room and lowered the music. When he reentered the dining room, Ebony was filling their glasses with wine. Leaning against the wall, he watched her move carefully around the table. Cleavage was flowing out of her black cocktail dress and dangly earrings and a thread-thin necklace complemented her elegant look nicely.

Ebony's picture-perfect style never ceased to amaze him. It didn't matter if she was wearing shorts and flip-flops, or a gown and stilettos; she was positively stunning. Mentally undressing her with his eyes, he felt his body temperature rise. Xavier's lust for Ebony knew no bounds. She was sexy and sultry and just watching her do something as tedious as setting the table was enough to get him hot. Impeding the urge to sweep her into his arms and carry her into the bedroom, he forced his eyes away. But staring at the oil paintings on the sage-colored walls did nothing to eclipse his thoughts. Thoughts of making love outside under the stars brought a slow, easy grin to Xavier's mouth. Absorbed in the errant wanderings of his mind, he didn't hear Ebony call his name until she was standing in front of him.

"You okay?" She touched his cheek with the back of her hand.

Embarrassed that he'd been caught daydreaming, he tried to laugh it off. "Me? I'm fine. Couldn't be better."

Before Ebony could quiz him further, he steered her back over to the table.

Unlike all the other times they'd eaten together, Ebony struggled to keep up her end of the conversation. She couldn't concentrate long enough to answer any of his questions and couldn't think of any of her own. But it wasn't her fault. Anticipation was wreaking havoc on her good sense. Ebony couldn't wait to see the look on Xavier's face when he saw his gift. She could see him now: mouth open, eyes wide, a look of disbelief marring the usual relaxed expression on his gorgeous face. This was going to be the surprise of all surprises. Anxious to get to the gift giving part of the evening, Ebony polished off her salad and the main course in record speed. She loved birthday cake as much as the next person, but she couldn't eat another bite. Or rather, she wouldn't eat another bite. Suspense overwhelmed her as she watched Xavier clean his mouth with his napkin.

He patted his stomach. "That was delicious, babe. Couldn't eat another bite."

"Does that mean you don't want dessert?"

"Not now, maybe later."

"Great!" Ebony jumped up from the table and dragged Xavier to his feet. "It's present time," she sang. "Ready?"

"I'm too full to make love, babe. Maybe in an—" He stopped when he saw the perplexed look in her eyes. "My birthday present isn't in the bedroom?"

Ebony shook her head. "Follow me." She took him by the hand and led him out of the living room. Stopping outside the garage door, she took a deep breath and then turned to Xavier. Sharing her feelings had never been easy, but Ebony was going to do her best to articulate what she was feeling inside. "I've never been in love so I don't know what it's supposed to feel like. I don't know for sure if heart flutters, sweaty palms and shaky knees are indicators of love, but that's exactly how I feel when I'm with you."

The twinkle in his eye told Ebony he was loving her impromptu speech. Sinful thoughts were written all over his face, and if he moved any closer she would be jammed up against the garage door. When he squeezed her shoulder affectionately, Ebony felt her confidence increase. "You mean a lot to me, Xavier, and I hope this is the first of many birthdays we share together." When she kissed him, she intended for it to be short and sweet, but when he pulled her closer and eased his tongue into his mouth, she couldn't resist throwing her arms around his neck and stroking his chest through his dress shirt. She forgot all about Xavier's birthday present, as his lips worked magic.

Infused with a sudden burst of energy, Xavier pinned Ebony against the wall and stuck his hand underneath her dress. He was surprised to find her naked underneath. No panties. No bra. No nothing. Ebony was as naughty as a girl could be. And he loved it. Making love to her the first time had transcended his expectations, and in the last three months she had managed to do the impossible: keep him guessing. He was her humble student and he enjoyed taking notes in the bedroom.

"Baby, we can't," Ebony protested weakly. The sensation of both his hands and his lips was almost too much for her to bear. She tried to steer his hands away, but it seemed like they were everywhere. And they were. On her face, her breasts, her butt. Her body was his playground, and he wasn't shy about exploring every single curve and slope. "W-we can't do this now…later…it's time…to open…your…birthday present," Ebony managed, between kisses. Using a gentle flick of his tongue, he covered her lips, then her neck, then her nipples.

"That's what I'm trying to do," Xavier told her, cupping her butt. Ebony might have been saying, "No, baby, we can't," but her body was screaming, "Yes! yes! yes!" Her nipples hardened under his touch and her eyes shimmered with desire. His erection pressed against the zipper of his slacks, dying for release. Strange things happened to Xavier whenever he touched Ebony. He broke out into a sweat. His heart felt like it was going to beat right out of his chest. And if that wasn't bad enough, his throat was so tight he could hardly speak.

Normally Xavier took his time loving her. He would lay her down on the bed, start with her ears, and then work his way down to her toes. Then he'd start the wickedly delicious pattern all over again. Xavier appreciated all the props Ebony set up—the candles, the music, the lingerie. But tonight, he didn't need the lights, the melodious voice of Keith Washington, or the red lace teddy; he just needed her.

Redoubling his efforts, he hiked up her dress and gripped her hips. He smothered her neck with kisses and traced his tongue along her collarbone. When he spread her legs just wide enough to slip a finger inside, Ebony groaned vociferously.

"Xavier—" Her words were swallowed by his kiss. His lips roamed over and around her mouth. Ebony bit down on her bottom lip to keep from crying out. She had never seen Xavier like this before. Aside from the living room couch and the occasional make-out session in her car, lovemaking had been confined to the bedroom. But tonight, it was as if he was reading her most private thoughts. Xavier palmed her breasts, grabbed her butt and whispered dirty words against her ear. Grinding himself against her, he sucked her breasts, making loud, slurping sounds that drowned out the music. Ebony loved every nasty minute of it.

The predatory expression on Xavier's face told Ebony there was no use trying to talk him out of it, so when he made a silent request with his eyes, she kissed him hungrily in response. Xavier entered her fast and furious.

Ebony met him thrust for thrust. Securing her arms around his neck, she rocked her pelvis forward and lifted her right leg high in the air. A guttural scream ripped from her mouth as he increased his movements and dug his fingers into her hair. Pressing herself against him, mumbling incoherently, she threw her head back in ecstasy.

Ebony wanted to tell Xavier that she loved him, that this was the best birthday she had ever had, that she didn't want anyone else, but the intensity of her orgasm robbed her speech. Pleasure waves tore through her body and the last thing she remembered was Xavier yelling her name.

Ebony woke up on the living room couch. Several pillows were positioned beneath her head, and a blanket had been thrown over her body. Her head was swimming and she had a cramp in her left calf. Ebony felt like she had died and gone to heaven. When she closed her eyes to relive the moment, she could still taste Xavier's kiss on her lips. His cologne clung to her skin and her hair, and the room was thick with his scent.

Ebony wondered where her Mandingo Prince was. She listened for a few seconds for sounds of him in the kitchen, but heard nothing. It wouldn't surprise her if Xavier was lurking behind a door or hiding in the closet. Last Friday, he had scared the skin off her and she had been on edge ever since. Ebony was dozing off on the couch, the TV blaring in the background, when she thought she heard the sound of a car pulling up in the driveway. Figuring it was just her imagination, she rolled over onto her back and buried her head under a pillow cushion. Ebony was tasting her first bit of sleep when she heard a faint knock on the front door. She looked through the peephole, but didn't see anyone. Cracking open the door, she peeked outside into the dark night. "Hello?" In one quick swoop, Xavier picked her up, locked the door behind him and took off down the hall to the bedroom. They had made love on and off for the rest of the night.

Ebony threw off the covers and heard a soft, jingly sound. A thin, diamond bracelet was hanging from her wrist. Three delicate charms were evenly distributed around the wristlet.

"Faith. Love. Trust," she read out loud. Ebony wasn't a diamond expert but she could spot the fake stuff a mile away. This was the real thing. This wasn't the first time someone had thought enough of her to buy a gift. Over the years she had received everything from expensive shoes to watches to purses. But this was the first time Ebony could actually feel the sentiment behind the gift.

Xavier cared about her. Maybe even loved her. Though she hoped and prayed for the latter to be true, she wouldn't waste precious time dwelling on the unknown. Once again, he had demonstrated that there wasn't anything he wouldn't do to make her happy, and that was more than enough for her.

Fingering the charm bracelet gently, Ebony felt her eyes grow moist. The urge to curl up on the couch and have a good cry didn't come from the gift itself. It came from the thoughtfulness behind it. A few weeks back while shopping with Xavier, she had admired a similar bracelet at Charleston Jewelers. When she had asked his opinion, he had glanced at the price tag and said, "It's overpriced, don't you think?"

Without a second thought, she had handed the charm bracelet back to the clerk and followed him out of the store and back into the mall.

Ebony stood. Xavier had to be here somewhere. She took a step toward the staircase, but that's as far as she could go. Her legs were still asleep. "Xavier! Where are you?" Ebony screamed so loud her throat burned. She heard the sound of someone running down the hallway, and then Xavier came charging down the stairs like the house was on fire.

"What's the matter?"

Shaking her charm bracelet under his nose, she said, "Grossly overpriced, huh?"

He gave her a teasing wink. "I changed my mind."

Ebony wasn't buying it. It had all been part of his plan. He had fed her that lie in the hopes that she wouldn't buy it. She turned the bracelet around her wrist, admiring it under the glow of the living room lights. "Thank you. I love it." As she stepped forward to kiss him, she heard another soft, tinkling sound.

"Oh my God!" Ebony bent down. Surprised that she hadn't felt the anklet on her foot all this time, she fingered the silver chain, paying close attention to the exquisite and unique design. Recalling the way Xavier had seduced her, she stood and coiled her hands around his waist. "That impromptu love-making session was just a ploy to get me into bed! You seduced me, so you could dress me in my gifts!"

Xavier's grin grew until it was eclipsing his entire face. "Guilty as charged."

Ebony kissed him hard. Feeling herself get hot all over again, she wisely drew back. "Did you peek into the garage while I was knocked out?"

Xavier chuckled. Ebony made it sound like she had been the other half of a boxing match. "No, Tyson. I didn't."

Laughing, and tinkling, she grabbed his hand and led him back down the hall. This time when they reached the garage door, she took a thick, black scarf from out of the closet. The blindfold was a soft, satiny material. After tying it around his eyes, Ebony opened the door, guided him down the steps, and then flicked on the lights. Releasing the blindfold, she yelled, "Surprise!"

Xavier blinked rapidly. "I…I—I don't understand."

Ebony laughed. "The BMW with the big red ribbon is yours!"

A shiny 325 BMW, with tinted windows, sat between Ebony's SUV and her convertible. Xavier shook his head. His eyebrows had climbed up to his hairline and his eyes were clouded with bewilderment. Stretching a hand toward the car, he said, "You bought me a car?"

Ebony's head bounced up and down like a bobble doll. She

spoke with childlike enthusiasm as she relayed the car's many features. "It has a hundred and eighty-four horsepower, a sunroof, navigational system, power everything, a leather interior, combined CD and tape player, a security alarm…"

Xavier's mind was too full to ask how, or why. It took several minutes before the shock wore off and he could collect himself enough to speak. He opened his mouth, then closed it. Unsure of what to say and scared he would sound like a bumbling fool if he attempted to speak, he rubbed his hands over his eyes to ensure this wasn't a dream.

When he opened his eyes, the car was still there.

"Well? What do you think?"

Xavier didn't know what to say. Didn't know where to begin. This was the last thing he expected from her. "I…I…I thought you bought me a mountain bike."

"Why? I never said I was getting you a bike."

"I know, but when we headed for the garage, I assumed…" Xavier dragged a hand over his head. "I can't believe you'd do something like this."

"Do you like it?"

"I love it," he admitted, taking a step forward and peering into the passenger window. "It's the right make and model, and the color is perfect—" He forced himself to calm down. No use getting excited over something he wasn't going to keep.

A long, uncomfortable silence settled over the garage.

Xavier took her hands. "I appreciate the thought, honey, I really do. No one has ever gone to such lengths to surprise me or bought me something this expensive, but as much as I love the car, and you for making my birthday a night to remember, I can't accept it."

Ebony didn't reply; she had expected Xavier to refuse the gift. In the last two months, she had discovered that Xavier Reed was as stubborn as an ox. He didn't ask for directions when he was lost, would rather struggle on his own than ask for help and he couldn't stomach being wrong. When she had asked him what he wanted for this birthday, he'd shrugged off the question. "Nothing. I have everything I need." Ebony covered her mouth with her hand to keep from laughing. Sometimes, Xavier could be so funny. It was his show of indifference that had led her to do some snooping. One night when he ran out to rent a movie, Ebony logged on to his computer and within seconds, found what he was pining after. By the time Xavier got back with the video, Ebony had printed off the necessary information, logged off his computer and returned to the bedroom.

Ebony kissed his cheek. "It's a gift, Xavier. You can't turn down a gift. That wouldn't be right."

"It's too much. I can't take it."

"You can and you will."

"No, seriously, I can't. I..." Xavier didn't finish his thought. What he wanted to say was, who had ever heard of a woman buying a man a car? And a BMW at that?

Ebony took a deep breath and blew it out. "Give me one good reason why you can't accept the car."

"Buying me clothes is one thing, Ebony, but shelling out thousands of dollars for a car is a whole other issue." He paused. "I wouldn't feel comfortable driving this car knowing that you paid for it. What would I say when my co-workers asked me where I got it from?"

"Tell them it's none of their damn business. Or tell them the truth. Tell them you have a wonderful girlfriend who helped you pick it out."

Xavier managed a small smile.

Ebony thought for a moment. There had to be something she could say to make him come around. She recalled late-night conversations they'd had in bed, secrets he had shared, and all the Sunday afternoons they had cooked together. Sundays. Church. *That's it!* "Remember a few weeks back when Deacon Wright testified about his house burning down and the church rallying around him and his family?"

Xavier played dumb. "No, not really."

"He said, 'I felt like a pauper when Pastor Henderson showed up at my in-laws' house and handed me that check, but my wife looked at me and said, "Fool, you better take that money before he changes his mind! It's a gift from God!"'"

"I can see where you're going with this, Ebony, but this situation is completely different. I'm not in need. I have a perfectly good car—"

"A gift is a gift, Xavier. The point Deacon Wright was trying to make was that—"

"I'm not taking the car," he said, interrupting her. The miserable expression on her face wrung at his heart, but instead of relenting, he added, "It wouldn't be right. I'm a man and—"

"So the only reason you won't take the car is because I bought it? You know what, Xavier, you're—" Ebony stopped herself from reaming him out. Calling him names wouldn't help any, either. "I just wanted to do something special for you. Is that so bad? You're always taking care of me and I wanted to do the same for you. Will you please reconsider?" When Xavier shoved his hands into his pockets and looked away, Ebony's shoulders sagged in defeat. "I thought we were building toward something, Xavier. I guess I was wrong." She unclasped the charm bracelet and pressed it into his palm. "If you can't accept my gift, then I can't accept yours."

After a long and lengthy pause, he asked, "How much was the down payment?"

When Ebony quoted the exact amount, his lips parted in surprise. "That's it? How'd you manage that?"

"I'm a master negotiator," she said, cupping her hands

around the back of his neck. "I've been a loyal customer of Motorworks BMW for years, and over the years, I referred friends, employees, clients and associates to the dealership. So when I walked in and told the manager his most loyal customer needed a new BMW 325, he gave me a deal I couldn't refuse."

Xavier had seen Ebony in action before and he didn't doubt for a minute that she was telling him the truth. Once she had convinced a store manager to give her a discount off a designer dress because it had a loose thread. Another time, she had scored gift certificates at a restaurant because her appetizer was cold. She was so polite and persuasive, most people didn't even realize they were being sweet-talked. He couldn't blame her for outconning a car salesman, could he? As he deliberated over what to do, something she had said earlier came back to him. "I'll take the car, but only if you agree to my conditions."

"Okay, let me see what you got." Ebony didn't want to return the car. Maybe giving Xavier a BMW for his birthday was a little over the top. In hindsight, the first class tickets to Paris would probably have been a better choice. But what was the point of having money if you couldn't share it with the people you loved? And buying Xavier the car would benefit them both. Ebony abhorred his rusted jalopy. It was a bucket with tires and she would have put a match to it weeks ago if she thought she could get away with it. It announced his arrival a block before he reached his destination and had more holes in it than a hockey net. The worst part was when Xavier put it in Reverse, it backfired so loud Ebony thought they were being shot at.

"You have to agree to let me pay you back half of the down payment." Xavier grinned when Ebony's lips tightened. She was so cute when she was angry. "Agreed?"

Fuming silently, she nodded.

"Very well, then. On to condition number two. You have to come with me to my parents' barbecue." Xavier watched her eyes dim. Convinced that she was going to reject his proposition, he cupped her hands in his palms and stared down at her. "You said you wanted to do something special for me. Meeting my family would be the best birthday gift you could ever give me, Ebony." Xavier kissed her softly on the lips, but she didn't respond with her usual heat. "Please?"

"Okay, I'll go."

He hugged her tight, and she melted into his loving embrace. After putting back on the charm bracelet, she handed him the car keys. "Here, these are for you."

Giving in to his excitement, he dangled the keys in front of her face. "How about we go for a spin in *my* new Beemer?" After another quick kiss, he dropped his voice to a conspiratorial whisper. "I say we find a secluded spot on lovers lane and christen the back seat."

"Now you're talking!" Ebony said, swiping the keys out of his hand and sauntering over to the car. "Get in. *I'll* drive."

Chapter 17

"Don't worry, sweetheart. My family's going to love you." Xavier helped Ebony out of the car and slammed the door behind her. After activating the alarm, he took her by the hand and led her up the narrow sidewalk. Her hands were clammy and Xavier had a feeling that fact had everything to do with meeting his folks and nothing to do with the record-breaking temperature. The air-conditioning had been on in the BMW the entire drive, and at one point Ebony had complained that she was cold, so he had turned it down.

Xavier gave her hand a gentle squeeze. "Nervous?"

Too preoccupied with her thoughts to answer, she shook her head absently.

"You look great, Ebony." He hugged her to his side, and dropped a kiss on her shoulder. His eyes moved leisurely down the slope of her curvy hips to her shapely legs. "When we get back home, I want to see what's underneath this dress."

His comment brought a lusty grin to Ebony's face, and momentarily eased her anxiety. Touching a hand to her freshly permed hair, she asked Xavier if he thought she looked okay. "You sure your mom won't think this dress is too tight? Or too short?"

"I'm sure," he told her. Xavier was glad she'd changed out of that unsightly brown dress and into something more stylish. It had taken all his self-control to keep from laughing when Ebony asked him what he thought of the shapeless, long-sleeved dress. It looked like it might strangle her. Xavier never thought he'd see the day when Ebony would look anything but beautiful, but in the high-necked, floor-grazing tunic-styled outfit, she had resembled a middle-aged Amish woman. The outfit had done her drool-worthy figure a disservice, and even someone as gorgeous as Vivica A. Fox wouldn't have made that dress look good. It reminded him of something he had seen her aunt Mae wear. *I wonder if*...Xavier quickly discarded the thought. Touched that she was going to great lengths to impress his family, but disappointed that she was trying to change who she was in the process, he had suggested she wear something a little less motherly and a little more sexy.

Xavier gave her a soft peck on the cheek. "Still doing okay?"

Ebony wished he would stop asking her that. His repeated questions and effusive concern were making her nervous. She viewed this visit to his parents' house with apprehension, but wisely kept her fears to herself. No sense upsetting the birthday boy. "I'm fine," she lied, her cheeks lifting into a small smile. "I'm not stressing and you shouldn't, either. Try and relax, Xavier. It's just a family dinner."

Xavier laughed. Ebony was imploring him to relax, but she was the one wearing a tight smile. Though conservatively clothed in a pearly-white dress and low-heeled sandals, she looked more like herself than she had in outfit number one.

Smoothing her hand over her hair for the hundredth time, she inhaled the sweet scent of summer. Birds chirped. Lawn mowers buzzed. Flowers permeated the air. The weather was seasonable for August—a mixture of hot days and humid nights—but it felt ten times hotter than when they had left her house twenty minutes ago.

The Reed family lived on a quiet street, close to a handful of parks, plazas and recreation centers. House number fifty-two featured fresh paint, an immaculate lawn surrounded by plants and flowers, and a tiny man-made pond. The sandstone brown house wasn't the biggest one on the block, but it was definitely the prettiest. A row of morning glory flowers adorned the stone walkway and a healthy fruit and vegetable garden stretched square around the house.

Even from several feet away, she could hear music and laughter. Ebony yanked down the hem of her dress and took a deep relaxing breath. *I can do this,* she told herself for what seemed like the hundredth time. For the next two hours, she was going to be on her best behavior. No suggestive jokes. No talk of work. And no making eyes at Xavier. For the rest of the day, she was going to focus on winning over his family, namely Jacqueline. If his sister gave them her approval, they were set.

Set for what? asked the quiet voice inside her head.

Ebony ignored the voice.

Xavier led her around to the side of the house. Mosaic stepping-stones created a colorful pathway to the sprawling backyard that accommodated a hammock, a flower bed and a picnic table covered in an assortment of barbecue-friendly foods. The sun, which had been shining brightly just moments before, retreated behind white, hilly-looking clouds. *I hope that's not a sign,* she thought, waiting for someone to answer the door. *God, I hope these people like me.* But when a willowy, dark-skinned woman with dimples as deep as a pocket flung her arms around Xavier and wished him a Happy Birthday, Ebony's fears dissipated. Mrs. Reed was nothing like what she had expected. There was nothing serious or somber about her. She was wearing red in various shades and even had her nails and toenails painted in the color. Red blush dusted the apples of her cheeks, and subtle tones of blond were in her neck-length, jet-black hair.

A woman this lively and bright couldn't hate anybody, could she? Ebony looked on incredulously as the woman rocked Xavier from side to side. He stood several feet above her, but he was being cuddled and kissed as if he were a five-year-old boy.

Ebony expected him to look embarrassed when they finally parted, but there was no sign of sheepishness on his face.

Mrs. Reed turned away from her son, and faced the striking-looking woman to her left. Her face spread into a welcoming smile. "Hello, there. I'm Xavier's mother, Gloria. You must be Tasha."

Ebony dropped Xavier's hand like she was discarding a piece of garbage. Staring up at him in disbelief, she envisioned her hands closing around his neck and squeezing the dear life out of him. Clasping her hands together, to keep from smacking the innocent smile off his face, she returned her gaze to his mother. Ebony fought to maintain her composure. Anger bubbled up inside her, but her countenance betrayed nothing. She opened her mouth to correct Mrs. Reed, but before she could get a single word out, the woman pointed a finger in her face and yelled, "Gotcha!"

Mrs. Reed chortled long and hard. "I'm just having some fun with you, Ebony. I wasn't expecting Xavier to come home with anybody named Tasha. He's told us all about you and I think I speak for the entire family when I say it's a pleasure to finally meet you."

Ebony picked her jaw up from the ground. Putting a hand on her chest, she said, "Please don't do that again, Mrs. Reed. You almost gave me a heart attack!"

All three laughed. Then, to Ebony's surprise, Gloria pulled her into her arms. The woman had such a strong upper body and squeezed her so tight Ebony thought she heard a rib crack.

"Now you bring your pretty little self in here and meet the rest of the family."

"Are Andrew and Jackie here?" Xavier asked. "I didn't see their van parked outside."

Gloria ushered them inside. "They're at Lamaze class, but Jacqueline said they'd try to be here by dessert."

Forty-five minutes after they arrived, Ebony was still working on her first plate of barbecue. Smiling politely at the elderly women staring over at her, she took a sip of her pink lemonade. The Reed family were nice people. Warm, hospitable, openhearted. Aunts, uncles, cousins and even small children had made their way over to where she was sitting in the dining room, and introduced themselves. Each family member had asked a ton of personal questions, but also supplied new information about Xavier. He was born three minutes after Jacqueline. In fifth grade he won the statewide spelling bee. He was the star of his high school basketball and baseball teams. But it was his mother who provided the piece of news that had left Ebony's mouth hanging.

"You know," she whispered, while Xavier was off tending to the grill, "you're the first woman he has brought home in years." Mrs. Reed chuckled when Ebony's eyes spread.

"B-b-but Xavier's had a lot of girlfriends."

"But none of them as smart or as pretty as you." With a wink, she added, "Xavier cares an awful lot about you, Ebony, and now that I've met you for myself, I can see why."

Her smile warmed Ebony's heart.

"Would you like to see some childhood pictures of Xavier?"

"I'd love to! I bet that boy was a handful," she joked.

Mrs. Reed laughed good-naturedly, and said, "He sure was," before hustling off. She returned seconds later, weighted down by an armload of photo albums, certificates and even a couple of Xavier's elementary school report cards. By the time Xavier returned from outside, Ebony was beginning to think he had planned the whole evening. His family was going out of their way to welcome her. They kept her entertained with stories of his childhood exploits and personal accomplishments, and soon the noise, the heat and the boisterous bursts of laughter didn't bother her. And after three animated and competitive games of dominoes and two glasses of wine, Ebony felt like a Reed herself.

"What are your intentions toward my boy?"

Ebony turned at the sound of the voice behind her. Xavier's father could easily have passed for his older brother if it weren't for the speckled gray hair, black-rimmed glasses and bushy mustache. Her boyfriend had obviously inherited his distinguished looks from his father and his warm, nurturing spirit from his mother. "Pardon me?" she said, noticing the living room was suddenly library-quiet. *Did somebody turn off the TV? What happened to the music?*

"Well, you've been dating Xavier now for what—three months?" When she nodded, he continued. "That's more than enough time to know how you feel about someone. I married my wife after our fifth date. Don't take long to know if you love someone." Mr. Reed thumped Xavier heartily on the back. "I guess what I'm asking is whether or not you see a future with my boy."

Ebony made no attempt to hide her shock. *Is he serious?* she thought, shooting a look at Xavier. Communicating with her eyes, she told him to do something. Instead of telling his father to back off, like she hoped, he popped a piece of shrimp into his mouth and shrugged his shoulders casually. "Answer the question," he mouthed.

Knowing Xavier as well as she did, she recognized the amused expression on his face. Ebony cleared her throat, then took a mouthful of her wine. Putting on her best smile, she told Mr. Reed, "Xavier's the best boyfriend I've ever had. He listens to me. He encourages me. He treats me like a queen. He's an all-round great guy!"

Mr. Reed's face broke out into a proud smile as if she was directing her praise at him. "That's my boy." He thumped Xavier on the back. "Yup, that's my boy!"

"But as for our future as a couple, I can't answer that because I don't know." When Ebony saw Mr. Reed's smile slide away and a frown work its way onto his thin lips, she quickly added, "Only God knows what the future holds, right?"

That seemed to pacify the older gentleman. "You know what, Ebony? You're right," he agreed, his tone suddenly jovial. Ebony Garrett could skirt around the issue all she wanted; she wasn't fooling anybody. He knew a thing or two about love and it was clear to him and everyone else in the room that she was in love with his son. Xavier's and Ebony's mutual devotion and affection were evident for all to see and Theodore couldn't be happier. Finally his son had found a woman to love. Ebony would make an affable daughter-in-law and a wonderful addition to the family. Cheered by his thoughts, he pointed at her near empty wineglass. "Would you like a refill?"

Ebony didn't want a third glass of wine, but she didn't want Xavier's dad asking her any more questions, either. "That would be nice. Thank you, Mr. Reed."

"Oh, enough of that Mr. Reed stuff," he scoffed, waving

away the title. "We're practically family now, so call me Theodore or Pops."

Ebony would rather call him Mr. Reed, but she wasn't about to argue. If he wanted her to call him by his first name, that's what she'd do. She sighed in relief when the music was turned back on and the chatter resumed.

Watching Mr. Reed weave his way through the jam-packed living room, Ebony hoped he would take his time coming back. Sighing deeply, she soothed her hands over her face. That had been a close one. Normally Ebony had the confidence to tell it like it was, but she didn't want to disappoint Mr. and Mrs. Reed. They clearly loved their son, but what was most noticeable was that the entire family was anxious for him to claim a bride. Ebony turned to Xavier. "I could've used some help, you know."

He coaxed a smile from her lips, by kissing her cheek. When he snuck a hand underneath the table and caressed her thigh, Ebony felt her frustration slip away. "I didn't interrupt, because I was curious to hear what you were going to say."

Ebony regarded him with pointed eyes. "Oh, you were, were you? What were you hoping to hear?"

"The truth."

"Did you hear the answer you were looking for?"

"Yes and no. You're right. We can't see the future, but God does take what we want into consideration. 'Make your requests be made known,'" he quoted. "That's what the good book says. What do you want for us, Ebony?"

You she heard a small voice say. Ebony spent some time mulling over his question. Xavier was a calm presence and had provided the stability she needed in her life. They were a perfect fit. Although Ebony was now open to the possibility of marriage, she wasn't ready for such an enormous commitment.

Inclining his head to the right, he searched her face for

answers. Xavier would have preferred to have this conversation at home, but he wasn't about to let this opportunity to discuss their future pass by. "I know what I want, Ebony. I want you." Flicking a finger between them, he said, "This is not just a summer romance. I know the thought of settling down and starting a family scares you, but that's where I see things headed."

The flash of panic in Ebony's eyes didn't go unnoticed. Caressing her cheek with his thumb, he watched her gaze drift fretfully around the room. They would be celebrating their four-month anniversary in a week, and although this talk was eight months too early, Xavier couldn't stop himself from sharing his heart. He was ready. Ready to propose. Ready to make her his wife. Ready to spend the rest of his life with her. Her distaste for marriage was the only thing stopping him from buying the ring and dropping to one knee.

Living together was another option, but not one he was keen on. "We're practically living together now," Ebony would say when it came up in conversation. "When we're not at my place, we're at yours, so why don't you just sell your house and move in with me?"

Good question often went unsaid. Xavier wanted to. He really, really wanted to. The thought of waking up every morning with Ebony in his arms would be a dream come true. He loved the thought of them living together, but as husband and wife, not boyfriend and girlfriend. Ebony deserved more than that. She ought to have the security that marriage provided, and so should he.

"Ebony, talk to me." He pushed aside his desire to kiss her, and touched the side of her face instead. He leaned in so his mouth was against her ear. "I want to know what you're thinking and how you're feeling and if you want me as much as I want you." There was so much more Xavier wanted to say.

He wanted to tell her that his best days were when they were together, his worst days when they were apart. The evenings that she had business dinners and staff meetings were the longest four hours of his life. He occupied the time by going to the gym, or hanging out with the guys, and although he enjoyed working out and spending time with his friends, he often felt like he was just killing time until she got home.

Xavier made small, light circles on her back. The heat of his breath against Ebony's ear gave her goose bumps. She looked cautiously around the room. No one was watching them, but she still didn't feel comfortable discussing their future at his parents' dining room table. "We can't talk about this now."

"When?"

"When what?"

Xavier could tell by the way Ebony was fidgeting with her charm bracelet that she was uneasy, but he didn't remove his hands from her face. "When are we going to talk about our future?"

"Later." Ebony was relieved that he didn't push her further. She said a silent prayer of thanks when Mrs. Reed emerged from the kitchen and announced it was time for dessert. Xavier left to grab them a few slices of pumpkin pie, leaving Ebony alone with his long-winded uncle. Uncle Posey talked animatedly about his stint in a county jail back in sixty-three. He had more hair on his arms than Alf and stammered excessively, but the more he drank, the less he stuttered. Ebony would have moved to another seat, but there was nowhere else to go. Friends and relatives were packed into the house so tight there was little room to breathe, let alone walk.

Ebony's gaze rested on Mr. and Mrs. Reed. They were sitting side by side, smiling, laughing, whispering to each other. Ebony had a strong suspicion she was the topic of choice. They'd been watching her off and on ever since Xavier's grand "confession." Ebony didn't mind that they were eyeballing her; she was just relieved that the afternoon had gone smoothly. The Reed family was incredibly warm, and spending time with Xavier's female cousins had given her insight into what he had been like as a teen.

Xavier returned and set a plateful of sweets down in front of her. Forking a piece of banana bread into her mouth, she noticed Mr. and Mrs. Reed kissing. *Cute,* she thought, trying not to stare. The uxorious man doted on his wife like they were newlyweds, rather than a couple with adult children. Mrs. Reed played the role of the submissive housewife perfectly. Her husband was the man of the house and Ebony guessed the arrangement suited Gloria just fine. She was old school with a capital O. During the course of the afternoon, she had waited on everyone, specifically the men and the children, and refused to sit down until everyone had a hot plate of food in their hands.

I wonder if that will be me one day, Ebony thought, glancing over at Xavier. A broad and content smile sat on his lips. *Who knows?*

Chapter 18

Ebony had had a wonderful evening. The food was delicious, the company pleasant and the time well spent, but now she was ready to go home. Her cheeks hurt from smiling and she was feeling tipsy from all those glasses of red wine.

Detecting a shift in her mood, Xavier lovingly rubbed the back of her neck. Her illuminating smile almost eclipsed the sleepiness in her eyes. "Ready?"

Ebony didn't want to take Xavier away from his family, but she could barely keep her eyes open. "Are you?"

When Xavier leaned over and whispered in her ear, she couldn't hold back her smile. The man had a gift when it came to reading her thoughts. It was as if he was focusing all of his energy and looking into her heart. "Yes, I'm hungry for you, too," she whispered, in response to his question, "but I don't want you to have to leave on account of me. If you want to stay longer, I can call a cab. I don't mind."

"No, we can go." Xavier suppressed a yawn. Then he patted his stomach and said, "I'm starting to feel a little sleepy. I think I ate too much."

"You did."

They both laughed.

Straining his neck toward the foyer, Xavier wondered out loud where his sister was. "Man, you've met my grandparents, my cousins and even Uncle Posey, but the one person I've been dying for you to meet isn't here."

Noting the frustration in his voice, she rubbed a hand across his back. "How about we invite Jacqueline and Andrew over for dinner on Friday? You can fire up the grill, I can order in some side dishes from Stella's catering and we'll make a whole evening of it. I'll invite Kendall, Turner, Opal and Spencer. It'll be a mini dinner party."

Xavier rewarded her thoughtfulness with a kiss. "That would be great."

Ebony spotted Gloria, and put some space between them. She wasn't about to ruin a perfectly good evening by getting fresh with Xavier at his parents' house. Aunt Mae had raised her better than that. "Do you need some help, Mrs. Reed?" Ebony offered, as the older woman passed by with an army of plates in her hands. She didn't wait for an answer. She stood to her feet. "Here, let me take some of these from you."

Gloria beamed. "I like her, Xavier. She's beautiful, mannerly and a successful businesswoman, too?" She turned back to Ebony. "Thank you, dear. Just follow me."

Ebony did as she was told. The kitchen was crawling with people, mostly women, griping about the problems they were having with their men and discussing hair and makeup. When the room emptied, and the counter was cleared of pots, Ebony and Gloria got down to work. The two women chatted easily, while they worked to get the kitchen back in order. When they heard a commotion in the other room, Gloria excused herself. "I'm going to see what all the fuss is about. Don't you move. I'll be right back."

Ebony heard Xavier say over the noise, "Happy Birthday, sis! I'm so glad you made it. I was beginning to think you guys weren't coming. How's my niece?"

"Xavier, stop that. The baby might hear you! We don't know if we're having a girl or a boy, but I know my body better than you do, and it's telling me that there's a boy in here!" Jovial laughter filtered into the kitchen.

That voice, Ebony thought, as she loaded the last of the dishes into the dishwasher, *I know that voice.* The squeaky childlike tone tickled her memory like a feather. Clients, business acquaintances and past colleagues ran through her mind at lightning speed. For some reason, she felt like this person was someway connected to her personal life. Allowing her mind to wander, she closed her eyes in concentration. Someone she went to grade school with? No. An old college friend? No.

No! No! No!

Ebony swallowed hard, her entire body quivering uncontrollably. *It couldn't be, could it? No. It can't be her,* she decided, unwilling to face her darkest fear. *It can't be!* She was so caught up in her musings she didn't hear Xavier call her name.

"Put those dishes down, and come over here and meet my sister, Ebony."

God, please, no! Don't let this be happening to me! She felt the heat rise up the walls of her chest, could actually hear the erratic beating of her heart. *It's…it's…it's…Malcolm's wife.*

"Jackie, this incredible woman…"

Ebony felt like everything was happening in slow motion. She turned around and ended up face-to-face with her past. The hairs on her arms and neck stood up. Her eyes swept over the woman's small delicate features. Xavier's sister was more cute than pretty. Chin-length bob, high, graceful cheekbones, button nose. With the woman standing hip to hip with Xavier, Ebony could easily see the resemblance between the two. Jacqueline had the same cocoa butter complexion and slight dimple in her right cheek that Xavier had.

In a yellow maternity dress and a multicolored scarf around her neck, Jacqueline resembled a walking traffic light. Looking about eight months pregnant, the mother-to-be certainly wasn't a threat, but the expression on her face gave Ebony the chills. Hate shone in Jacqueline's eyes and if looks could kill, two medics would be carrying Ebony's corpse outside.

Grinning like a circus clown, Xavier looped his arm around Malcolm's wife. Or rather, ex-wife. *Maybe she won't recognize me. After all, it's been, what, six years?* Reality quickly set in. *Of course she'll recognize me. A wife never forgets the other woman.*

"What is *she* doing here?"

The light in Xavier's eyes dimmed. "You guys know each other?"

"Of course I know who she is!" Jacqueline's temper flared. "That's the bitch who stole my husband!" Her voice rose to dangerous heights. If it wasn't for the animated conversations and riotous laughter coming from the living room, the whole house would've heard her.

Xavier had never heard Jacqueline curse, and her tone was sharper than a piece of jagged glass. Ebony was...the other woman? The woman Malcolm had been sleeping with? Xavier felt like all the air in his body had been sucked out of his lungs. This had to be a misunderstanding. Or a case of mistaken identity. "Jackie, are you sure—"

"Of course I'm sure!" she snapped. "Do you think I'd forget the woman who stole my husband?"

Xavier paled when he saw Ebony lower her head. There was nothing worse than the two women you loved fighting, but before he could diffuse the situation, he had to calm himself. He had to step in, but he'd be no good to anybody if he acted on his emotions. After taking a deep breath, he offered Jacqueline some words of comfort. "Jackie, you have Andrew and the baby and—"

She cut in. "Leave me alone, Xavier. This doesn't concern you." Jacqueline stared at Ebony with an almost violent hatred. She balled her hands into tight fists and stepped deeper into the room.

For a second, Ebony thought Jacqueline was going to hit her. The mother-to-be might be petite, but like Ebony's marketing director, Sabrina, it was apparent she was a fighter.

In a very controlled voice, Jacqueline said, "The day I caught you *screwing* my husband was the worst day of my life. I thought I was going to die. Malcolm and I had a few problems, but we were working things out. That is, until *you* came along." She jabbed her index finger at Ebony's chest with such force, Ebony was certain it would leave a bruise.

The best thing Ebony could do was to take the high road. Let Jacqueline get it all out. Permit her to say all the things she'd been holding inside all these years. Ebony would have followed the route of her thoughts, had it not been for Xavier listening in. What they had was far too precious to be ruined by vicious lies. Jacqueline could call her everything in the book, but Ebony didn't want Xavier to think she had wilfully and deceitfully ruined her marriage.

Intent on clearing up the past, Ebony said, "I didn't wreck your marriage, Jacqueline. I didn't know—"

"You're pathetic, you know that? Utterly pathetic. You're a home wrecker. A sleazy gold digger who doesn't have what it takes to find her own man, so she goes after happily married men. 'I didn't know Malcolm was married,'" she mimicked. "Bullshit! You knew…you just didn't care!"

Ebony willed herself not to cry. Not here. Not now. She wanted to fight back, wanted to clear her name, wanted to make things right, but arguing with Jacqueline would only make things worse. Eyes glazed with pain, she spoke in a low, contrite tone. "I swear to you, I didn't know. I'm sorry if—"

"Shut up!" Jacqueline yelled, cradling her stomach protectively. She clutched her brother's arm and forced him to look at her. "Stay away from her, Xavier. I know her type. She's nothing but trouble. I wouldn't be surprised if she's slept with other married men. I bet she intentionally seeks them out to help finance her extravagant lifestyle."

"That's not true!" Ebony protested. She started to say more, but when she saw the wounded expression on Xavier's face, she closed her mouth. He looked like he'd been kicked in the stomach and then rolled over and pummeled in the back. His face was blanketed with hurt and he couldn't even bring himself to meet her eyes.

Ebony would be the first to admit that she had made some bad choices in life. There was a time when she didn't care about anyone or anything. She had dated men who were all wrong for her. Spent ridiculous amounts of money. Partied more than she should have. But with the help of aunt Mae, and the support of her girlfriends, she had cleaned up her act. Through intense counseling, she had come to terms with her bitter childhood and the untimely death of her parents.

Ebony wasn't the same naive twenty-five-year-old who had been seduced and deceived by Malcolm Pleiss. She had changed and the past was long behind her. If she had the power to turn back the hands of time, she would. But she couldn't.

"Women like you make me sick. You screw around, spreading diseases and breaking up happy homes. You have no consideration at all for the families left behind to pick up the pieces!"

Ebony wasn't going to take any more of this abuse. She wasn't going to stand aside while Jacqueline bashed her good name and humiliated her in front of the man she loved. Poking out her chest, she straightened her shoulders and lifted her chin defiantly. It didn't matter what Jacqueline thought of her; she knew the truth and that's all that really mattered. Clearing the anguish from her voice and resting the dishrag on the counter, she directed her comments to Xavier. "I'm leaving."

Ebony fled the room before Xavier could reply. After collecting her purse from one of the back bedrooms, she hurried down the hall toward the foyer. *You can't leave like this!* The voice in her head sounded like aunt Mae. Leaving the barbecue without saying goodbye to Xavier's parents would be rude. Mr. and Mrs. Reed had opened their home to her, and made her feel welcomed. Regardless of her hurt, she had to extend her heartfelt thanks to the couple. Ebony found them in the backyard, playing a game of spades with another couple.

"Thanks for everything," she said, when they looked up and acknowledged her presence with a smile. "I had a lovely time."

"You're leaving now?" Gloria attempted to stand. "Well, the least I can do is see you and Xavier off."

"No!" Ebony stripped the panic from her voice, and mustered a smile. "Xavier's not leaving. He's going to stay and visit with his sister for a while. I'm taking a cab."

"Are you sure?" Mr. Reed asked. "Gloria and I can run you home and come right back."

"No, I'll be all right. I don't live too far from here."

"Oh, okay." Gloria gave her a hug. "Don't be a stranger, you hear? I expect to see you at all the family gatherings from now on. Understand?"

Ebony hated lying to the woman, but she had no choice. After promising to come by next week for Sunday dinner, she tore out of the backyard and down the walkway.

Chapter 19

Depending on her mood, Ebony had the ability to play the sultry siren, the coy cutie, the sexy bombshell, or the no-nonsense businesswoman. She could be mysterious and seductive one minute, hard-hitting and outspoken the next. Tonight, she was playing a role Kendall had never seen: the distraught ex-girlfriend.

When Kendall picked her up on the corner of Garfield and Seventh Boulevard, she could tell that Ebony had been crying. Her eyes were red, her cheeks were puffy and her shoulders were hunched. Ebony wasn't a crier. Aside from the occasional movie or heart-wrenching Oprah moment, she didn't tear up. Kendall could count on one hand the number of times she had seen her best friend cry, and over a man? Never. She had encouraged Ebony to talk about what happened, but she'd looked away and stared out the window.

Kendall couldn't make sense of her best friend's behavior.

Ebony was a woman of action. If she didn't like the way things were going, she made changes. No whining. No complaining. No pity parties. But when Kendall pressed her for answers, she said in a sad, pitiful voice, "I can't believe I was stupid enough to believe Xavier loved me." Name-calling was completely out of character for Ebony; Kendall had never heard her best friend chastise herself. With tears in her eyes, Ebony recounted what happened at the barbecue. Kendall could understand why she was upset, could understand why she was feeling so low, but she couldn't stomach Ebony calling herself names.

Kendall tried to reason with Ebony, but it was no use. She wouldn't listen to what she had to say and lashed out whenever Kendall tried to comfort her. Sensing she wouldn't be able to handle this situation on her own, Kendall called for backup.

Opal arrived fifteen minutes after Kendall called. Setting her sunglasses down on the counter, she said, "I got here as fast as I could." She closed her arms around Ebony's shoulders and held her tight. "Do you want to talk about it?"

Ebony didn't know why, but her eyes filled with more tears. If she started crying in front of Opal, she would never have peace again. Mother Hen would insist she come and stay at her house and wouldn't back off until she agreed. Ebony pressed her eyes shut to ward off the tears. She needed another good cry, but now was not the time. Later, alone, in the privacy of her bedroom, she would let it out.

"Has Xavier called?"

Ebony shook her head.

Opal took a seat. "Why didn't he say anything when his sister was going off on you? Why didn't he tell her to back off?"

That very question had been circling in Ebony's mind ever since she left the Reed house. What bothered her the most wasn't facing off with Jacqueline or even the malicious things she'd said. It was Xavier's reaction. Or rather, lack of reaction. Jacqueline's accusations didn't trouble her half as much as his betrayal. He never once jumped in or came to her defense. He just stood there, watching, passing judgment with his eyes.

During the course of their relationship, Xavier had convinced her that she was special; that she mattered to him. Over the last few months, he had done all the little things men did to express their love. He brought her dinner when she was stuck behind her desk. She received three, sometimes four calls a day. Text messages and e-mails crowded her message box on a regular basis. But tonight, when she needed Xavier the most, he wasn't there for her.

What would have happened if Jacqueline had tried to hit me? Would he have hung back and cheered her on? Ebony took a sip of her tea. *Now, I'm just being silly. Xavier wouldn't let his sister beat on me, would he?* Sighing deeply, she stared down at her hands. Aspirin had alleviated her headache, but it did nothing to dilute the pain in her heart. The bubble bath had soothed her mind, relaxed her body and washed away the stench of the afternoon. She was still upset over what happened, but at least she wasn't bawling all over herself anymore. "Xavier didn't come to my defense because he believed what his sister said. Shouldn't surprise me. He's been judging me ever since day one."

"You don't mean that," Kendall said to her.

"Yes, I do. If Xavier truly cared about me—" she pinched two fingers together "—even a bit, he wouldn't have let his sister disrespect me like that. He would have stepped in."

"Don't say things like that, Ebony. You know that man loves you. Think of all the things he's done since you started dating." Kendall paused, as she thought back to yesterday. The excitement was clear in Ebony's voice when she called and told her about their romantic birthday dinner. And last week when Xavier showed up at the office with lunch for all of the staff, Ebony had kissed him in front of everyone. Her friend was still very much her own woman, but she had made room in her life for Xavier to come in. Kendall found herself amazed at the difference in her business partner. Ebony wasn't bopping around the office with a ridiculous grin on her face, or singing in the rain, but she was more patient and understanding with her employees. The staff was secretly hoping that the boss's new relationship would lead to marriage, because a happy boss meant a less stressful work environment. Kendall urged Ebony to be patient. "Wait until you've talked to him before you make any decisions. Don't discard a perfectly good relationship just because you're angry. Talk things out—"

"What's there to discuss?" Ebony asked, her voice devoid of any emotion. "We had our fun and now it's over. Xavier alluded to the fact that he loved me, but after what happened this afternoon, I'm sure any love he may have felt for me is gone."

Opal disagreed. "Love isn't like a faucet, Ebony. You can't turn your feelings off and on. Jamal and I have been divorced for years, but there's a big part of me that still loves him. Every time he picks up the girls, everything I ever felt for him comes rushing back. I'm with Kendall. Give Xavier a chance to explain. He needs to hear your side of the story, too. What happened between you and Malcolm was years ago. Xavier's a good man, he won't hold your past against you."

"Why bother? It's my word against hers. You don't have to be a genius to figure out who he's going to believe. Jacqueline painted the picture and he bought it." She snorted, "To hear her tell it, I'm a whore who only goes after happily married men."

"It doesn't matter what she thinks," Kendall told her. "The people who love you know the truth. You just have to make Xavier see that."

They sat in silence for several minutes, the tick of the grandfather clock the only sound in the room. A rush of cool air gushed through the kitchen window, filling the space with a soft breeze.

"I met with Yolanda this morning."

"Oh?" Since Kendall and Ebony couldn't agree on what to do with the district manager, they had suspended her without pay until they could reach a compromise. After checking in with the employees who worked under Yolanda and hearing all the admirable things they had to say about her, they had decided to give her one last chance. Yolanda had practically gotten down on her knees when she heard the news. Firing her would have been a mistake of epic proportions. The boutiques under her care had the highest sales, the most satisfied employees and the most creative merchandise displays. She was a talent, and they were convinced that she would do better.

"She came in to help us fine-tune the Women of Sensuality promotions and ended up giving us a few slogans, as well," Kendall said, sure the news would lift her partner's spirits.

"What did you come up with?"

Kendall filled her in. By the time she finished bringing Ebony up to speed, she had perked up a bit. "Sabrina wants us to get together on Wednesday to go over the budget, but I told her to pick another night. You have Changing Lives Through Meals in the evening and—"

"Wednesday's fine."

"But what about—"

Ebony reiterated, "I said, Wednesday's fine, Kendall."

"So, that's it," Opal concluded, refilling their mugs with tea, "you're not going to try and work things out?"

Rubbing the tenderness underneath her eyes, she said, "I'm going to go about my business and forget I ever met Xavier

Reed." Ebony stared down at her cup, wrestling with the feelings in her heart. Pushing aside her insecurities about the future, she took another long sip of her tea. "I'm not going to lose any sleep over what happened. I learned a lot from him, we had some great times together, but it's over and I'm okay with that." Kendall and Opal stared at her like she had just told them she was going to travel to South Africa and live in the jungle. "I'll be fine, you guys. Stop looking so worried. God, you two are acting like Xavier's a Greek god or something. He's no different than any of the other guys I've dated."

Ebony was lying, and Opal and Kendall both knew it.

Kendall looked long and hard at her best friend. Ebony loved Xavier with everything she had. He was the only man who had ever been given unlimited access to her house, her cars and even her finances. In turn, she had keys to his house, equal closet space in his bedroom and now had met his family. That alone was proof enough of his commitment. A man didn't bring a woman home to meet his mother unless he was in love.

Kendall was struck by another interesting fact. Since Ebony had started dating Xavier, she had called in sick or left early for "personal reasons" a dozen or more times; last year, Ebony hadn't missed a single day of work. Kendall thought of sharing this staggering fact with her friend, but decided against it. Ebony might take exception to it, and Kendall didn't want to do anything to upset her further. Besides, she was thrilled with the changes Ebony had made in her life. For the first time ever, she had found a happy medium between work and play. She still took work home in the evenings and came in on the weekend, but the overtime hours had ceased and she delegated more tasks to her assistant. "Why would you want to stop dating someone who's made you so happy?"

"His sister hates me. Jacqueline is the most important person in Xavier's life and though I want to be with him, I can't put him in a situation where he'd have to choose. That wouldn't be fair."

Opal covered Ebony's hand. "Talk to him. Tell him how you feel and then go from there. I know you're hurting and it may seem like things are over, but don't make any rash decisions until you've talked to him."

Kendall thought for a moment about the problems she had encountered with her husband's side of the family when they first started dating. "Remember when I moved in with you?"

Ebony did. The few days Kendall had said she would be staying had turned out to be three weeks. Ebony hadn't minded the company, though. It was nice having someone around, and her best friend could throw down in the kitchen. "That was the weekend Turner's parents visited, right?"

"And were they ever surprised to find a half-naked black woman frying bacon in their son's kitchen!" Kendall giggled, despite the anguish that had surrounded the situation. "They told Turner if he married me, they were going to disown him. He told me he didn't care what his parents said, and begged me to stay, but I knew the best thing I could do for both of us was give him the space and time to think about what he wanted." Her words came out powerfully. "Ebony, I had Turner's entire family to convince, and I'm still working on it, years later. You only have one person to win over—Jacqueline. You said yourself that the rest of his family welcomed you with open arms, so quit focusing on the negatives. Reach out to his sister. Go to her and tell her the truth. Do whatever it takes to change her mind." Kendall had one more thing to say. "And take it easy on Xavier. The brother's in a tight spot."

Ebony gave some thought to Kendall's words. She had been so busy feeling sorry for herself, she hadn't considered what Xavier must be going through. Her friend made a valid point. *This has to be a difficult time for him, too.*

Opal spoke next. "Things will work out, Ebony. I'm sure of it." She checked her watch, then stood. "I wish I could stay longer, but I left the girls at my neighbor's house and it's past Tessa's bedtime. I'll give you a call once the girls are in bed, okay?"

Ebony nodded.

"I should go, too. That husband of mine is probably wondering where I am." Kendall rubbed a hand across Ebony's back. "If you wake up in the morning and don't feel like coming in, stay home. After the day you've had, you deserve some R&R."

After another quick hug, Ebony walked her friends to the front door. Guilt pricked her heart as she watched Opal slip her feet back into a pair of her sandals. She had been so busy chasing after Xavier the last few months, she hadn't been much of a friend. Opal, who had been battling her weight all her life, had shed what appeared to be a good twenty pounds. Her face had thinned out, the flesh around her stomach was gone, but the most drastic change was the way her clothes fit. The clingy material of her powder-blue sundress hit the slope of her hips and showcased her slim thighs. Her loose, flowy micro braids were held together with a silver barrette, and added a soft feminine touch to her summer look. Ebony infused her voice with humor. "Looking good, Momma," she teased. "What have you been taking and where do I get some?"

Opal giggled.

"Doesn't she look hot?" Kendall asked Ebony.

"She does." Then to Opal, "How much weight have you lost?"

"Ah, give or take about eighteen pounds."

"You go, girl! I'm scared of you!" Ebony chuckled. It felt good to laugh again. This time, it was Ebony who threw her arms around Opal and squeezed tight. "Keep at it, girlfriend. I like the new you."

"Me, too." Swallowed by her career, her children and being there for her friends and family, Opal hadn't even noticed that an entire year had passed without a single date. Sure, she went out with male friends and co-workers, but it was never anything serious. No more waiting by the phone for Jamal to call. She was wasting her time waiting for him to come to his senses and ask to come back home. Opal was going to get out there and see what the dating world had to offer.

After agreeing to meet for lunch later in the week, Kendall and Opal left. Ebony watched her friends get into their respective cars, and waved goodbye.

Ebony closed the door and returned to the kitchen. As she entered the room, she spotted Opal's sunglasses sitting on the counter. Ebony snatched up the glasses and sprinted back down the hallway, in the hopes of catching her best friend before she drove out of the cul-de-sac. She flung open the door, but instead of entering a wide-open space, ran smack dab into Xavier.

Chapter 20

Ebony didn't want Xavier in her house. Didn't want him in her personal space, asking all sorts of questions, trying to get all up in her business. Her friends had cheered her up, given her the support she so desperately needed and helped to restore her self-confidence. Xavier being here would just complicate matters.

Her heart had shattered into a million pieces when Jacqueline humiliated her, and now Xavier was here to stomp on what little of her pride she had left. *I'm not going to let you hurt me,* she vowed, crossing her arms over her chest. Casting aside the advice she'd been given by her friends, she stepped back to create some distance and usher in some fresh air. "What do you want?"

Xavier stood firm. He had some hard questions for her and he wasn't leaving until he got answers. She had lied to him, maybe not point-blank, but neglecting to tell him she had once dated his brother-in-law was inexcusable. "We need to talk."

Anticipating her response, he added, "And I'm not leaving here until we get everything out in the open."

Ebony shivered as the wind flowed into the foyer. Rubbing the cold from her shoulders, she thought of what to do next. Ebony definitely wasn't in a talking mood and she didn't want to be badgered about her past. Exhausted didn't begin to describe her emotional state, and the sooner Xavier vacated the premises the sooner she could go to bed.

"Xavier, I want you to leave."

Pretending he didn't hear her, he closed the door behind him and slipped off his shoes. Not bothering to wait for an invitation, he stalked into the living room and sat down on the couch. Xavier waited for Ebony to join him, but when she didn't, he patted the empty space beside him. "Come here."

Ebony didn't know if she could. Being in such close proximity of him might end up working against her. What if he tried to kiss her? Or touched her hand? Pushing his kisses and soft touches out of her mind, she stood there quietly.

"Please?" The soft pleading of his eyes did her in.

Ebony ambled into the room and took a seat. Inhaling deeply, she waited for the interrogation to begin.

"Why didn't you tell me about you and Malcolm?"

Her lips pinched. "Tell you what, Xavier? How was I supposed to know you knew who Malcolm Pleiss was?"

"You didn't know he was married?"

"No!"

"Really?"

Ebony didn't know why, but she couldn't bring herself to meet his gaze. Maybe it was because of the skeptical look on his face or the way he was studying her. Xavier was implying that she knowingly took up with Malcolm. He couldn't be further from the truth. Making no effort to hide her displeasure, she said, "Malcolm told me he was separated."

His voice was thick with insinuation. "And you believed that?"

"There was no reason not to." She offered an explanation before Xavier could probe any further. "Malcolm had a two-bedroom apartment on Thomas Avenue, he was available whenever I needed him and he never once mentioned his wife in my presence. I didn't even know her name."

Ebony read the question in his eyes. "When I heard you and Jacqueline talking in the living room, I recognized her voice but I couldn't place her right away. All I knew was that she was somehow connected to my past."

"How did you get involved with Malcolm?"

Ebony hesitated. This was the question she had been dreading. What she said from here on out would definitely change the way Xavier saw her. Thoughts of Malcolm Pleiss came creeping in, and try as she might, she couldn't shake them. Normally Ebony stayed far away from men with baggage. She didn't date single fathers. Or divorcés. Refused to give her number to men who weren't gainfully employed, regardless of how fine they were. But with his confidence and won't-take-no-for-an-answer approach, Malcolm had easily won her over. Ebony had contacted five different construction companies about renovating one of her boutiques that had suffered flood damage. On top of guaranteeing the renovations could be done after store hours so that business wouldn't be disrupted, Malcolm had quoted an estimate five thousand dollars less than his competitors. Ebony would have been a fool to turn it down. "I met Malcolm at a low point in my life. My parents had just died, I was busting my ass trying to get my business off the ground and I was living on a meager three hours of sleep a night. Every time my head touched the pillow, I had a nightmare about my parents' car accident. It was those nightmares that ultimately brought Malcolm and me together."

"How so?"

"One morning when I showed up at the boutique looking haggard, Malcolm brought me a cup of coffee and offered his ear. We ended up talking for over an hour. He told me about the plane crash that ended his father's life and—" Ebony broke off when she noticed the harsh look on Xavier's face. His vacuous stare only added to her uncomfortableness. "What?"

"Malcolm's father isn't dead."

Ebony felt her face pale. She closed her eyes for a moment, trying to think. "But Malcolm told me his dad died in a TWA plane crash back in 1989. He even showed me the newspaper clipping he kept in his wallet."

"Malcolm Pleiss Sr. is very much alive. The last I heard, he was living in Vegas with a twenty-year-old showgirl."

"Like father, like son," slipped from Ebony's mouth. Shutting her eyes to block out the pain made it seem less real. In her mind's eye, she saw Malcolm holding her in a comforting embrace and telling her he knew what it was like to feel alone. "You're not alone, Ebony," he'd said in a deeply tender voice. "You have me now. I'm here for you. We'll get through this together."

Ebony shook her head in wonder. Besides being a cheat and a schemer, Malcolm Pleiss was also a pathological liar. He would say and do anything to get a woman into bed. Ebony wondered if anything he had told her was the truth. *I'll be thirty-three on my next birthday…I manage several contracting companies…I don't have any children…I love you, girl.* It was a marvel that Malcolm had the time to work with all the time he spent lying and juggling various women.

Regret filled Ebony's heart. And the more she thought about his deceit, the angrier she got. Malcolm might have regarded himself as a twenty-first-century Casanova, but he was a dirty, mangy dog in her book. "What kind of guy invents a story about his father dying just to worm his way into a woman's life? I can't believe this! He made up that whole story just to soften me up!"

"That's what it sounds like." Xavier actually felt sorry for her. When Ebony had told Jacqueline she didn't know Malcolm was married, he had mumbled under his breath. She sounded like the typical mistress. "Don't hold me accountable for my actions. I didn't know. I didn't know," were the first words out of an adulteress's mouth. But hearing what his ex-brother-in-law had done gave new credence to Ebony's claims. Cracking his knuckles, he pictured himself driving down to Prospect Park and paying the lowlife a visit. He didn't know his house number, but it wouldn't be too hard to find. There weren't too many Jaguars in Minneapolis and none had personalized plates that read Smokin'. Xavier shelved the thought for now. "What happened next?"

Ebony thought back to the first time Malcolm had taken her out for dinner. The man had wined and dined her to the tune of a two-hundred-dollar meal, plus tip. The pismo clam chowder and Maine lobster entrée had been the best meal Ebony had ever had. After date number one, they began seeing each other sporadically. A movie here, a dinner there. Nothing serious. Malcolm was an average looking guy with kind eyes and an easy smile, but she wasn't attracted to him. She didn't have fantasies about becoming his wife or having his babies. She enjoyed his company. She liked having someone she could talk to. Confide in. Vent to. Ebony considered Malcolm more of a confidant than a lover, so when he invited her to his thirty-third birthday party at the Marriott Hotel, she didn't think anything of it. That is, until she got to the suite and discovered she was the only guest. Swept up in the soft lights, Luther's velvety voice, and the champagne, she had allowed Malcolm to kiss her. He was in the middle of undressing her when the hotel door busted open and a hysterical woman screamed at the top of her lungs, "Get off my husband, you tramp!"

The sound of Xavier's voice brought Ebony out of her thoughts. She cleared her throat and manufactured a smile. "Did you say something?"

"Were you in love with Malcolm?"

"No."

Xavier was shocked by her prompt response. Ebony had been struggling to answer his questions ever since they sat down, but she had responded to the last one easily. Xavier swallowed. He hoped she would answer his next question with the same speed. "Did you guys sleep together?"

Ebony took her time answering. Jacqueline had done a venerable job of seeing to it that Xavier didn't trust her anymore. The seeds of doubt had been planted and there was nothing she could do to change that. Xavier's words played back in her mind as she considered her options. *There's no one in this world I'm closer to than Jackie.* There was a slim chance he'd forgive her if she told him the only reason she'd slept with Malcolm was because he'd pressured her. Xavier had been raised in a loving, supportive and deeply religious family; she had raised herself. Cliché as it might sound, blood was thicker than water and Ebony knew this was one fight she just couldn't win. Causing a rift in Xavier's relationship with his sister was the last thing she wanted to do. "I don't want to talk about it."

"I'll take that as a yes."

Ebony threw her hands up in disgusted resignation. "Take it any way you want. I'm not going to dredge up my past just to make you feel better." There was a lot more she wanted to say but she held her tongue. Everyone deserved a second chance, regardless of their past, but it was clear Xavier didn't see things that way. It was too late for them, but his eyes needed to be opened to his own prejudices. "We can't change our mistakes," she told him. "We can beat ourselves up all we want, but it won't change anything. Yes, I'm sorry about some of the things I've done, but I wouldn't be who I am today without those experiences. I never once questioned you about your past because it didn't matter. We—"

"What do you want to know?" Xavier demanded, raising his voice. "Go ahead and ask. I don't have anything to hide. My life is an open book."

"Your past means nothing to me. I don't care how many lovers you had before me, or how many times you've been in love, or if you used to watch porn." Ebony couldn't resist touching him. Her fingers caressed his cheeks, and then outlined his lips. When he managed a small smile, a frisson of hope filled her heart. If Xavier could find it in his heart to give her another chance, she would make sure he never regretted it. "Baby, all that matters to me is the man you are today. Your past has no bearing on our future and neither should mine," Ebony's voice faltered at the end and she had to stop a moment to control it. "The only thing I care about is us, right here, right now."

Her words pierced him to the core. Ebony had a damn good point. This wasn't the first time he'd been admonished to let go of the past and look to the future. He had heard it countless times before at Jubilee Christian Center. *If anyone is in Christ, old things have passed away, and new things have come.* As Xavier reflected on the power of the scripture, he was reminded of something his great-grandmother used to say. "Don't go stirring up old ghosts," she would warn, swaying in her wooden rocking chair, "because once you do, there's no turnin' back." His grandmother's words made sense, but his curiosity was burning a hole in the back of his head. It didn't matter that Jacqueline was happily remarried and awaiting the birth of her first child. He loved Ebony—mind, body and soul—but he couldn't move on until he knew every single detail of her affair with Malcolm.

Xavier's mind wandered. He envisioned Ebony in Malcolm's arms. They were in a seedy motel on the outskirts of town, and the busted neon green sign flashed across her clear and radiant brown skin. She was wearing a pink lace garter set, high heels, her jet-black hair a volume of springy curls. Xavier saw Malcolm's grubby hands pawing her breasts, and then gliding down the length of her stomach. Half drunk, they tumbled onto the battered queen-size bed. Pressing his eyes shut, Xavier gave his head a good shake. He wouldn't go there. He wouldn't allow his imagination to run rampant. It would eat him up inside if he thought about Ebony's relationship with his ex-brother-in-law. But instead of turning his mind from the past, he asked, "How many times?"

It took Ebony a second to catch his meaning. She stood and walked away from the couch. "Xavier, it's time for you to leave."

"That many, huh?"

She paused. Not long, maybe all of ten seconds. Blinking away the tears stinging the back of her eyes, she put a hand to her chest to steady the volatile beating of her heart. "Why are you doing this to me? Why are you hurting me like this?"

The sound of her injured voice made him reach for her. Hurting the woman he loved was not his intention. Xavier went to her. He found it in his heart to push away his anger, and take her in his arms. "Ebony, you know I love you, don't you?"

She slowly nodded. His gentle words were just what her heart needed to hear and his touch was welcome, even if it was just for a moment.

"You're perfect for me in every way and despite what happened tonight, I still want you in my life. But in order for us to get there—"

"You need to know what happened with Malcolm," she finished.

"Exactly." When Xavier asked Ebony if he could ask one final question, she grudgingly agreed. Holding her in the crux of his arms was the greatest feeling in the world, and though they were at odds, this was exactly where he wanted to be. "Why didn't you go to Jacqueline and tell her the truth?"

Ebony's eyebrows drew together, but Xavier didn't let the hard expression on her face stop him from getting to the bottom of things. "If what you say is true, that Malcolm lied to you about being married, then why not track down his wife and explain?"

Ebony pulled out of his arms. He was doing it again. Judging her. Their future hinged on her response, and that scared her. They had fun together, shared jokes, and even in the silence that sometimes plagued their conversations, she felt loved. Ebony didn't want to lose Xavier, but there was nothing she could do to make him stay.

"I don't know."

"You're going to have to do better than that, Ebony."

"I was young," she said, pushing the words out of her mouth. "After Jacqueline busted into the room, Malcolm threw on his clothes and ran after her, leaving me all alone. I had every intention of tracking her down and telling her what really happened, because I knew Malcolm would lie, but I got scared. A week passed, then two, and before I knew it, six months went by."

When Xavier parted his lips to respond, she waved her hand in his face. "No more questions."

He held up an index finger. "Just one more."

Later, when Ebony reflected on their conversation, she would regret ever giving him such leeway, but in the moment, he wanted to erase the pain in his eyes. During their relationship Xavier had been the one to make her laugh. And smile. Tears of happiness had flooded her eyes too many times to count. It had been his sweet, compassionate nature that had opened her heart to love. Xavier made her feel good about who she was and what she had accomplished in her life. He encouraged her to do better, and in the time they had been dating, he had proven to be a shoulder she could lean on.

Friends, family, co-workers and even employees had commented on her improved outlook on life, and she had credited her newfound peace to her growing faith and her relationship with Xavier. Their love was embedded in security and loyalty, and the raw, deep-seated attraction they shared only intensified their bond. Ebony wanted to return to the safety of his arms, rest her head on his chest and listen to the soft beating of his heart, but knew she couldn't.

Bracing herself for the worst, she held her head high and met his gaze. "One last question, Xavier. And then I want you to go."

"Did you continue dating Malcolm after you learned he was married?"

Ebony flinched as though he had slapped her. "Do you think that little of me, Xavier? Do you think I would continue seeing him after all the stress he put me through?" Tears filled her eyes and when she rubbed them away, her eyes filled with more. She loved Xavier with every fiber of her being, but she wasn't going to let him hurt her any more than he had.

The inky darkness of the evening, which had enclosed the room, mirrored what Ebony was feeling inside. There was an undertone of sadness in her voice when she finally spoke. "After the incident at the Marriott, I never saw or heard from him again." Ebony opened the front door. "Now, if you don't mind, I'd like you to leave." Conflicting emotions left her feeling confused. She wanted Xavier to leave, but secretly hoped he would stay with her.

Xavier stopped in front of the open door, unsure of what to do. Ebony wasn't to blame for what happened with Malcolm. The man was a womanizer who preyed on innocent women searching for love and acceptance. Xavier had disliked the businessman on sight. And when Jacqueline announced they were engaged, after dating a mere seven months, the entire family was outraged. But his sister was a grown woman and there was nothing anyone could say to change her mind. The ink on the wedding license hadn't even dried when the young newlywed started suspecting her husband of having an affair.

Jacqueline had confided in him about her marital problems, hoping he could give her some advice. Malcolm was coming home all hours of the night or not at all. He was squandering their money on lavish dinners that she wasn't a part of. And he grew angry when she questioned his whereabouts. Despite Xavier's protest, Jacqueline began leaving work early and trailing Malcolm around town. After three weeks, she discovered that he was spending copious amounts of time with a young, dark-skinned woman. But it wasn't until Jacqueline stormed into his hotel suite and found him in bed with his mistress that she filed for divorce.

Xavier remembered that afternoon with acute clarity. Jacqueline had called him at work, sobbing. The more he tried to calm her, the harder she cried. Xavier had signed out at the office and left the school immediately. He spent the rest of the night, and the weeks following, comforting his sister. He helped Jacqueline move out of the house she shared with Malcolm and into his place. One of the women at Jubilee Christian Center, who was also going through a divorce, took Jacqueline to a women's support group, and six months later, she was back to being her old self. As luck would have it, she met Andrew soon after at a church fellowship service.

The faint lights of the wall sconces cast an angeliclike ex-

pression on Ebony's face, although bitterness underlined her
eyes. In the time they had been dating, she had never given
him any reason not to trust her. Men approached her con-
stantly, offering dates and even gifts, but she didn't respond
to their advances. She was his woman, his love, his life and
he wanted her with him on a permanent basis. But first, he
had to talk things over again with Jackie. "Ebony, I love you
with all my heart, but if Jackie isn't going to be okay with us
being together, then…"

"Why does *she* get to decide *our* future?"

"Because she's my sister!"

Ebony couldn't believe what she was hearing. *He's willing
to throw away what we have because his sister has a problem
with it? I haven't seen or spoken to Malcolm in years. I've
moved on and changed my ways. Doesn't that count for something?* Ebony wasn't going to sit around and wait for Xavier to
come to his senses. He either loved her enough to stand up to
his sister, or he didn't. "Don't bother talking things over with
Jacqueline, Xavier. I'll make the decision easy for you. It's over."

"Wait! Let me—"

"No, you wait! You've been judging me since day one and
I'm tired of trying to win your approval. We tried to make a
go of a relationship, and we failed. No hard feelings." But the
harshness of her tone suggested otherwise.

"I'll call you in a few days and we'll—"

"Don't bother. We have nothing to discuss." Ebony
shrugged a shoulder nonchalantly. "I guess you were right all
along. We are too different for each other."

Xavier studied her face. Since they'd begun dating, he'd
learned to look beyond the surface and search for the truth in
the depths of her eyes. He wanted to dispute her claims but
decided against it. Besides, what Ebony said made no difference. Over the next few days, he would talk things over with

Jackie and then go from there. There was nothing Xavier wanted more than to have Ebony in his life, but his sister's feelings mattered to him, too. In one last attempt to smooth things over, Xavier stepped forward and reached for her.

"Don't," she warned, narrowing her eyes. Ebony glanced down the hall, thinking about all the packing she would have to do. Movies were stacked in the entertainment unit, nutrition books lined the last row of the bookshelf, and T-shirts, pants and sneakers crowded the spare bedroom. It all belonged to Xavier. "I'll have your things ready tomorrow. Pick them up before I get back from work and leave my keys on the kitchen counter."

"Don't do this, Ebony," he said, touching her cheek. Xavier wanted to take her into his arms, which he'd grown accustomed to doing, but if he gave in to his desire he knew there'd be no turning back. And now, more than ever, he needed to think clearly.

"Don't do what? End a relationship that you don't want to be a part of?"

Xavier wanted to argue with her, yell at her, tell her she was wrong. How could Ebony insinuate that she didn't mean anything to him? He loved her and he knew that she loved him too, so why was she doing this? Why was she willing to throw away what they had? Xavier was stunned to learn she had had an affair with Malcolm, but nothing had changed. His feelings for her were still intact. Xavier didn't know how to keep the peace in his family and have Ebony in his life, but he would do everything in his power to have both.

"I don't want to waste any more time discussing this. Kindly lock the door behind you when you leave." Tears of frustration blurred Ebony's vision as she trudged upstairs. In her bedroom, safe from hurtful words and accusations, she collapsed on her bed and cried. A full minute passed before she heard the door slam, and then the house fell quiet.

Chapter 21

By the time the sun crept over the horizon the following morning, Ebony was behind her desk, hard at work. Staying home had never crossed her mind. Work had to be done and no amount of crying or pondering over what could have been was going to bring Xavier back. He was gone, they were over and the best thing she could do was focus on her business. Ebony had a vaulting ambition to take Discreet Boutique worldwide, and now that Xavier was gone, she could focus all of her time and energy on making her dreams a reality.

Unable to shut off her thoughts long enough to get some rest, she had tossed and turned for the better part of the night. Thoughts of happier times had played over and over in her mind like a PowerPoint slide show. Quiet, moonlit drives through downtown, picnicking in Xavier's backyard, cooking exotic meals and then feeding them to each other were just a few of the memories that touched her heart. And then the were the thoughts of making love. All the times Xavier touched every square inch of her body and the way he would slide himself between her legs at the perfect moment were welcome memories. And so was their birthday romp outside the garage door.

Filing away all thoughts of her ex, she gave her head a shake. Then a sudden, intense panic gripped her. *What if Xavier finds someone else? What if one of those well-meaning but interfering church mothers throw their daughter or grand-daughter at him?* Xavier had given Ebony every little thing her heart desired, and she knew it was just a matter of time before he found happiness with someone else. Ebony pushed away an errant strand of hair, thoughts of him swarming her mind.

God, I miss him.

It hadn't even been twenty-four hours since they spoke, but it felt like days. Several days. Ebony longed to be back in Xavier's arms. She missed the feel of his fingers in her hair, hankered for the taste of his lips just one last time. Ebony wanted to hear his voice, but calling him was out of the question. Washing her mind of all thoughts of Xavier, she did a mental check of what she had to do that afternoon. She was taking Lydia out for lunch to celebrate her new apartment. "It's not the Hilton or anything," Lydia had said when she invited her over last Wednesday after Changing Lives Through Meals, "but it's mine."

"That's right," Ebony agreed, giving her a wide smile. "You should be proud of yourself. You've accomplished a lot in a short time." Lydia's stint at the women's shelter had gone far better than either of them expected. Smoking was a habit she had yet to break, but she was trying her best to quit. Despite her past, it quickly became apparent to the staff at the New Hope Women's Shelter that Lydia Miller was going somewhere with her life. Under the advice of her counselor, she enrolled in adult education classes at a local high school and began volunteering at a day care center three afternoons a week. In her spare time, she spent generous amounts of time at the public library, poring over fashion magazines. Lydia was bent on being a makeup artist and Ebony was already pulling strings to make her dreams come true.

When Kendall poked her head into her partner's office at eleven-fifteen, Ebony was staring off into space, her fingers intertwined, resting in the crux of her hands. Polished looking as she was in a conservative charcoal-colored suit, an opaque blouse, and sporting a new wavy hairstyle it was hard to believe that Ebony had been crying her eyes out last night.

"You all right?"

"Just fine," Ebony lied, snapping out of her thoughts and casting her eyes on the spreadsheets in front of her. "How did the meeting with Mrs. Toliver go? Any promising news or was she her usual evasive and surly self?"

"Things look grim," Kendall confessed. "She all but said the loan would be denied." Flopping down on the leather couch, she released a sigh of frustration. Ebony's mind wandered back to last Wednesday. Xavier had surprised her with lunch from her favorite Italian restaurant. She had jumped to her feet, wrapped him in her arms and properly thanked him with her lips. After locking her office door, she'd straddled him in the middle of the couch and helped him out of his track suit. The seafood spaghetti, garlic cheese sticks and potato salad were forgotten as they satisfied a hunger of another kind. Ebony closed her eyes. Six days later, she could still feel the heat of his lips on her neck and his hands on her breasts. Xavier had done things to her on that couch that she would never forget. And that night in bed, he had given her a repeat performance that left her body writhing in ecstasy.

"Are you listening to me?"

Ebony's eyes flickered. Caught daydreaming, she smiled at her partner ruefully. "Sorry, Kendall. What were you saying?"

Kendall shot her a sympathetic look. She wanted to ask Ebony if she wanted to talk about last night, but decided against it. Her partner didn't like the staff discussing their personal affairs during work hours. No matter how grave the situation. "The bank is going to turn us down."

Ebony wasn't surprised by the news. First National Bank had been giving them a hard time all year. They had made good on their loans, were professional and thorough in their dealings, and the boutiques were making more money than the projected figures. Racking her brain for the next step to take, she tapped her ballpoint pen absently on her desk. *There has to be something we can do.* She eyed the picture frame propped up against the computer. Opal and Spencer were in the picture, along with her and Xavier. His eyes were alight with excitement and he had a hand draped across her shoulder. The shot had been taken at Q's Joint and they were the picture of happiness. "That's it!" she yelled out loud.

Kendall sat up. "What's it?"

"I know who can help us. Kale! A few years back he hosted the First National Bank Charity Ball. Who knows, maybe he can pull a few strings for us." Ebony buzzed Jocelyn and asked her to get Kale Washington on the line. "If anyone can give us a hand, it'll be Kale. I'll see if I can set something up for this week. What day works for you?"

Jocelyn stuck her head in the door, preventing Kendall's response. "Mr. Washington wasn't in but his secretary said she'd have him call you back when he returns. He's expected back within the hour."

"Thanks, Jocelyn."

Ebony checked her appointment book. She wanted to be ready with a date and time when Kale returned her call. The only day she was available to meet was Thursday afternoon. She told Kendall.

"I can make it, as long as we're finished by four. I have an appointment at Garden Square at five and you know how crazy rush-hour traffic is."

"Must be a pretty important appointment if you're willing to blow off this meeting," Ebony noted.

Kendall was quiet. She wanted to share her news, but she didn't know how it would be received. Ebony was going through a rough time, and she knew from experience that when her partner was in a mood, she didn't want to hear anybody's good news, especially if it had to do with a man. "I wasn't going to say anything, because I know you're bummed out about Xavier…but…um, I think I'm pregnant. I'm not a hundred percent sure, but—"

The rest of her sentence was drowned out by Ebony's screams. She abandoned her chair and ran around the desk. "When? How? Well, I know how," she joked, "but I thought Turner was dead set against having children right now."

"He was, but I took your advice, and he—" When Ebony's eyebrows sank, she said, "No baby, no nooky. Remember? I just flipped the script on that husband of mine. Since he was the one worried about getting pregnant, I told him *he* should be the one using birth control. Needless to say, it didn't go over too well.

"Turner tried to keep on top of things, but failed. Then he told me that if we got pregnant it was God's will. My period was late, but I didn't think anything of it because I'm *always* late. But four days later, I knew something was up. I was waiting for the results of the home pregnancy test when you called. When I heard you crying, I raced out of the house, forgetting all about the test."

Ebony fidgeted with her charm bracelet. She couldn't

believe she had cried all over herself like that. "I never did thank you for coming to get me."

"You don't need to. That's what friends are for."

Ebony smiled. "Well, what happened with the test?"

"When I got back home, Turner met me at the door with the applicator in his hand. 'Two pink stripes. I guess that means we're pregnant!' I bawled my eyes out!" she said, a smile of pure joy on her lips.

"I'm so happy for you!" Ebony gave Kendall a hug. Kendall was more than her business partner and friend, she was the sister she had never had. Sometimes they called each other names, and back in college, they had even gotten into a shoving match, but no matter what she went through, Ebony could always count on Kendall to be there for her. Her eyes teared and her face twitched like she was about to sneeze. Being a mother meant the world to Kendall, and Ebony couldn't think of anybody more deserving of the honor. "Kendall, you're going to make a terrific mother!"

Kendall felt guilty for not wanting to share her news with Ebony. Her friend was genuinely excited for her. She broke into laughter when Ebony touched her stomach and said she could already feel the bulge. Her stomach was as flat as an ironing board, but she was looking forward to the weight gain, the intense cravings and even the sleepless nights.

Ebony listened quietly as Kendall chattered about the baby names she had picked out, the colors she was going to paint the nursery and the furniture she was going to buy. Sabrina and Jocelyn came into the office, carrying a tray of coffee and muffins, and suggested they take a break. Kendall told them she was pregnant and was plied with more hugs and kisses.

Questions whirled in Ebony's brain. *I wonder what our kids would have looked like? Would we have had a set of twins?* Thoughts of Xavier, and their love, left her speculating whether or not she would ever find such happiness again. Her eyes pooled with water. Ebony wiped a tear away. She refused to shed another tear over the demise of their relationship. It was over, done, history. And brooding over what could have been wasn't going to bring Xavier back.

Kale Washington loved the dog days of summer. Not because of the heady scent of the season or the additional hours of sunlight. There was one reason and one reason only why he looked forward to the summer: the women. The greater the heat, the less women wore outside. Miniskirts, cleavage-baring tops and booty shorts came out the second the temperature soared above seventy-five degrees.

Kale loved his wife passionately and would kill any man who touched her, but marriage had done nothing to curb his appetite for other women, especially sultry and provocative females like the one sitting across from him. Ebony Garrett had more going for her than just her good looks. She was the prototype of what he desired in a mistress. Secure, career-minded, intelligent and self-sufficient. There wasn't anything he could do for her that she couldn't do for herself. He admired that. In his experience, businesswomen made the best girlfriends. They didn't ask for too much of his time, weren't interested in taking his wife's place and had no inhibitions in the bedroom. The confidence they had in their abilities carried over into their intimate lives as well. As far as Kale was concerned, dating a professional woman was a win-win situation. He got all the sex he could stand and she received companionship and romance.

Tilting his head back to finish his wine, he let his eyes linger over the seductive curve of Ebony's mouth. He liked that she was a very together businesswoman and sure of herself. If it weren't for the fact that his wife was on friendly terms with the boutique owner, he would have stepped to her a long time ago. For now, he had no choice but to admire her beauty from afar.

"It's a shame Kendall couldn't join us," he said. "It's been months since I saw her. How is she doing?"

"Great. She had an appointment that couldn't be rescheduled, but she sent her greetings." Ebony took a generous bite of her steak. It was moist and succulent, just the way she liked it. "I really appreciate you agreeing to meet with me, Kale. I know how busy you are running the club and satisfying all the other commitments you have."

Kale gave her a winning smile. "It's no problem. I'm always here to help." His smoky-gray eyes bore down on her like a lynx stalking its prey. His mouth drew back into a toothy smile. "Have I told you how stunning you look tonight?"

Ebony returned his smile. She considered Kale a friend, but this was still a business meeting, so she had wisely dressed down in a black V-neck dress and sensible pumps. Wanting a smart and professional flair, she had curled the ends of her hair lightly. Ebony knew Kale was attracted to her, but she wasn't going to do anything to suggest the feelings were mutual.

Tonight, he had traded in his customary Armani suit for a black mock-neck dress shirt and tan slacks. Although he'd set hearts racing when he strolled into the Indigo Lounge, Ebony wasn't impressed. He was handsome enough, but there was only one man she desired.

She took a bite of her sautéed potatoes, and took her time chewing. "This is my first time here, but it won't be my last," Ebony told Kale, as her eyes passed over the room. The contemporary and attractive restaurant was sequestered behind tall hedges of ficus trees and boasted a dazzling view of the city. Slightly upscale, the main floor level housed sleek furniture, muted tan walls and glistening hardwood floors. In addition to the delectable Southern cuisine, and extensive wine lists, the restaurant had a live jazz band that wooed patrons on Friday and Saturday nights. Ebony had wanted to eat somewhere less flashy, but she had allowed Kale to pick the time and the place, and he had chosen the Indigo.

"Amelia just loves it here. She says their Margarita Mama is the best drink on the face of the earth." Kale chuckled easily. "Speaking of drinks, would you like me to order you one? Looks like you could use something stronger than water. You know, something with a little kick in it."

His grin had sexual overtones to it, but Ebony pretended not to notice. She picked up her glass. "No, water is fine for me. I don't drink on the job." They both laughed. After some pleasant conversation, Ebony told Kale why she was anxious to meet with him on such short notice.

"The expansion project has hit some rough spots, huh?"

Ebony nodded, and then gave him a brief overview of previous discussions with the branch manager at First National Trust and Kendall's meeting with Roxanne Toliver earlier in the week. "Mr. Oakwood assured me that the project would be approved. But now that he's been replaced, we're left wondering where we stand. And my repeated attempts to get in touch with him have gone…"

Kale had a difficult time keeping up with the pace of the conversation. Her heady, scintillating perfume was working him over. It took all his effort to remain in his seat. Willing his body to remain calm, he rubbed a hand over his stubble-free chin. A steady stream of diners, mostly clans of young, single women, had been sashaying in and out of the restaurant all night, but up until now he had been too preoccupied with Ebony to notice.

"Go on, ask him. I'm sure that's Kale Washington," whispered a female voice behind him.

Normally he loved being recognized, especially when he

was out on a date. It made him feel like a superstar. He had been retired for the past three seasons, but it hadn't diminished his popularity with baseball fans. When Kale was out on the town, he soaked up the attention he received. He'd sign autographs, pose for pictures, and on occasion he even joined fans for a round of drinks. But tonight, Kale didn't want anyone cutting in on his time with Ebony, so he glanced over his shoulder and shot the two less-than-attractive women a leave-me-alone look.

"Jerk!" he heard one of them say.

"Sorry about that," he said to Ebony, when he turned back around. "Continue."

Ebony finished the piece of steak in her mouth, then washed it down with some more ice water. "Why do you think the bank is stalling? Why won't they approve the project?" She hated to play the friend card, but this was important to her and she desperately needed his expertise. Not only had Kale cleaned up Q's Joint and made it the hottest place in town, but he had investors on both the East and West Coasts anxious to bring the club to their cities.

"Well, I don't have an MBA in business or finance, but my professional opinion is that First National Trust feels the expansion idea has substantial risks." Ebony started to speak, but Kale held up a hand before she could interrupt. "Granted, Discreet Boutiques is hugely popular and the revenues generated in the past seven years are impressive, but there's no guarantee that opening additional stores will be a lucrative venture." Kale paused to drink his brandy, and noted that Ebony had the kind of eyes a man could get lost in. They were one of the most captivating things about her. "In the last meeting you had with Ms. Toliver you made known your intentions to expand to Michigan and possibly Philadelphia. That was a bad move. You shouldn't have mentioned your future plans. It likely scared them off."

Ebony didn't speak. Her comments weren't meant to sound boastful or arrogant, but she could see how the bank manager could interpret them that way. "What should we do now?"

A lewd thought popped into Kale's mind, but when he opened his mouth to share it, the deep, slumberous voice of the restaurant manager drowned him out. "Is everything to your liking, Mr. Washington?" The Italian man, aged about sixty, had a large stomach concealed by a tacky gold and black silk dress shirt. His square face was a terrain of wrinkles, eclipsed by a bumpy nose and light brown eyes the size of marbles. This was the man's third trip over to the table, despite Kale telling him he wanted to enjoy a quiet meal with his friend.

"Everything is great, Mr. Ambrosia."

The manager's untimely interruption gave Ebony the chance to regroup. Kale had been flirting with her ever since they sat down. Normally she laughed off his comments and jokes, but tonight there was something in his grin that made her uneasy. Ebony needed his help, but she wasn't going to do anything to compromise her integrity.

"Anything else I can get you? Wine? Coffee?" the manager queried eagerly. "We've introduced new dessert menus since the last time you were here, Mr. Washington."

Kale forced a polite smile. His voice was terse when he declined the offer.

"Well, if you change your mind, let Tina know and she'll bring it right out."

Kale nodded courteously and the man departed. "Where were we?"

"You were about to give me some advice."

"Right. The first thing you need to do is revise your proposal. Lay out exactly what you intend to do to ensure the success of the new boutiques and come up with a…"

Ebony's heart jumped up into her throat when Xavier walked into the restaurant. It was as if time stopped. She no longer heard Kale's voice or the amiable chatter and laughter whirling around the room. All of her senses and emotions were focused on her ex. He walked tall, proud, confident. And in a cream polo shirt, khaki slacks and open-toed sandals he looked absolutely delicious. Ebony recognized the shirt as one of the pieces she had bought him during one of their many shopping sprees. The man looked hot. A certified ten. And she obviously wasn't the only woman who felt that way. A feeling of protectiveness washed over Ebony as she noticed other female patrons ogling him too. *Back off, vultures!*

Ebony watched Xavier scan the restaurant and prayed he wouldn't see them. Sighing in relief when he turned back and spoke to the hostess, she guzzled down the rest of her water. *Who is he waiting for? Is he on a date?* She didn't have to wait long to find out the answer. Straining her eyes toward the lobby, she saw Xavier sling his arm around a fair-skinned woman who was rocking back and forth on her heels. Ebony gripped the side of the table, gasping for air: Jacqueline.

"Are you okay? You look like you've seen a ghost."

I have went unsaid. "I'm fine. Just a little warm. This place sure filled up fast." Ebony used the next few minutes to gather her wits. *How could this be? Why did Xavier and Jacqueline drive halfway across town to come to the Indigo?*

Ebony needed a plan—and quick. If Xavier saw her with Kale, he'd assume the worst and she didn't want him to think any less of her than he already did. It wouldn't matter that Kale was a husband and father and a prominent and respected figure in the community. Jacqueline would poison Xavier's mind with lies and that would dash all hopes of them ever getting back together.

I thought you were going to be about your business and forget you ever met Xavier Reed, a voice in her head said. *Thought you were moving on.*

"I am."

"You're what?"

Ebony cleared her throat. She had spoken out loud and now Kale was staring at her like she'd been possessed by an evil spirit.

"Are you sure you're all right?"

"Fine." It was an outrageous lie, but she couldn't very well tell Kale that her ex-boyfriend was here and she was terrified that he would get the wrong idea if he saw them together. Ebony was confused and all broken up inside, like a puzzle missing some pieces. On one hand, she was happy to see Xavier; on the other hand, she wished he was anywhere but here. She faced the window. It was going on eight o'clock and the sun would soon be making its descent, but for now it hung boldly in the sky, flaunting its beauty.

I have to find a way to get out of here without Xavier seeing me! For a split second, Ebony thought of going to the women's bathroom and climbing out the window. *Don't be ridiculous! That's insane!* But when Xavier stepped into the dining area for a second time, and did another quick sweep of the room, her heart leaped into her mouth. Ebony politely excused herself from the table and hurried toward the bathroom.

Chapter 22

"Xavier, let's go somewhere else. We've been waiting for almost thirty minutes," Jacqueline whined, scrounging around in her purse. She pulled out a sandwich bag filled with animal crackers. Munching on one, she rested her hands on top of her stomach. "The baby's so hungry he's punching me!"

Chuckling, Xavier patted his sister's jean-clad leg. "Come on, Jackie. The hostess said we're next in line and besides, you're craving ribs and the Indigo makes the best ribs in town." He winked. "Next to mine, that is."

Jacqueline laughed. After a brief pause, she stared over at her brother. "How have you been? Have you spoken to *her* yet?" The words came out of her mouth with supreme disgust. Another animal cracker went into her mouth and disappeared.

Xavier didn't want to get into this with Jackie. The last seven days without Ebony around had been like living without the sun. Last night at Changing Lives Through Meals, everyone wanted to know where Miss Lady was. He'd had no choice but to tell them she went out of town on business. Xavier hated lying, especially in church, but he didn't think he could stand people asking him where she was when Friday night rolled around. "No, but I'm going to call her tonight."

"You're making a mistake, Xavier. Trust me. She's nothing but a—"

"Save it, Jackie." He raised a hand to silence her. "I've thought long and hard about this and there's nothing you can say to change my mind. What happened between Ebony and Malcolm was years ago and if I've learned anything from being involved with Changing Lives Through Meals it's that people *do* change."

Jacqueline shook her head. "Not everyone. There are some people who never change, despite all the efforts of their family and friends." She could tell he wasn't listening to her, so she put a hand on his shoulder and forced him to look at her. "That woman is completely wrong for you! And you and I both know women like *her* don't change. How do you know she's not going to hurt you the way Malcolm did me? How do you know she won't cheat on you?"

"Because I trust her." Xavier's voice was louder and firmer than he'd intended. His sister just didn't get it. She didn't understand how much Ebony meant to him. His footing in life somehow felt more secure with her beside him. She was his sounding board; he could say anything to her without feeling like he had to explain himself. Ebony always seemed to understand where he was coming from. The decision to return to graduate school had been an easy one after talking things over with her, and she had even taken the time to help him fill out the necessary forms.

Xavier could kick himself. He had had a good woman behind him, and because of his insensitivity, he might have lost her forever. Ebony had awakened his heart with her sharp wit, uncompromising opinions and erotic sex appeal, and if she forgave him, he would spend the next thirty or more years making it up to her. Xavier wanted Ebony Denise Garrett as his lawfully wedded wife and he would go to any lengths to make it happen. Her commitment fears were rooted in her past—her parents' lackluster marriage, her own insecurities, her fear of abandonment—but that wouldn't stop him from loving her. Or making her Mrs. Xavier Reed.

"I'm going to marry her," he told his sister, "so get used to her being around. Ebony means the world to me. I love her. Don't hold her past against her, Jackie. Give her a chance. I don't expect it to happen overnight, but I hope one day you'll find the courage to let go of your hatred for her.

"Malcolm didn't love you. I know that's hard to hear, but it's the truth. I believe Ebony when she said she didn't know he was married. The more I thought about what she told me, the more it made sense. I know her, Jackie. She's not the type of person who would intentionally hurt anyone. I love her and these past few days have been pure agony…" He trailed off.

Jacqueline regarded Xavier. His voice was thick with emotion, and for a second she thought he was going to cry. She took a few minutes to take a critical look at what he was saying, but she still couldn't share his faith in Ebony Garrett. Her brother was blinded by lust and he couldn't see the truth staring him in the face. Jacqueline wished Xavier would find someone else to love. Someone who didn't have a wild past. But she loved him dearly and wanted him to be happy. She would never truly accept his relationship with Ebony, but she wouldn't stand in his way.

Standing, he shoved his hands into his pockets. "I'm going to go find out what's going on with our table. Be right back."

Xavier was a foot away from the hostess when he spotted

Ebony. She was sitting at the corner of the restaurant—alone. If
it weren't for the hostess cleaning up a spill on that side of the
room, he wouldn't even have noticed her. Xavier's feet turned
to jelly but when Ebony's shiny come-kiss-me lips parted, he
bypassed the hostess and headed straight for her table.

Ebony counted to five, and then pushed the air out of her
lungs. She had three minutes to talk, give or take a few seconds,
depending on how long Amelia kept Kale on the phone.
"You're the last person I expected to see here," she said, when
Xavier reached her table. "It's Thursday night, don't you have
a basketball game?"

"It got canceled. The coach of the opposing team had a
family emergency," he explained, inhaling her scent. Ebony
was wearing the perfume he had picked out for her. It was
called *Love Spells* and its fruity, aromatic scent evoked thoughts
of the last night they had spent together. The wine, the music,
the insatiable lovemaking. Xavier wrestled with his thoughts.
There would be plenty of time to reminisce; right now, he had
to make amends. He took in Ebony's tense facial expression and
shifting eyes. She looked like she wanted to dive underneath the
table. *Has it come to that already?* Xavier pushed away his fears
and kept his tone light. "How have you been?"

Ebony sat back in her chair. She wanted to tell Xavier the
truth, but she didn't know if she could trust him. When her
friends asked how she was coping with the breakup, she responded with false enthusiasm. "I'm great," she would say.
"I couldn't be better," and, "I don't need a man to make me
happy." All day long she pretended that life was perfect and
cited reason after reason why: she had a thriving business; a
beautiful home; money in the bank. But Ebony knew those
things weren't enough. She wanted someone to share her life
with. Deep down she was hurting bad. The pain was so deep
and so raw Ebony didn't think she would ever heal. She longed

to open her heart and tell him that she was dying without him in her life, but she lacked courage. Baring her soul would only leave her feeling more confused than she already was, so she put a bright smile on her face and said, "I've been busy. We have our last meeting with First National Trust in a week and we have a lot of work to do between now and then. I've been slacking off the last few weeks, so now it's time to burn the midnight oil."

Was that a shot at me?

"How was Changing Lives Through Meals last night? I couldn't help thinking about Old Man Griffin as I ate my dinner." *Alone,* Ebony wanted to add, but didn't.

"It's not the same without you," Xavier admitted, helping himself to the chair across from her. Without thinking, he took her hands in his own. Fighting the urge to caress more than just her fingers, he held her gaze. Her lips were moist, slightly glossy, just the way he liked them. Xavier wanted what they used to have. He missed their playful banter, the sound of her laugh, the closeness and passion of their lovemaking, but most importantly, he missed talking to her. "Ebony, I can't stop thinking about you. I can't eat, I can't sleep and every time I hear a John Coltrane song, I feel like I want to…" Xavier stopped himself from saying more. It wasn't ever cool for a grown man to admit that a song made him cry. He searched Ebony's face for clues, but found nothing. His heart was racing, his throat was dry and he could feel perspiration crowning his forehead. When the silence became unbearable, he squeezed her hands. "Say something, anything. Tell me what's going on in your mind."

"I don't know what to say." That was another outrageous lie. Ebony wanted to be back in his arms. His embrace had always held warmth, comfort and security, and now more than ever she needed—no, wanted—his love.

"Xavier," she began, unsure of what to say. Feelings of love and anger mingled as Ebony reflected on what had led them to this point. "Does Jacqueline know you're over here talking to me?" Ebony needed affirmation that his sister wasn't going to interfere in their lives anymore. If they were going to be a couple again, Xavier was going to have to put her feelings above those of everyone else. Just like she had done with him.

"The check's been taken care of, Ebony. We can leave anytime you're ready." The sound of Kale's deep, masculine voice made Xavier's face turn to stone. He dropped her hands and stood abruptly.

Ebony directed her eyes at Kale. *Why couldn't you have stayed on the phone!*

Tension hovered over the trio, ebbing and flowing like a great, mighty river.

Kale recognized the fair-skinned man. He remembered Ebony leaving the club with him the last time she came in. Extending his right hand, he said, "Hi. I'm Kale Washington."

"I didn't realize you were..." Xavier couldn't finish. Couldn't make his tongue say the words. His gaze wavered between the couple, disbelief masking his face. "I better get going. Enjoy the rest of your *date*." The last word rolled off his tongue like a four-letter curse word.

"Wait! Let me explain!" Oblivious to the inquiring glances from patrons at nearby tables, Ebony jumped from her seat and threw down her napkin. She hated the sound of her voice, hated that she was afraid and hated that they had come so close to reconciling without it happening. Pushing aside her feelings, she smoothed a nervous hand over her dress. Ebony couldn't let Xavier leave. If he walked out of the restaurant feeling and thinking the way he did, she might never see him again.

"Can you give me a moment, Kale?" Ebony didn't bother

waiting for a response. She rushed after Xavier, almost plowing over a waitress carrying a tray of palatable desserts.

"Xavier, at least give me the chance to explain!"

Keep it together, she willed herself, as she trailed him out of the dining area. Xavier was practically running to get away from her; Ebony had to take long strides to keep up with him. If the situation weren't so precarious, she would have laughed to the point of tears. Grabbing his forearm, she said, "What's *your* problem?"

"What's *my* problem?" Xavier turned around. Luckily they were the only two people in the waiting area and there was no one in hearing distance. "What's my problem? I'm not the one out on a date with a *married* man." His eyes curved dangerously. "You're something else, you know that? We haven't been broken up a week but you're already dating someone else. A dried-up athlete at that."

"First of all." She glanced back and motioned with her head to Kale, who was chatting it up with a leggy blonde wearing a too-tight shirt. "We're not on a date, it's a business dinner. Secondly I would never think of taking up with Kale or any other married man. *Got it?*"

Her explanation sounded believable enough, but doubts stabbed his mind like fiery darts. Xavier had seen the way Kale Washington looked at her that night at the club and he hadn't liked it one bit. And tonight when Kale swaggered over to the table, it was apparent that he had more on his mind than just "business."

Ebony watched Xavier, her mind rolling back to last Sunday, to the showdown with his sister. "Why do you care what I do with my time or whom I go out with? You dumped me like yesterday's trash, remember? 'I need to talk to Jacqueline and see if it's all right to date you.'" Ebony did a horrible impersonation of him, but she made her point. She forced the shakiness out of her voice. "I'm not the one who chose my family over you, so don't you dare try to turn me into the bad guy. This meeting with Kale is business. That's it."

Now Xavier was good and angry. She was playing the victim role. Carrying on as if she was innocent. His eyes narrowed on her face. "You know what your problem is? You hide behind your work and your deprived childhood to keep people from getting close to you. You push people away because you don't feel worthy of their love. That's why you fear commitment and marriage. It's not because you don't think you're cut out for it, it's because you're scared I'll leave you, just like your parents did." Xavier broke off when he saw Ebony's face crumple. He had never seen her look so shaken, but if they were ever going to have a future together, she had to hear the truth. Hoping to soften the blow of his words, he reached out for her.

Ebony jerked her hand away. "Don't touch me."

Xavier softened his voice. "You can't control our relationship the way you control your company. Love makes no promises and it has no guarantees. You might get hurt if you give your heart to someone, and then again, you might not. Love is a risk you just have to be willing to take."

Ebony didn't miss a beat. Recovering quickly from the shock of his scathing words she straightened her shoulders and lifted her head high. His cutting remarks had pierced her heart, but she wasn't going to run away like she did with Jacqueline. "I'm not the only one with a problem, *Xavier.* You're intimidated by my success. It's eating you up inside that I'm more interested in building an empire than being a housewife. I love what I do and despite what you think, I am more than comfortable with who I am. And I don't need you to take care of me, because I can take care of my *damn* self!" Ebony spun on her heel and walked full speed back inside the restaurant. Tears fell

fast and hard down her cheeks. Ebony hurried to the ladies'
room. When she yanked open the door, she startled Jacqueline,
who was shuffling out. Mumbling a halfhearted apology, she
brushed past her and escaped into the bathroom stall.

Chapter 23

Xavier was going to lose his mind if another person came up and asked him where Ebony was. From the moment he'd opened the church doors and welcomed the regulars inside they had been asking about Ebony's whereabouts. "Where's Miss Lady?" "How come she ain't been around?" "When is she coming back?" It was difficult for Xavier to put Ebony out of his mind when her name kept coming up in conversation.

Who am I trying to fool? he thought, serving some wild rice onto a plate and handing it to the plus-size man waiting in line. *Forgetting Ebony would be like forgetting to breathe.*

Xavier couldn't put Ebony out of his mind long enough to do anything. Sleep evaded him at night, his basketball game was in serious trouble and his mind was too crowded to do any work on his graduate school essay. And then there were his parents. His sister promised not to say anything to his parents about the whole Malcolm-Ebony-Marriott Hotel incident, so they had no idea what was going on. As a result, every time his mother called, she encouraged him to bring Ebony by for dinner. Just that morning, Gloria had asked for Ebony's home number so she could extend an invitation to Jacqueline and Andrew's Jack and Jill baby shower.

"It's on the twenty-seventh? Shoot. Ebony won't be able to come. She's in her cousin's wedding." Xavier didn't know where the lie had come from.

Xavier searched for a seat. The basement was packed and the only seat available was at Old Man Griffin's table. He would rather stand than sit with Old Man Griffin. Not because of Chester's and Mariana's poor eating habits, but because conversation would eventually turn to Ebony. Bracing himself against the wall, he dug his fork into his Caesar salad. Xavier caught Sister Bertha watching him, but avoided making eye contact.

"There's an empty seat over here, son." Sister Bertha pointed to the empty chair to her left. "Come on over!"

Xavier gave her a smile he didn't feel. "I'm all right over—"

"Boy, please! Everybody knows that your food won't digest properly if you eat standing up."

For a half second, Xavier thought of correcting her. The myth was probably something a mother had made up years ago to get a disgruntled child to sit down, but Xavier thought better of challenging Sister Bertha. He sat down at the table and fixed his eyes on his plate. Stuffing more salad into his mouth, he felt himself relax as he listened to the humorous exchange between two of the newest program members. They were talking about growing up on Chicago's dangerous streets. Sister Bertha asked them about the city, and even Chester shared fond memories about his hometown. *See, no one is even thinking about you and Ebony,* Xavier told himself. *I was worried for nothing.*

"When's Miss Lady comin' back?" Old Man Griffin asked,

as if reading Xavier's thoughts. He dipped a butter biscuit in his spaghetti sauce and swirled it around the noodles before shoving it into his mouth. "Sure do miz her company," he said, his lips slapping together. He finished chewing what was in his mouth, then guzzled down a glass of fruit punch. Using the collar of his plaid shirt as a napkin, he scratched his head with his free hand. "Thought she was comin' back this week."

"Miss Lady—I mean, Ebony—has a lot of work to do. She doesn't have time to volunteer anymore." Xavier's conscience pricked his heart, but he ignored the sting.

"Is she going to come by and at least say goodbye?" Sister Bertha asked, resting her elbows on the table. She thought a moment. "I hope she does because I wanted the recipe for her sweet and sour meatballs."

"Dem my favorite," Old Man Griffin said with a nod of his head.

Mariana took a second butter biscuit from the half-empty basket sitting in the middle of the table. "Miss Lady must be busy trainin' Lydia. The girl ain't too good with numbers. Used to shortchange me all the time."

Sister Bertha turned to look at Mariana. "Training who?"

"Lydia," she answered, pointing at the chair that used to be occupied by her friend. "Lydia's workin' now."

Xavier put down his glass. "Last week when I asked you where Lydia was you said she went back home."

"Did I? Naw, I said she found a home. She has a little apartment, it's no bigger than a shoe box, but the rent is cheap and it's in a decent neighborhood. Miss Lady got her a job at some swanky store where they be sellin' women's intimates. Panties and nighties so expensive I would need to put them on layaway!" She guffawed loudly, drawing the attention of others.

"Isn't that nice," Sister Bertha said sweetly. "Ebony sure

is a gem. First she donates all new appliances to the church and then—"

"She did what?" Xavier's head snapped up. *Where was I when she was doing all these things?* he thought, with a heavy heart. Ebony used to tell him everything. It was a sobering thought to know he wasn't her confidant anymore. Before long, another man would take his place and he'd be forgotten. Xavier directed his next question to Sister Bertha. "How do you know Ebony donated appliances to the church?"

She raised a sculptured eyebrow at him. "Pastor Henderson announced it at church last Sunday. Apparently she ordered the appliances a few months ago, but there was a mix-up at the store and the order was never sent out. But now everything's been straightened out and the appliances will be here next week. Ebony gave Pastor strict orders not to reveal her name, but he couldn't keep her secret." Sister Bertha looked Xavier over. "You were sitting right there in the front row when he made the announcement, how come you missed it?"

Xavier had been there in body, but his mind had been at 2735 Valley View Road. He had a vague recollection of the announcement, but couldn't remember any specific details. The first thing he was going to do when he got home was call Pastor Henderson. His pastor would tell him everything he needed to know.

"Miss Lady sure is sweet," Sister Bertha said affectionately. "Never met such a generous soul in my life." Her voice dipped at the end in reverence, like she was talking about a saint. "Miss Lady and I were having girl talk a couple weeks back and I mentioned me and Willy were days away from celebrating our thirty-seventh wedding anniversary. The following Sunday, she walked over, gave us a hug, and handed me a card. I opened the card on the drive home—it was one of those real expensive Hallmark cards—and inside was a gift certificate for the Radisson Plaza Hotel. Can you believe that? Three whole nights in the honeymoon suite! Willy ain't never taken me to no big, fancy hotel, let alone spent that kind of money on me. Damn shame if you ask me! A man ought to…"

Xavier excused himself from the table as Sister Bertha jabbered on about how husbands didn't know how to romance their wives anymore. After wrapping the leftovers with cellophane and helping himself to another glass of mango punch, he leaned against the sink, deep in thought. Somewhere between Mariana's and Sister Bertha's tales about his ex-girlfriend, he had lost his appetite. Xavier couldn't say that he was surprised to hear that Ebony had donated appliances to the church and was helping Lydia get back on her feet. Next to his mother, she was the most munificent woman he knew.

Unnerved because Ebony had never shared her plan to employ Lydia, or donate to the church, or give the Jenkinses an anniversary gift, he sulked. Xavier's mind wandered back to the first time he had met Ebony, right here in this very church. *Man, was I ever a jerk!* When the whole pregnancy fiasco came back to him, he actually groaned in self-disgust. Shaking his head, he washed his glass and put it on the rack to dry. *I've hurt her so many times, but she still gave me a chance.*

"You don't look too good, son. Why don't you go? We can handle it here."

Xavier turned at the sound of Ms. Hawthorne's motherly voice. "Are you sure?"

She nodded. Then she leaned over and gave him a kiss on his cheek. "Tell Ebony we miss her and we're praying for her."

"I will."

"And just for the record, I think the two of you make a nice couple."

Xavier started to lie, but stopped himself. If there was one thing he had learned in life, it was that you couldn't pull the wool over the eyes of a mother. "Thank you, Ms. Hawthorne. Good night."

Five minutes later, Xavier was in his BMW, cruising down Hennepin Avenue. The air-conditioning was on full-blast, cooling his body's heat, and on the CD player, Yolanda Adams was reminding him of God's faithfulness. It was late evening and the sun was low, making for a picturesque scene. Instead of driving in the direction of home, Xavier made a left turn on Washington Avenue. Going home, to where memories of Ebony crowded every square inch of his house, would only depress him. His thoughts of her were beginning to border on obsession, so the only thing Xavier could do was find somewhere to hide for the next few hours. Every Friday night, the guys on his basketball team crammed into Leroy's House of Ribs to shoot pool and run their mouths. The fellas would provide the perfect distraction.

"I told you to watch out," Darius chided, devouring his BLT sandwich. He finished the food in his mouth and continued. "See, you wouldn't heed my warning and that's why you're crying now."

"Shut up, Darius." Xavier picked at his plate of curly fries. Since his arrival, his teammates had tried pulling him out of his funk by sharing their women problems. His friends were dating females who lied and schemed and demanded money. Ebony did none of those things. She wasn't perfect, but she treated him with the utmost respect and valued their relationship. Xavier had all but lost his mind when he realized Ebony was at the Indigo with Kale. The thought of her with another man—a pretty boy athlete at that—was killing him inside.

"I thought Ebony was *the one*. Being with her, loving her,

sharing my life with her all just felt right. She has a kick-ass sense of humor, is feminine and girly without being irritating and she doesn't let me get away with smack. She does a good job keeping me in line," he joked. In his mind, he could see Ebony staring at him with a hand fixed to her hip and a smirk playing on her lips. The hip-hop music blaring from the sound system throbbed in his ears, but he could still hear Ebony's contagious laugh. "I've never been with a woman who made me laugh as much as she does." He hastened to add, "And she's smart, too. We can talk about anything for hours. Sports, religion, sex, you name it."

"If that's how you feel about her, then go get her," Darius advised, wiping his sticky, barbecue-coated hands with a wet nap. He held up his empty beer mug, and after the freckle-faced waitress filled it to the brim and he took a sip, he said, "Sometimes a brother has to be man enough to admit he was wrong. If I were you, I would go get that woman. She's hot!" He held out his hand. "No disrespect, bro."

A grin turned the corners of Xavier's mouth. Darius was right; she was hot. And charming, too. Ebony had impressed his parents, which was no easy task, and aside from Jacqueline, everyone in his family thought she was wonderful.

"I got down on my knees and begged Keke to take me back," Juan confessed.

Xavier's eyes spread. Juan on his knees? The image was a powerful one. His friend talked more smack than anyone else, so it was staggering to learn that a woman had brought him to his knees.

"Remember when I cheated on her and she heaved my stuff out the window?"

Xavier nodded. How could he forget? Juan had roused him out of bed at three in the morning and begged for a ride to his brother's house. It was the middle of February and five inches of snow had been dumped on the city that afternoon. By the time Xavier had dug his jalopy out of the snow and got it started, Juan had already soothed things over with his girl-friend and returned inside the house.

"Well, not too long after that the girl I cheated with started spreading lies that we were still kicking it." Stroking the stubble on his pronounced chin, he shook his head. "That skank would call the house and tell Keke I skipped work and spent the entire day in her bed. Or drive by our condo screaming insults at my girl. One day, Keke got fed up and told me to pack my shit and get out." Juan took a swig of beer. His gaze slid across the room to the curvy Jamaican woman dancing suggestively on the dance floor.

"It took me two weeks to convince her to take me back. Two weeks! I had to show her my time card to prove that that bitch was lying, but it took a long time for her to trust me again. I'd never even think of cheating now." Turning his head away from the dance floor, he said, "Not for anyone. I don't care if the woman looks like a Playboy bunny and has breasts the size of cantaloupes, I'm keeping it in my pants from now on."

Xavier and Nathan chuckled. Neither one of them had ever heard Juan sound so contrite. "Keke must be the *bomb* if she's got you ready to turn over a new leaf," Nathan said, smacking his friend on the back. "Tell your girl I said thanks. With you out of the game, that leaves more women for me!"

"Go on, bro. But one day you'll see that I was right. A good woman is hard to find, right, Xavier?"

"Right."

Nathan laughed. "Forget ya'll! I'm going to go find some booty!"

Xavier watched his friend stroll over to the dance floor with as much subtlety as Billy Dee Williams. It wasn't long before he was dancing with a blonde in a red one-piece pantsuit.

Beckoning the waitress back over to the table, Juan asked Xavier if he wanted a drink. "Want a beer? It'll help clear your mind. You know, relax you, take your mind off your woman problems."

Xavier shook his head. "Naw, man, I'm cool."

"Keep your head up," Juan told him, returning to his sandwich. "It's not *that* bad."

Yes, it is, the voice in Xavier's mind said. For the next three hours, Xavier hung out with his friends. And when Leroy's shut down, he took Juan up on his invitation to play a game of cards. Xavier wasn't much of a card player, but he'd rather suffer through a game or two of poker than go home to a cold, empty house.

Chapter 24

Ebony debated whether or not to reheat her food. She'd been so busy daydreaming, she'd missed the timer going off, and now her chicken teriyaki tasted like cardboard. *Just great,* she thought sourly, popping the plate back into the microwave and setting the timer, *now my food is dry and overcooked.*

Her eyes returned to the window. It was the perfect night for stargazing. The sun had fallen behind the clouds some time ago, leaving a clear, cloudless sky, and a calm breeze whistled mellifluously through the trees.

Thoughts of Xavier turned over in her mind and every time Ebony relived their argument, she cringed. Over the course of the last two weeks, she had picked up the phone to call him but lost her nerve each time. A lot had happened in the time they had been apart but she missed him more and more each day.

Despite all the work that had been put into the revised proposal, the loan petition had been denied. Oddly enough, Ebony wasn't disappointed. The Women of Sensuality campaign was a glowing success and sales at all six Discreet Boutiques locations had shot through the roof.

"Maybe this is God's way of telling *one* of us to slow down and enjoy our success," Kendall had said wisely.

Ebony had agreed but in the back of her mind she was already planning their next move. The rejection was a minor setback. They had been doing business with First National Trust for six years, and had always appreciated their first-class approach of doing business. But they weren't the only bank in town. Yesterday, Ebony had called a half dozen other financial institutes and received some promising news. She wasn't going to make any decisions right away, but it gave her something to think about.

The Women of Sensuality campaign was more than enough to keep her busy. And when she wasn't working, she was going to spend more time with the people she loved. Attending the Reed barbecue had reminded her just how important family was. Iyesha was going through the terrible-teen phase and Ebony remembered what a confusing time that had been. She didn't have anyone to talk to and even if Ingrid had been willing, Ebony wouldn't have felt comfortable opening up to her mom. Opal was a fabulous mother, but Iyesha needed someone else to talk to. Someone who would listen to her and validate her feelings without passing judgment. Ebony and Iyesha had a strong relationship and maybe if she made more time for her goddaughter, she wouldn't act out as much.

Her relationship with Xavier was over, but the time they'd spent together had changed her forever. Her aggressive in-your-face approach to dealing with the opposite sex was a thing of the past. She didn't have to be the star of the party or the loudest person in the room to get noticed, either. Xavier had shown her that much. He stood out in a crowd because of hi quiet confidence and likable nature. He genuinely cared about people and it was evident in everything he said and did. Ebony's feelings for him would be there for as long as she lived.

The kitchen curtains flapped in the wind, and the breeze brushed across her face. *I wonder where he is?* On days like this, Xavier liked to ride his bike down to his parents' house or jog around his neighborhood park.

You're doing it again, said a voice.

Ebony slanted her head to the right. *Doing what?*

Thinking about him.

When Ebony thought about all the times they had cooked together or watched *Jeopardy!* or made love in the backyard under the stars, she felt warm all over. The sound of the microwave prevented her from retreating deeper into the past. After filling a glass with ice and drowning it with water, she put her plate on a wooden tray and went into the living room. Previews flashed on the TV, while Ebony fluffed pillows and spread out her blanket. Her new high-definition TV had been worth every penny. If it weren't for the blanket and the pillow, Ebony would swear she was at the movie theater. Hushing the light on the lamp, she increased the volume and prepared for the movie to start. The doorbell chimed just as the title of the movie was displayed on the screen.

It's Opal, Ebony surmised, shaking her head. *Now that she has a new body, she wants to show it off every chance she gets.* When Opal had stopped by the office last night, Ebony had made it clear that she didn't want to go out this weekend. She missed having male companionship but she would rather stay home and watch *Scary Movie 3* than go to some overpriced club.

After spending the last week in meetings, Ebony just didn't have the energy to get dressed up, let alone dance. Truth be told, she just wanted to be left alone. No noisy clubs, no obnoxious jerks gawking at her. Tonight, she was going to enjoy a quiet evening at home and there was nothing Opal could say to change her mind.

The bell chimed again and Ebony had to restrain herself from yelling. *Why is Opal banging on my door like a raving lunatic? Is she trying to get arrested for disturbing the peace?* Ebony hit Pause on the remote control. Tossing the duvet cover off to the side, she stuffed her feet back into her slippers and stood.

"Hold on, I'm coming," she called as she headed down the hall. Ebony opened the door. "Are you out of your—" The rest of her sentence fell away when she saw who the caller was. Ebony wanted to close the door and open it again because it was obvious her eyes were playing tricks on her. That, or Jacqueline Reed was standing on her doorstep.

"Hi."

Ebony would recognize that voice anywhere. Jacqueline's stomach was jutting out of her orange baby doll dress, her face was plump and she was breathing heavily. It was hard to believe her due date was weeks away; she looked like she could give birth any second now.

Ebony eyed her with interest. *What is Jacqueline doing here? Oh God, Xavier must be hurt!* He had been in a car accident. His car had flipped over five or six times. He had been rushed to the nearest hospital but the doctors didn't think he was going to make it. Heart racing and mouth dry, she asked, "Is Xavier okay?"

"Not exactly."

"Not exactly? What is *that* supposed to mean?" *God, it's worse than I thought!* "Is he alive?"

Jacqueline saw the horror in Ebony's eyes and suddenly understood her unusual line of questioning. "He's fine. I came here so we could speak in private." She stood there quietly. Jacqueline had traded in her chin-length bob for dozens of floss-thin braids, and fingered the ends as she waited to be invited inside. When several seconds passed, she asked, "May I come in?"

Ebony wanted to tell Jacqueline to get lost, but instead, stepped aside. Feeling a tad underdressed in her robe and needing time to organize her thoughts, she offered Jacqueline a seat in the living room. "Can I interest you in something to drink?"

Jacqueline eased down onto the sofa. "A glass of juice would be nice."

After bringing her a glass of orange juice and a plate of aunt Mae's hazelnut cookies into the living room, Ebony hurried upstairs to change.

Ten minutes later, she returned wearing a blue tank top and denim shorts. Once the curtains were closed and the two floor lamps were turned on, Ebony took a seat on one of the leather chairs. Standing would imply that she was uninterested in what Jacqueline had to say and anxious for her to leave. Ebony was both, but she was wise enough to use the good graces she had been taught.

"Would you like anything else?" Ebony wasn't trying to be hospitable; she was trying to move the conversation along so Jacqueline could be on her way. The quicker they got down to business, the sooner the mother-to-be could waddle her way on home.

Jacqueline rested her glass on a coaster. She smiled politely. "No, thank you, I'm fine."

The two women sized each other up.

Ebony didn't know how she felt about Jacqueline Reed. Part of her hated her for being the main source of her problems with Xavier; the other part of her felt sorry that she had been married to a man like Malcolm Pleiss.

Jacqueline had no business butting into Xavier's life and Ebony resented her being in her house. But this time around, there would be no insults or accusations. This time, Ebony had the upper hand. This was her sanctuary, her domain, her safe haven. Nobody was going to disturb her peace. As soon as Jacqueline crossed the line, she and her big belly would have to go.

"You're probably wondering why I'm here."

Damn, Skippy! Ebony tasted her drink.

"Xavier's a mess!"

Water spewed out of Ebony's mouth. Wiping as the liquid dribbled furiously down her chin, she set down her glass and grabbed a napkin from the napkin holder.

"Okay, okay, so maybe I spoke in haste but the whole family is worried about him. He's stopped going to church, he's been partying with his friends and one night last week I had to go pick him up from the bar because he was too drunk to drive home."

Ebony kept her tone light. "What does all of this have to do with me? After what happened at the Indigo, I'm quite sure I'm the *last* person Xavier wants to see."

"He never did tell me what happened that night. Do you want to talk about it?"

Yeah, but not with you.

As if reading her mind, Jacqueline set out to dispel her fears. "I'm embarrassed about the way I treated you, Ebony. That's not who I am. Ask anybody. They'll tell you I'm the sweetest person you'll ever meet. When I saw you in the kitchen, all the painful memories came rushing back. But that's no excuse for my behavior. I had no right to embarrass you and I'm sorry." Fingering the gold wedding band dangling on the chain around her neck, she rounded her eyes on Ebony, a sympathetic look on her face. "I'd like it very much if we could put the past behind us and start over."

Jacqueline thought back to last night. When she dropped by her brother's house to check on him, he was inside the kitchen, hard at work, proofreading his graduate school essay

"I'm applying to schools on the West Coast," he had told her.

"Why, when we have perfectly good schools here?"

"I need a change of scenery."

Xavier had never mentioned leaving Minneapolis before. He loved the city. All his friends were here and he liked living close to their parents. Jacqueline suspected loneliness was the driving force behind his decision to relocate, but when pressed, he denied it. Jacqueline didn't want Xavier to leave. She wanted him present for every birthday, graduation and all the other milestones in her child's life. E-mail, Web cams and camera phones made it easy for loved ones to stay connected, but it wouldn't be the same as having her brother close by.

While Xavier tended to dinner, Jacqueline had gone to the bathroom. "Nature calls," she'd joked. But instead of going to the bathroom, she ducked inside his bedroom and raked through his drawers. Jacqueline had found what she was looking for on his nightstand. It had taken her three-quarters of an hour to find Ebony's house, and now that she was here, she had no intention of leaving until she got what she wanted.

"You don't have to tell me what happened at the Indigo. I'm not here to get into your business. I'm here for Xavier. He misses you and he wants you back."

Uneasy with Jacqueline's stare, Ebony looked away. "I don't think Xavier and me getting back together is a good idea."

"What's there to know? Xavier's in a funk because of *you*, Ebony. You're the one he wants. He loves you and you love him, so what's there to think about?" Jacqueline didn't understand Ebony's reluctance. She would never find a man who loved her the way Xavier did. Unless— "Are you seeing someone?"

"No, there's no one else."

"Then what is it?"

Ebony held Jacqueline's gaze. If she revealed her thoughts, this peaceful meeting would quickly change tones. Finishing what was left of her drink, she struggled to find a nice way to say what was on her mind. "It's you."

Jacqueline's hand flew to her chest. "Me!"

"Yes, you. I love your brother and I'd give anything to have him back, but I don't want to live the rest of my life on tiptoes because you hate me."

"I'm going to be honest," she said. "If I was looking for a woman for my brother, I wouldn't pick you."

Ouch!

"You're completely wrong for him."

No, I'm not!

"He's laid-back, quiet. You're loud and, well, loud."

Ebony's jaw set in anger. Jacqueline had a lot of nerve talking to her like that. If it weren't for the fact that she loved Xavier, she would have shown his sister the door a long time ago.

"But it's not up to me who Xavier chooses to love."

Thank God. Ebony wanted to tell Jacqueline she was wrong about her, but held her tongue. There was no use arguing. Not when they were finally starting to get somewhere. Ebony disguised her anger with a smile. She stretched her mouth so wide her lips hurt. "So, you're okay with us dating again?"

"It's fine by me."

Ebony was so happy she was trembling. She couldn't wait to see Xavier. The anticipation was so great, she felt like she was going to burst. Reaching for the phone, she said, "I'm going to call him."

"He's not home."

"Oh." She pulled her hand away from the receiver. "Where is he?"

"Nathan's been pursuing some 'dancer' for months now and she finally agreed to go on a double date with him. She's bringing her sister, and—"

"Nathan's bringing Xavier," Ebony finished.

"I just thought I should warn you. I hate to call anybody names, but LaDonna Jeffries is a tramp. She's fast and loose and if her sister is anything like her, Xavier could end up with more than he bargained for. In the mood my brother's in, he's going to be easy prey for the Jeffries sisters."

Now it all made sense. Jacqueline didn't drive all the way over to her house to bury the hatchet; she didn't like her for Xavier, but she disliked Nathan's choice of women even more. "Where are they?"

"Q's Joint. Heard of it?"

Ebony nodded absently. She was thinking about the afternoon Xavier had taken her to Spring Lake Amusement Park to play a round of miniature golf. Ebony had learned a lot about Xavier that afternoon. He loved sports. His middle name was James. And the most startling news of all, he had once been engaged to his college sweetheart.

Nathan was the one who had arranged the first date with Xavier and his ex-fiancée! That man is nothing but trouble! What's wrong with him? Why is he always dragging my man out to meet other women? Xavier is my man and no one is going to take him away! A mischievous smile crept over her face as a plan formed in her mind. It didn't matter how beautiful or how sexy his blind date was; the woman didn't stand a chance.

Ebony didn't want to be rude, but Jacqueline had to go. "Looks like I have a date to go ruin," she announced, standing to her feet. "Forgive my manners, but—"

"No apologies necessary, girl. Go and get your man!"

The two women laughed and for the first time since Jacqueline's arrival, Ebony felt herself relax. She and Jacqueline might never become friends, but at least they weren't enemies anymore. After seeing her guest off, Ebony raced down the hall and sprinted upstairs.

Chapter 25

Dressed to kill in a black body-skimming dress and three-inch sandals, Ebony bypassed the line of people waiting to get inside Q's Joint. Her anklet jingled as she made her way toward the front of the queue. Straightening her back, she lifted her head high and clutched her purse. Her fitted halter dress played up her enviable hourglass figure and drew stares from the crowd.

Ebony didn't recognize any of the bouncers, and the man guarding the door looked like Rocky Balboa. Hard face, pursed lips, muscular build, rigid stance. *I hope he can track down Kale,* she thought, approaching the front of the club. If not, she would have no choice but to join the others in the slow-moving line. Luckily for her, Kale was standing by the entrance signing autographs. When he saw her, he tapped one of the mobster-looking bouncers on the shoulder and signaled to him to let her pass through.

"I didn't know you were dropping by tonight," Kale said, kissing Ebony on the cheek. "I would have saved your favorite table if I knew you were coming."

"No problem," Ebony told him.

"Amelia is here. She'll be so happy to see you."

After a few minutes of idle chitchat, Ebony promised to save Kale a dance and entered the packed-out club. Ebony decided to check the lounge area first. It was a secluded and intimate spot for people who wanted to talk. Her eyes swept the room and came up empty. Ebony was about to walk into the restaurant when she caught sight of Nathan and a busty redhead making out near the washrooms.

Xavier's got to be around here somewhere.

Ebony walked farther into the lounge. She found Xavier on the opposite side of the room, in a booth obscured by a massive floor plant. His date had friendly eyes, curly hair and a slender frame. She looked like the type of woman who would make a great mother. For a half second, Ebony reconsidered what she was about to do. *Now's not the time to back out,* she told herself. *A lot is at stake here. You can't give up now!*

Ebony stalked over to the unsuspecting couple. She eased into the booth beside Xavier and squeezed his forearm. "Hey, baby. Sorry I'm late but traffic was crazy."

Xavier's jaw fell.

Ebony turned to his date and extended her right hand affably. Just because she was about to dash the woman's hopes didn't mean she had to be cruel about it. After all, this wasn't personal. This was business. Ebony was in the business of getting her man back and this poor, clueless woman was in the way. "Hi. I'm Ebony. Xavier's *fiancée.*"

The brunette cleared her throat. "Did you say fiancée?"

"Uh-huh." Ebony grazed her lips across his cheek, and nestled against his shoulder. "We're getting married next month."

If she had glanced over at Xavier, she would have seen his bug-eyed, openmouthed expression and probably would have burst out laughing. That would really have thrown the brunette for a loop.

Xavier's date swiped her purse off the table and slid out of the booth. "I thought you were different," she snarled. She sounded like she was on the verge of tears. The woman stomped away, and Xavier turned to Ebony.

"What the hell was—"

Ebony kissed him hard on the lips. She ran the length of her tongue over his mouth and pressed her body against his. Soon the kiss picked up speed. It was as if they were trying to make up for lost time with their lips.

Xavier cupped Ebony's face in his hands. It was an intimate and touching gesture that brought tears to her eyes. If she had any doubts about Xavier's feelings, they diminished when he broke the kiss and whispered, "I love you" in her ear.

Ebony could have spent the rest of the night kissing Xavier but they had to talk. She pulled out of his arms and wiped all traces of her Copper Glitz lipstick from his mouth. With a coy and sexy smile, she said, "Now, that's what I call a homecoming!"

Xavier chuckled. "What was that all about?" he asked, motioning toward the vacant seat.

"That? Oh, nothing. I'm just staking my claim. You're my boyfriend, remember?"

"You told my date I was your fiancé."

"Aren't you?"

"I don't know, *am* I?" Xavier's eyes twinkled. "I'm not going to name any names, but I remember a certain somebody saying she didn't want to get married or have kids."

Ebony gasped. "Why would someone say something like

that?" Closing her eyes, she dropped her head on his shoulder. "I missed you, Xavier."

"It's been miserable for me, too," he admitted.

"I heard." Ebony told him about Jacqueline's visit. "I almost fainted when I opened the front door and saw her there!"

"I bet you did." Silence followed. There were a lot of things Xavier wanted to say, but he didn't know where to begin. He had landed more than just a lover; in Ebony he had found a confidante and a friend. Seeing him out with another woman had brought out her claws, but he needed to know if the only reason why she wanted him was that he was with someone else. But first, he had to apologize. "About the things I said to you at the Indigo—"

She cut him off. "We both said things we didn't mean."

"I know, but I hurt you and I'm sorry. I lost my head when I saw you with Kale."

"My loyalty has always been to you, Xavier. First, last and always."

He kissed her forehead tenderly.

Fighting off the tears gathering in her eyes, she sat up. *What is wrong with me? When did I become a weepy female who cries at the slightest act of affection?*

"Some of the things you said were true," she told him. "Deep down, I guess I never thought I was good enough to receive my parents' love. That's why I pushed myself extra hard in school." She added, "That's why I push myself today."

"Ebony, I'm sure your parents loved you the best way they knew how. And if they were still alive, I know they'd be proud of you. Not because you run your own business or because you're successful." He tilted her chin, "They'd be proud of you because of who you are. You're generous and compassionate and sweet and—" he cocked an eyebrow "—you're a great kisser."

Ebony laughed.

"I have a confession to make," he told her. "I am a little intimidated by your success. It's not that I don't want you to succeed, it's just that I don't want anything to come between us."

"You're right, Xavier. I *am* afraid of rejection. That's why I work around the clock and push my employees so hard." Remorse flickered across her face, then quickly vanished. "I want us to work, Xavier, even if it means I have to slow down a bit."

Love was etched on his face when he said, "You'll never have to worry about me walking out on you, Ebony. I'm not going anywhere. I promise." Xavier drew a deep breath. There was a deep-seated bond and before he even opened his mouth, Ebony knew what he was going to say. Xavier had never been more nervous, but her smile of encouragement eroded his fear. "I love you, Ebony, and I want you to be my wife."

Silence.

"Did you hear me, Ebony? I want to marry you. I want you to be my wife."

Her face shone with ebullience. Sniffing back tears, Ebony reached out and touched a hand to his cheek. "Okay."

Xavier blinked. "Okay?"

"Okay."

"Just like that?"

"Just like that." Ebony brushed her eyes tenderly over his face. There was nothing to think about. Xavier was the one. The *right* one. He improved her life dramatically. Not in financial means but in the ways that mattered most. Spiritually, emotionally and mentally. She had never defined her self-worth by a man, but Ebony had never felt more beautiful than when she was with Xavier. And there was no doubt in her mind that the day she became Mrs. Xavier Reed was going to be the happiest day of her life. Anticipating his next question, Ebony pressed an index finger to his lips to quiet him

"I'm sure about this. I love you and I want to be with you for always. I know that sounds corny as hell, but it's true." They sealed their reunion with another kiss.

When they broke apart, Ebony spotted Xavier's date at the bar. The woman was watching them, a funny expression on her face. "I should go over there and apologize to that poor girl. She probably hates you!"

Ebony watched in stunned silence as Xavier raised his glass in the direction of the bar. Smiling, the brunette gave him a small wave.

"Th-th-this…this was a setup!"

Xavier neither confirmed nor denied her suspicions.

"You sent Jacqueline to my house with that pitiful *'Xavier is miserable without you'* story just to lure me over here!"

"No, that part of the story was true!"

Ebony pointed a finger at the brunette. "Who's that?"

Xavier struggled to keep a straight face. "My co-worker, Sandy, she teaches English."

"But how did you know I'd show up?"

Brimming with confidence and smiling generously, he said, "I just did."

"You tricked me!" Ebony gave him a shot in the arm. "You liar!"

"Now, is that any way to talk to your *future husband?*"

Epilogue

Six months later

"So, how does it feel to be an old married woman?" Opal asked, once the waiter left to place their orders. "Have your feet touched the ground yet or are you still floating on clouds?"

"Girl, please," Kendall scoffed. "Girlfriend doesn't even remember how to walk!"

Ebony laughed. Shaking her head wistfully, she admired her glittering pear-shaped diamond ring. "Who knew marriage could be this sweet? I'm so happy I don't know what to do with myself!"

Opal and Kendall cracked up.

"I tried to tell you, but you wouldn't hear it," Kendall told her, rubbing her hands over her protruding belly. She was seven months pregnant, and in a clingy white turtleneck sweater, her stomach looked twice its normal size. "I'm just thankful Xavier stuck with your stubborn behind."

More laughter.

"Ladies," the waiter said in a diluted German accent, "here are your drinks."

"So, how was the honeymoon?" Opal asked, once the waiter left. "Did you guys have a chance to do any sightseeing or were you too busy doing *other* things?"

Ebony and Xavier had returned late last night from St. Lucia. After grabbing some groceries from Big Stop Foods and moving some of his boxes from the garage into the house, they had collapsed into bed exhausted.

"What do you think?" The playful expression on Ebony's face brought giggles from her two friends. She took a sip of her Long Island iced tea, and then said, "We expected the island to be swarming with tourists because of the holiday season, but it was fairly quiet. We basically had the place to ourselves."

"Did you leave your hotel room or what?" Kendall asked.

"That husband of mind wanted to stay in bed all day, but I reminded him it was *our* honeymoon, and there was a lot I wanted to see—outdoors." Ebony chuckled at the memory of Xavier's crestfallen face when he learned they wouldn't be spending all day and all night in their honeymoon suite. "Our first stop was Pigeon Island—an absolutely breathtaking natural park with several historical sights and statues. I loved it there. Later in the week, I dragged Xavier to the Marquis Estate. He complained the whole way there, but once we reached the plantation house and finished the tour, he was glad we went. The lunch they served was to *die* for and the staff shared some amusing island folk tales with us. On our last night we went on a romantic boat ride and even managed to sneak in some shopping." Ebony turned to Opal. "I got some stuff for the girls and some adorable tie-died outfits for

Andrew, Jr. I can't wait until Jacqueline and Andrew come over tomorrow night. He's probably grown a foot in the two weeks we've been gone!"

Kendall pushed her chair back and swung her purse over her shoulder. "Be right back, ladies. If the food comes while I'm gone, start eating without me."

Opal tasted her drink. "How are things going with Jacqueline? She looked happy at the wedding."

"I doubt that we'll ever be best friends, but we're cool. Did I tell you that she dropped by the Calhoun Square Boutique the day before the wedding?" When Opal shook her head, Ebony continued. "Yeah, she tried on a few items from the new Women of Sensuality line but didn't buy anything. So I bought the silk pajamas and accompanying robe that she tried on and gave them to her as a gift."

"That was thoughtful."

Ebony glanced outside and was surprised to see large snowflakes falling from the sky. It had been snowing off and on since last night. "I think we'll be okay." She added, "As long as I keep supplying her with expensive lingerie."

Both women laughed.

Kendall returned and their lunch entrées soon arrived. Conversation was put on pause as the server got the orders straight and refilled their drinks.

"How are things going with Doc? Are you and Charles an official couple now?" Ebony took a healthy bite of her jerk chicken and chewed slowly. After all the food she had eaten on her honeymoon, it was a wonder she could still fit into any of her clothes. "I kept my eye on you guys during the reception. You looked *mighty* cozy."

Kendall examined Opal with her eyes. "They were, weren't they?"

"We're taking things slow. Charles might not be tall, dark

and handsome, but he's cute, honest and sincere. A woman can't ask for much more than that."

Kendall and Ebony nodded in agreement.

Opal smiled. "It's funny, I was sweating bricks over inviting Charles to the wedding because I was nervous about him meeting the girls. But it turns out I had nothing to worry about. Iyesha thinks he's cool because he drives a Hummer and Tessa stole the stars from the man's eyes! The two of them have a better relationship than Charles and I do! Actually I'm a little jealous."

"Maybe we'll be planning another wedding before the end of the year," Ebony said, wiping crumbs from her mouth with a napkin.

"And this time I won't look like a beached whale in my bridesmaid's dress," Kendall added, staring down at her stomach.

All three women laughed.

"Oh." Kendall put down her fork and rummaged around in her purse. "I almost forgot. Here are some of the proofs from the ceremony."

Ebony took the envelope being offered and flipped through the stack of pictures. Her wedding had taken place two weeks ago, but the magic and excitement of that day still lingered in her heart. Ebony studied each picture as if it were under a microscope. When she came across the picture of Xavier tossing her over his shoulder as they walked down the church steps, she threw her head back and laughed.

The Garrett-Reed wedding had been an intimate, elegant affair attended by only their closest friends and family—less than eighty people in all. The couple spared no expense for the event. A five-piece orchestra, an extravagant six-course meal and tables outfitted with bottles of champagne and personalized thank-you cards for each guest had made the reception a memorable night for all.

"There wasn't a dry eye in the church when Xavier recited his vows."

Kendall took a sip of her hot chocolate. "I think I even saw some of the men crying."

"What can I say? Not only did I pick the most handsome man in the world, but he's thoughtful and sensitive, too. My baby is a ten in more ways than one!" Giggling, Ebony fanned herself with her napkin. "As far as I'm concerned, the man can do no wrong."

Opal didn't want to burst her best friend's bubble, but she couldn't stop herself from saying, "Ebony, get real. You guys are newlyweds. Everyone thinks like that until they have their first real argument. The honeymoon doesn't last forever, girl-friend." She returned to her penne pasta. "Count yourself lucky if it lasts six months!"

Kendall nodded. "I'm surprised Xavier let you out. He wasn't ticked that you took off to have lunch with us?" She took a sip of her water, before she finished her thought. "I mean, you're not due back at the office until Monday. Your poor husband probably wanted to spend the entire weekend with you."

Ebony laughed. "Girl, please. Xavier was the one who encouraged me to come! He kissed me goodbye, walked me out to the car and told me not to hurry back. He's at home unpacking as we speak. By the time I get home, he'll have the house spick-and-span."

In the two weeks that Ebony and Xavier were in St. Lucia, twelve inches of snow had been dumped on the city. Roads were slick, sidewalks were icy and there was the constant sound of screeching tires and plastic shovels scraping against the pavement. The arctic-type temperatures and periodic snowfalls throughout the day were creating havoc all across the city. Ebony walked cautiously up the steps, appalled to see that her new husband hadn't shoveled the walkway as promised. The bitter, shiver-down-your-spine wind was so fierce, Ebony was scared it would blow her away.

Once inside, she slammed the door and turned the lock. Ebony didn't care who called to invite them over for dinner tonight; they were staying in. After kicking off her boots and hanging up her jacket, she dropped her keys on the table and headed into the kitchen. Ebony swiped the thick stack of bills off the counter, and then set out in search of her husband.

"Xavier!" she called as she went. Pushing open the bedroom door, she said, "Sorry it took so long for me to get back. Traffic was backed up for—" Ebony gasped.

Hangers, clothes and toiletries were sprawled across the unmade bed, and dress shoes, belts and sneakers lined the carpet, making it virtually impossible for her to walk any farther into the bedroom.

Wait until I get my hands on him! Ebony chucked the mail on the only patch of the dresser that wasn't covered with Xavier's junk. Her bedroom—her beautiful, clean, peaceful sanctuary—looked like a tornado had ripped through it, and to make matters worse, there were dirty dishes on the nightstand and an empty carton of orange juice.

Ebony stomped back downstairs. The exhilarated voice of Marv Albert greeted her as she entered the basement. Xavier's size twelve feet dangled casually over the edge of the couch and a stack of pillows were piled behind his head. *Why is he lounging around watching basketball when the house is in shambles?*

Ebony stormed over to the couch. "Xavier, why does it look like Mother Nature unleashed her fury in our bedroom? I almost broke my neck trying to get up the walkway! You said you'd shovel the snow. What have you been doing since I left?" She tossed a look over her shoulder at the TV. "Besides watching basketball, of course."

Xavier stood up. He tried to kiss her, but she turned away. Steeling herself against his kiss, she pressed both hands against his chest. "You promised you'd finish unpacking before I got home."

Ebony heard a low humming sound. "What's that?"

Xavier brought his arms from around his back. A tiny white terrier with big brown eyes and a thick coat of fur was cradled in his hands. He held up the puppy for his wife to see. "Surprise!"

"It's a terrier."

"Just like the one you used to have."

"Where did you get her from?" Ebony took the dog from Xavier. Stroking the top of its head, she spoke quietly in the puppy's ear. "She looks just like—"

"Lace. I know. That's why I bought her."

Amazed that Xavier remembered the story she had shared with him on their first date, Ebony smiled up at him. Her husband was wonderful in every sense of the word. Kissing him lightly on the cheek brought a self-satisfied grin to Xavier's lips. Ebony cuddled the puppy to her chest. "What's her name?"

"Strawberry."

"Strawberry?"

Nodding, he let his eyes drift lazily over his wife's body. Xavier's hands reached out to explore. He pulled Ebony into his arms and kissed the side of her neck. "After what we did last night with that bowl of fruit, I think the name'll stick. Don't you?"

Xavier pawed Ebony through her dress and she replied by planting a body-tingling kiss on him. Her tongue pushed its way into his mouth and she rubbed her body sensually against his. Just before they reached the point of no return, Ebony pulled away. Tapping his chest, she said, "Work before play, baby," and then turned and raced upstairs, with Xavier hot on her trail.

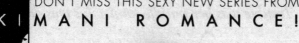

Trouble was her middle name...his was danger!

Elaine OVERTON

His Holiday Bride

Fleeing from a dangerous pursuer, Amber Lockhart
takes refuge in the home—and arms—of
Paul Gutierrez. But the threat posed by the man
who's after her doesn't compare with the peril to
Amber's heart from her sexy Latin protector.

THE LOCKHARTS
THREE WEDDINGS AND A REUNION
FOR FOUR SASSY SISTERS, ROMANCE CHANGES EVERYTHING!

*Available the first week of October
wherever books are sold.*

KIMANI™
ROMANCE

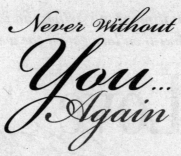

Never Without *You... Again*

National bestselling author
FRANCINE CRAFT

When Hunter Davis returns to town, high school
principal Theda Coles is torn between the need to
uphold her reputation and the burning passion she still
feels for her onetime love. But her resistance melts in
the face of their all-consuming desire and she can't stop
seeing him—even though their relationship
means risking her career...

"Ms. Craft is a master at storytelling."
—*Romantic Times BOOKreviews*

*Available the first week of October
wherever books are sold.*

KIMANI™
ROMANCE

National bestselling author

ROCHELLE ALERS

No Compromise

In charge of a program for victimized women,
Jolene Walker has no time or energy for a personal
life...until she meets army captain Michael Kirkland.
This sexy, compelling man is tempting her to trade
her long eighteen-hour workdays for sultry nights
of sizzling passion. But their bliss is shattered when
Jolene takes on a mysterious new client, plunging
her into a world of terrifying danger.

"Alers paints such vivid descriptions that when Jolene
becomes the target of a murderer, you almost feel as
though someone you know is in great danger."
—*Library Journal*

Available the first week of October
wherever books are sold.

ARABESQUE®

Will one secret destroy their love?

Award-winning author

Janice Sims

One fine Day

The Bryant Family trilogy continues with this heartfelt story
in which Jason Bryant tries to convince lovely bookstore
owner Sara Minton to marry him. Their love is unlike
anything Jason has ever felt, and he knows Sara feels
the same way...so why does she keep refusing him,
saying she'll marry him "one day"? He knows she's
hiding something...but what?

Available the first week of October
wherever books are sold.

ARABESQUE®

www.kimanipress.com

*I*t happened in an instant.
One stormy December night, two cars collided,
shattering four peoples' lives forever....

Essence Bestselling Author

Monica McKayhan

The Evening After

In the aftermath of the accident that took her husband,
Lainey Williams struggles with loss, guilt and regret over her
far-from-perfect union. Nathan Sullivan, on the other hand, is
dealing with a comatose wife, forcing him to reassess his life.

It begins as two grieving people offering comfort and
friendship to one another. But as trust...and passion...
grow, a secret is revealed, risking the newly rebuilt
lives of these two people.

The Evening After is "another wonderful novel
that will leave you satisfied and uplifted."
—Margaret Johnson-Hudge, author of *True Lies*

*Available the first week of October
wherever books are sold.*

sepia™

www.kimanipress.com KPMM0371007

GET THE GENUINE LOVE
YOU DESERVE...

NATIONAL BESTSELLING AUTHOR
Vikki Johnson

Addicted to COUNTERFEIT LOVE

Many people in today's world are unable to recognize
what a genuine loving partnership should be and
often sabotage one when it does come along. In this
moving volume, Vikki Johnson offers memorable
words that will help readers identify destructive love
patterns and encourage them to demand the love
that they are entitled to.

Available the first week of October wherever books are sold.

NEW SPIRIT
TM

www.kimanipress.com

KPVJ0381007